LAVINGTON'S HOLE

LAVINGTON'S HOLE

A Tallyforth Mystery

Bob Bibby

PIERREPOINT

PRESS

First published in Great Britain by Pierrepoint Press 2013.

A CIP record for this book is available from the British Library.

ISBN 978-0-9533196-9-5

Cover design by Clare Brayshaw

Typeset, printed and bound in Great Britain by:
York Publishing Services Ltd
64 Hallfield Road
Layerthorpe
York

YO31 7ZQ

Tel: 01904-431213

Website: www.yps-publishing.co.uk

To republicans everywhere

Acknowledgements

I would like to thank Tony Giles, former Chair of Bridgnorth and District Historical Society, and Peter Wooldridge, former Editor of *The Shropshire Review* for enormously helpful comments on preliminary drafts of this novel.

Other books by Bob Bibby

Travel Writing
Grey Paes and Bacon:
From the Heart of the Black Country
Dancing with Sabrina: The River Severn –
A Journey from Source to Sea
Special Offa: A Walk along Offa's Dyke
On the Wall with Hadrian

Walking Guides
The Shropshire Cakes and Ale Trail
The Worcestershire Cakes and Ale Trail
The Warwickshire Cakes and Ale Trail
The Staffordshire Cakes and Ale Trail

Crime Fiction
Be a Falling Leaf
Bird on the Wing
The Liquidator
The Llareggub Experience

Fiction
Known Unto God

For fuller information, go to www.bobbibby.co.uk

PROLOGUE

Bridgnorth. April 20.1646

My dearest love,

You were not at our trysting place yester evening and I can only conjecture that you have been apprehended by your father and that he has locked you in your chamber so that you can never see me again. Is that so? Has he made you confess that we have been meeting? Have you told him what I am, that I am a soldier in the Parliament's army, his sworn enemy? Does he upbraid you for loving one who is his enemy, one who seeks only justice for all men from this tyrant King whose cause he has espoused?

This silence from you does make me feel grievous sore, lest it is of your choosing and not forced upon you by your father. I fear you love me no longer, for that I have made you a victim of this conflict, setting you against your own father and causing you to forsake him. Is it even so, my sweet? Has some great thought struck you in the night

and set you to revoke that love which you
did swear to me as I the same forswore
to you? Have you taken your father's side,
thinking perchance that you are in debt to him
in memory of your mother and that allegiance
to me, nay love for me, were foolish and a
dishonour to her name?

O my love, that were not so. Whatsoe'er
your regard for your father and your dead
mother, it is not they who will be at your
side throughout life's struggles. Do you not
see that your father is aging and, although
you love him and fear to disrespect him, he
will not be there to protect you throughout
your life? Do you not see that this world is
changing around him and that this castle he
does govern shall fall soon enough, and too
that men have cast off their shackles and will
no longer be constrained by the old lords of
the counties when they have been fighting so
long for freedom? Trust me when I tell you
that a new order is coming in this country
of ours whose shape I know not but whose
voice I have heard around the campfires and
on the battlefields and in the sounds of men's
shoes as they march. We are surely close
to that time when the King must perforce
recognise that he does not command this
country any longer. All over the Parliament's
troops are beating back those armies of the
King, are besieging all towns where the King's
garrisons are situated, and taking dominance of

all places where once the King's supporters
held sway. This war, this mighty civil strife
we have been engaged on for many years, this
endless bloodshed, has almost run its course.

And what of us, my lovely Venetta, for only
now dare I pen your name as no longer wary
of our discovery, which I fear has already
occurred? What of our love? Will you not
come to me in the night, as we have so often
promised ourselves when locked in embrace
and when our kisses so inflame us? Will you
not come with me in the night and we can
flee, just as we once swore to do? I yet have
the name and household of that sea captain
in Portsmouth whereof we might purchase
passage to New England and I have garnered
enough silver whereof to pay for such a
passage for the two of us. I know where we
may find a horse to speed us on our way, I
know the secret paths through this county
and through some others where we would not
be apprised and besides, this war is drawing
to its conclusion and there is little to hinder
us by way of obstructions if we were to ride
so to Portsmouth.

I needs must tell you that these words I
write to you are not mere empty vessels,
writ to persuade you of the truth of my
argument, but have greater substance than
you might dream of. For, beneath the castle
in which you sit with your father Sir Robert

ix

and those other gentry of the county, as well as all their soldiers and those others of the household, beneath the castle I say there is a work of great moment now being enacted. For an engineer of our troops is even now with his men digging a tunnel through the rock underneath Bridgnorth Castle, purposing, as he has been ordered, to reach a place directly below the church within the castle walls where it is known your troops do store their ammunitions. These engineers have been digging now for several days and it will not be many more days ere they come to the place they intend, for Colonel Lavington has so computed that place. There they will place a huge mine that will so destroy the rock above it that it will cause the ammunitions in that chapel to explode and therefore the whole of the castle grounds will be torn apart in that explosion.

My sweet Venetta, there is not time to spend, disputing your father's words or considering those of mine. Very soon, unless your father does relent and make that surrender which Colonel Lloyd has so desired of him on two times already, then all within the castle grounds will suffer grievously. You must make good your escape now. I will await you at our trysting place on the Stone Way each morn at cock crow and each e'en as the sun sets, praying that you will come to me and that we can so begin our life together. Be not afraid, my love, for I have the protection of the Parliament's army wherever we go in England. I have a letter here in my purse that I did entreat my Master Pierpoint to obtain for me, that guarantees us safe passage. It is signed by Master Cromwell, who men say is our greatest commander in the field and many do say will be the one who will make sure that freedom be not extinguished again, when that this strife does end.

My love, my body aches for you, wishing your arms e'en now were clasped around me and we were riding through the countryside intent on reaching Portsmouth and the longed for passage to a new life together. My soul cries out for your love and begs God in all earnestness to allow you to escape without harm from the castle and from the King's garrison. I pray that you will receive this letter and that our hiding place in the rocks has not been discovered and some other may take this letter and reveal it to your father. I can only hope. I will be waiting as I promised. Pray God we will soon be one.

Yours evermore, my sweetest Venetta,

Henry Tolliver

ONE

'Lavington's Hole!' called out the balding man who was stood up at the head of the table, a fellow of late middle age with ruddy complexion and gleaming eyes.

'Lavington's Hole!' repeated the assembled members of the Lavington Society, standing at their seats around the table and raising their glasses.

Draining their glasses and noisily seating themselves again, the 'Old Lavs', as they jokingly referred to themselves, resumed their animated conversation. George Elliott, hair newly trimmed in a fashionable spiked style, took another sip of her chardonnay and looked around the table. There were a dozen of them gathered there, some couples, some singles, and her. All were in roughly the same age bracket of between forty and sixty, all comfortably off, all dressed in similar semi-casual clothing, none thinking that an evening such as this which would end up costing them the best part of forty pounds a head was extravagant. A sign of the affluence of the times, she thought to herself. An indication of the prosperity of so many people's lives nowadays, even under a Labour government.

They were in the garishly decorated back room of The Habit, which had until a few years ago been The Ball Hotel but had then been converted into a stylish restaurant to meet the changing needs of the aspirant middle classes of the old market town of Bridgnorth. The Habit stood near the end of East Castle Street, a street whose name reminded all visitors that once a proud castle had guarded this rock by the fast-flowing River Severn.

1

George Elliott turned towards her sister who was sitting beside her.

'Who's he then?' she asked with a smile, reaching for her wine glass.

'Who?' rejoined Donna Latham, a largish woman who sought to disguise her size with an extravagant, dusky-yellow, chenille pashmina. 'Lavington? The man with the hole? God knows! You'll have to ask Andrew. He's the local boy. I'm just an illegal immigrant, as you know only too well.'

George Elliott laughed with her sister.

'I suppose I should have asked before but you told me this was just a social occasion. I didn't realise there was some point to it all. I thought it was connected with Andrew's old school or something of that nature.'

'Lavington's Academy for Young Gentlemen, you mean?' cut in Andrew Latham himself, who was sitting opposite her and had just caught the drift of the two women's conversation. He was a tall, handsome-looking man, with dark hair lightly tinged with silver above his ears, piercing blue eyes and a nose that had in an earlier life seen too much service in the middle of rugby scrums. 'Sorry, nothing like that at all. Lavington played a most important part in the history of this town.'

'Oh, bore, bore,' interrupted Donna, stifling a feigned yawn. 'This bloody town and its bloody history. Pass the cheese, George, and top my glass up please. If I'm going to have to listen to Andrew's rewriting of the history of the British Isles, I'm going to need something to keep my mouth occupied. That Camembert looks deliciously dripping. Thanks.'

Andrew Latham smiled indulgently at his wife, as she cut herself a generous hunk of cheese and reached for sesame crackers. He was used to her manner and knew that what others might take for criticism was no more than the well-rehearsed persona Donna had appropriated when still at university in London, where incidentally they had met, as a way of coping with the apparent super-confidence of all those other LSE students she had been set amongst.

'Colonel Lavington,' he began, reaching for his own glass of red wine and taking a restrained sip, 'or Levington or

Livington or Lavingstone – remember this was before the good Doctor Johnson and his chums sought to regularise the English spelling system – was an engineer in the Parliamentary army at the siege of Bridgnorth.'

'The Civil War?'

'The same,' continued Andrew. 'It's about the only time that Bridgnorth featured in the history of this country, so everyone here knows all about it. Hasn't Donna shown you what's left of the castle?'

'No.' George Elliott glanced briefly at her sister.

'Oh, come on, Andrew,' spluttered Donna, showering biscuit crumbs on to the table, 'George has only been with us a couple of hours. She's here for a break, remember, not to collect another notch in her *I Spy Book of Castles*. Give the girl a break. We're only here tonight because you said you couldn't cancel, so then I couldn't dip out and I certainly couldn't leave George on her own, for God's sake!'

Andrew Latham smiled indulgently again at his wife but ignored her protestations. He leaned forward across the table to make himself heard more clearly in the hubbub of conversation.

'I'll take you tomorrow morning,' he said, smiling at George. 'In fact, if it's still dry when we leave here, we could go tonight. It's only just down the street. It won't take long. There's not very much to see.'

'Just a pile of old stones, really.' Donna helped herself to some more cheese, a varicose-veined Rocquefort this time. 'And we're not walking back that way tonight, Andrew, please. I've got heels on. I don't think I could make it.'

'Well, you could go home and put the percolator on for some coffee. I'll take George and show her the castle ruins. How about that?'

'Sorry, you've lost me here.' George Elliott looked quizzically at Andrew, beginning to wish she hadn't asked her question in the first place given the ensuing friction that she seemed to have precipitated between her sister and her brother-in-law. 'What's the big deal? I was just curious what this Lavington's Hole was.'

'That's the whole point,' said Andrew, warming to the task now. 'Colonel Lavington was ordered by the commander of the Parliamentary troops to end the siege of Bridgnorth by digging a tunnel under the east side of the hill on which Bridgnorth Castle stood. The plan was to dig the tunnel until they were right underneath the church that was in the middle of the Castle grounds and where the Royalists had their gunpowder stored and you can guess the rest.'

'So that's why there's only a bit of the Castle left?'

'No, not so.' Andrew chuckled. 'Fortunately, the Royalist soldiers could hear the Parliamentary engineers digging underneath and the Governor of the Castle decided that there wasn't much future in being blown sky-high, so he surrendered.'

'So why is there no Castle now then?'

'Well, like just about every other fallen-down castle in the country, Bridgnorth Castle was actually in a state of massive disrepair at the time anyway. After the Royalists surrendered, the Parliamentary commander ordered that what was left of the Castle should be pulled down and that's what happened. What's left is the bit they couldn't blow up, I guess.'

The muted conversation around the long table suddenly rose in volume, not in anger but in mirth, as one of the Old Lavs completed a tale that he had been regaling others with for several minutes. George turned towards the noise, noting the appreciative smiles on people's faces, the sense of warm companionship and the sheer comfort all clearly had with each other. These were people who knew each other well, who revelled in each other's company and were prepared to forgive individual idiosyncrasies for the sake of the greater pleasure of sharing a mutually enjoyable evening.

'So what's the origins of this Lavington Society? Is it some ancient practice that's been handed down for centuries?'

Andrew laughed, as did a couple of his companions sitting either side of him who overheard her query.

'The Old Lavs?' butted in Donna with a sneer. 'You must be joking! They only go back to nineteen ninety-seven. Andrew and his pals thought it would be a way of celebrating Blair's first election victory. Now it's just an excuse for an annual piss-up.'

'Which you don't seem to mind attending,' said George testily, feeling a trifle sorry for the constant verbal battering that her brother-in-law was receiving from her sister.

'Pay no attention to her,' laughed Andrew. 'You can bet your life that Donna will never miss the opportunity for a booze-up. No, we thought that Lavington was a symbol of the people's fight for democracy, a blow in the eye for the toffs, a smack in the face for the aristos. That's why we started the Lavington Society. Just a reminder, with a Bridgnorth face, of our heritage. Nothing too political really, just a night out to celebrate the social good.'

'And to get sloshed.' Donna raised her newly topped-up glass to the heavens. 'Here's to the Old Lavs. May they all get stuffed up Lavington's Hole!'

TWO

George Elliott, more properly known as Detective Inspector Georgina Elliott, had come to visit her sister and brother-in-law in Bridgnorth. The previous weekend George had split up from Larry Powell, the black police colleague who'd been sharing her life for the past couple of years, and decided on the spur of the moment to visit her sister. It was some time since she had spent time on her own and her apartment had felt empty all week. That was manageable while she was working, since the hours were inevitably irregular and she had deliberately immersed herself in work in order to stave off thoughts about the immediate future. Returning to her apartment late in the evening, she had had little time for more than a quick check of the day's post, a hastily-microwaved meal and sleep. Then Friday had arrived and the suddenly unwelcome promise of an empty weekend on her own, so on a whim she had telephoned Donna and, without going into detail, explained about the split from Larry.

'Come now.' Donna had insisted. 'You need a change of scene, girl. Get your stuff together and get yourself here.'

Donna and Andrew Latham had moved to the Shropshire hill-town of Bridgnorth a few years previously when Andrew had been appointed as headteacher of the Jack Mytton High School. For him it was a homecoming, as Bridgnorth had been the town he was born and grew up in, though for Donna it was more of a challenge. Much as she approved theoretically of farmers' markets, of free range produce, of hand-made clothes and shoes, and of local shops, in practice she missed the city stores she had grown up with in Manchester, experienced even as a penniless student in London, and then enjoyed in Sheffield, Leeds and Nottingham, as Andrew's career had advanced.

'It's just down the end of the road,' said Andrew, taking George's arm to steer her in the direction of the Castle Gardens and the remains of Bridgnorth Castle that he had promised to show her.

'And watch he keeps his hands to himself,' called Donna after them as they left her at the doorstep of the handsome Georgian house which had been their home in recent years. 'I could tell you a thing or two about what they get up to in those gardens at night. I don't want Andrew leading my little sister astray.'

George Elliott smiled at the thought of herself, aged forty, being led astray by her middle-aged brother-in-law. She glanced sideways at him. True, he was wearing well. Despite the indubitable stresses of the job he had, there were still plenty of laughter lines on his face, still a spring in his stride, still a sense of... what would she call it?...yes, joy wouldn't be too strong a word. Andrew was one of nature's optimists, a man who, whatever the cloud, always saw the silver lining.

'Pay no attention,' he laughed, as they negotiated the unevenly-slabbed pavement. 'You know your sister's mucky mind as well as I do, I guess. And the alcohol does tend to release even the mildest inhibition in her.'

He paused momentarily in his stride to glance at the elegant Georgian houses they were passing along the curving East Castle Street. George paused with him and shared his admiring view.

'I love this street. I always wanted to live here when I was a child,' Andrew continued. 'In one of these beautiful houses with their outlook over the Severn valley. It was like a dream come true when we could afford to buy one.'

'How long is it now? Five years?'

'No, seven,' he corrected her. 'Remember I was appointed just before the first Blair government in 1997. That's how the Lavington Society came about. When we moved in, I was amazed to find that several of the blokes I'd been at school with years ago in Bridgnorth were still here. Even more remarkably, given the natural small 'c' conservatism of small market towns like this, where even the arrival of a new Indian restaurant causes great excitement, so many of those old mates of mine were still lefties. That's how the Old Lavs came about.'

They had reached the end of the road and were now outside the honey-coloured stone of St Mary's church. Andrew steered his sister-in-law to the right and through the dark churchyard to the wall overlooking the grey mass of what is left of the keep of Bridgnorth Castle. In the darkness of the night, with a paper-thin moon giving a faint glow behind it, the stone keep, leaning scarily at its pronounced seventeen-degree angle as it had done for over three hundred years, looked ominous. How much more so must the whole castle have looked when it still stood before those Parliamentary forces pulled it down, George thought to herself.

'The story is that it has a more pronounced incline than the leaning Tower of Pisa.' He mirrored the incline with his left hand, as if he still found it unbelievable. 'Ever been there?'

'Yes,' she replied, recalling with a slight pang of regret the weekend break she had enjoyed there with her then lover, the now-retired Detective Chief Inspector Tallyforth. She still had the photograph he had taken of her, grinning inanely at him with her hands positioned as if she were holding up the Tower of Pisa that leaned demonically behind her.

'So that's it,' said Andrew, turning away from the grey-black shape that loomed behind them. 'Not much to see, is it? It's a bit parky out here, even at this time of year, isn't it? I could use another drink. Fancy one?'

'Sure thing,' replied George. 'And I don't think coffee will be sufficient.'

'Agreed. Let's see what we can rustle up. I'm sure we've still got some of that Laphroaig. That suit?'

THREE

'So, What d'you make of Andrew's castle then, eh?' quizzed Donna, sitting on the floral-patterned sofa with her legs curled underneath her ample bottom. 'Something else, isn't it?'

The room was large, with wooden window shutters pulled across the sash windows, a deep-stained oak floor on which sat a brightly-coloured Persian carpet, and a carved stone fireplace with a cast-iron basket in which the remains of a log fire glowed warmly. Several greying photographs in wooden frames decorated the magnolia walls and a range of knick-knacks sat on the mantelshelf and on other exposed surfaces in the room.

'M'm?' said George, surprised at this apparent change of interest in her sister's words.

'I'm joking,' spat Donna. 'It's a bit pathetic that all these people think that what they've got is some ancient monument to rank alongside the Pyramids and the Parthenon. It's just a bit of old stone that they failed to blow up at the end of the Civil War. Period. End of story. It's nothing to gloat about.'

Just then the tall figure of Andrew Latham entered the lounge of their home, bearing a silver tray with three glasses of yellow Laphroaig whisky.

'Donna enjoys mocking our small town pretensions,' he said, presenting a glass to each of the women. 'She'd like everyone to think that she was the world's greatest expert on metropolitan life, just because she grew up in Manchester.'

'Up yours too, matey,' responded Donna, taking a slug of whisky and resettling herself on the sofa, having moved up to allow her sister to sit beside her. 'Mister-bloody-dogooder-of-Shropshire.'

Andrew shifted uncomfortably in his leather armchair, opened his mouth to speak then thought twice about what he had been going to say, before trying again.

'I don't think we need to bore George with all that,' he said lamely.

'Why not?' asked Donna, with a ferocious gleam in her eye, like a lion poised for the kill. 'It's all you've been on about for the past week. Tell her. Go on. You know you can't resist it. Tell her.'

'What?' asked George Elliott, wide-eyed in suppliance trying not to inflame the argument that her older sister seemed intent on causing.

Andrew Latham sighed and crossed his legs. He still didn't want to go down this route, though he sensed that his wife was going to force him to do just that any moment now.

'Andrew has got this kid in his school that he accepted after he'd been kicked out of another school. Only this little toerag isn't grateful that he's been given another chance. Oh no, straightaway he's back in trouble at Andrew's place. Swearing at teachers. Dealing drugs. You name it, he's done it.'

'So?' queried George, aware from her colleagues in the Mercian force of the high frequency of drug-dealing in schools nowadays. 'Nothing unusual in that, I'm afraid. It's rife in Birmingham. Everywhere.'

'It's not just that,' said Andrew quietly, reluctantly allowing himself to be drawn into the discussion. 'This youth is a nasty piece of work all right and he's up before the governors on Wednesday week for his drug-dealing. I'd be surprised if we didn't exclude him as well, though there will be some special pleading on his side, because of his circumstances.'

'Bloody circumstances!' interjected Donna. 'Bloody excuses you mean.'

'What d'you mean?' queried George.

'His father was in Iraq,' Andrew sighed again.

The evening suddenly seemed colder. The blackened bits of log in the fireplace no longer gave off any heat and shadows had invaded the corners of the large room. George Elliott knew that what she had thought to be the regular stream of banter between Donna and Andrew now had a chillier undercurrent.

'Army?'

'Yes. And I'm afraid that's not all. The father was at Camp Breadbasket. He was one of those suspected of being involved in the abuse of Iraqi prisoners.'

George replaced her glass of Laphroaig on the polished table. The evening's merriment seemed a long way off. How could the two of them have moved so swiftly from then to now? Did they even realise that this was a matter of deeper importance than Andrew's enthusiasm for Bridgnorth's history? Or were they so tied into their call-and-response pattern of behaviour that they could no longer distinguish the significance of any matter that they discussed?

'You saw the pictures on the telly, didn't you, George?' said Donna Latham, almost gloating with excitement now at the prospect of revealing the gory details. 'Forcing those poor geeks to simulate cocksucking, giving them electric shocks, stripping them and humiliating them, standing on them and posing for photographs. If he was one of those soldiers, he really was some kind of weirdo. It's no wonder his son's turned out a bad 'un.'

'So what's the problem?' asked George Elliott, who could see the suggested connection between the father's misdemeanours and the son's misbehaviour, but not why this case was so exercising her sister and brother-in-law or why they had wanted to bring it to her attention.

'The problem is,' replied Donna waspishly, giving her husband a withering glance, 'that St Francis over there took pity on this kid, because of the father's circumstances, and brought him here one weekend to try to show him the good life. Some chance!'

George Elliott looked at the two of them sitting together there on the sofa, locked in this mutual battle of words that had become their *modus operandi* for as long as she could remember. She had not visited them for some time and had forgotten the wordy battles they were always engaged upon. It was a way of living together she did not envy but, she

11

thought, at least they were together and had stayed together for over twenty years. It was more than she had managed to do. She thought again of the four men who had featured large in her life – Andrew the PE teacher from her first posting in Coventry, her fellow-officer Roger Miles who had once threatened her with a knife, DCI Tallyforth her long-time partner-in-crime, as they used to jokingly refer to themselves in the good days, and more recently Larry Powell, whom Tallyforth had insisted on calling Enoch.

'What happened?' she asked.

'Tell her, St Francis,' insisted Donna Latham, grinning with the anticipated pleasure of hearing her husband recount an incident that made him look foolish.

Andrew sighed again and took a long sip from his whisky.

'The boy's name is Ryan Blakeway,' he began wearily and warily. 'What Donna's told you is absolutely correct. I did take him into my school when he'd been excluded from his previous place. I did know his father was in the army and serving in Iraq, though at that stage I didn't know about the Camp Breadbasket allegations. And I did bring him over here for a weekend when I first heard about the charges against British soldiers in Iraq.'

'Why?' asked George. She knew her brother-in-law had a strong sense of social justice and was much stronger in his belief that all humans were redeemable. They had argued much in the past. He would never accede to her view that there were good 'uns and bad 'uns, and there was not much you could do about it. They came from opposite ends of the spectrum in terms of human expectations.

'Because I knew more than he did at that stage. His social worker had alerted me to the fact that Blakeway senior was at this Camp Breadbasket where the soldiers involved in the abuses were stationed. And I knew from previous information I'd had that Blakeway senior was no angel; in fact, he had a record for fighting and violence before he joined the army. It was likely in my view and in that of the boy's caseworker that the father was involved in the abuse allegations.'

'But to bring him over here? What was all that about?'

'Exactly!' cut in Donna, relishing her husband's discomfort.

'I know, I know,' said Andrew, holding up his hands in mock surrender. 'Everything in my training and experience told me it was not something I should even have considered. But just listen to this. In the year he'd been at Jack Mytton High, Ryan had sworn at two of my staff, he's been caught selling cannabis to younger kids, and he's been given Grade A's for his English and Art coursework for GCSE and has won a prize for an essay he entered for a competition run by the local Rotary Club. It was a defence of Lenin. God, I'd never even heard of Lenin at his age. Does that tell you something of why I broke all my rules? This boy is a real one-off. I suppose I naively thought I could save him somehow.'

'And how did he repay you, St bloody Francis?' pressed his wife.

'OK, he stole some jewellery from our bedroom.'

'And?'

'And he was caught swapping the jewellery for drugs in the town.'

'And...?'

George saw that Andrew's body had sagged as his wife pressed home her questions. His shoulders had drooped, his arms had lowered themselves, like wet rags, between his legs and his handsome face had become grey and drawn.

'And, even after I'd sorted all that out with the local police and got him released with a caution, he found something even more wicked to do to get himself into trouble,' continued Andrew, aware that he was looking more and more foolish to his sister-in-law, the highly-trained and highly-experienced Mercian Police Force detective inspector. 'He stole a gun from the town museum in the Northgate.'

Donna was nodding to herself, as if this was the final piece of evidence needed to convict her unwise husband.

'What sort of a gun?' asked George Elliott.

'Oh, it's not just any old gun,' he replied. 'It's a pistol from the seventeenth century, muzzle-loading and with a wheel lock, which apparently dates it quite precisely to the period of the Civil War. It has the initials 'RH' scratched on it. It was apparently found in the old Governor's House, just up East Castle Street, about fifty years ago under the floorboards of one of the bedrooms, wrapped in Italian brocade.'

'Do we know who 'RH' is or was?'

'They think he was Sir Robert Howard of Clun who was the Governor of Bridgnorth Castle at the end of the siege of the town.'

'He was the one who surrendered when they heard Lavington's engineers digging under the Castle?'

'Yes, the same.'

This was getting more and more serious. Their voices had started to echo in the room, as if the house itself was expressing its apprehension. She was aware of Donna squirming on the sofa as the conversation moved away from her husband's error to more of the story of Bridgnorth in the Civil War.

'And the pistol? Did it work?'

'Well, after a fashion. Though I'm pretty sure that wasn't why Ryan took it.'

'So?'

'The pistol is a symbol for Ryan. In his warped mind, it stands for oppression.'

'See what I mean?' interrupted Donna triumphantly, delighted that she could once again act the scold. 'Complete twaddle! The boy's a thief and a toerag. That's all there is to it. You brought him into our home. He made off with my pearl necklace, tried to sell it for drugs, and then nicked a gun from the Northgate museum. He needs putting away.'

George Elliott put her hand on her sister's arm to hush her.

'Go on,' she instructed. 'I'm curious how an act of theft can come to be seen as justifiable.'

'OK, I screwed up,' admitted Andrew, with another long sigh. 'I shouldn't have brought him here. It was a mistake and I should have known better. But this kid is not, believe me, a run of the mill yobbo. I'd talked to him beforehand when I was trying to sort out his problems at school and the boy has a very unusual intelligence. Yes, it's misplaced. Yes, it's cock-eyed. But it is definitely there. Most teenage boys when they get into trouble either adopt a sullen stance, saying nothing, or they tell a pack of lies, or they blab on their mates. Ryan Blakeway does none of those. He argues with you.'

'What d'you mean?'

'Well, for instance, when I had to see him over this swearing incident, he didn't deny it, like many of them do, or say he was provoked. No, he started telling me that the obscenities he had been mouthing were only considered obscenities because of the hangover of Victorian attitudes in schools, that they were words that could be heard every single night on British TV, and that he bet I swore myself on occasion.'

'Too true,' cut in Donna, scratching her left ear absent-mindedly. She was enjoying this. 'Especially when you're using your famous DIY skills.'

He looked at her as if he was about to respond, then changed his mind before continuing.

'For another instance, when I had to deal with the drug-dealing, he started arguing that tobacco and alcohol were far more poisonous drugs than cannabis but it was okay for me and my staff to smoke on the school premises and to go to the pub every night.'

'And the pistol?' asked George.

'Well, Sir Robert Howard was the Governor of Bridgnorth Castle and leader of the King's forces, therefore, according to Ryan, he was oppressing the citizens of the town. To liberate his pistol from the museum was to show that the ordinary people were superior.'

'That's a bit weird, isn't it?' said George, stretching her legs out and folding her arms behind her neck.

'It's back there now. He handed it in at the police station and said what I've just told you. You should speak to him.' Andrew Latham reached for his whisky, grateful that he had reached the end of his tale and of his wife's sarcasm. 'He's a very unusual boy.'

No, she would not like that, she thought. This was a trivial crime, not the sort of thing that engaged her professionally nowadays. Besides, hadn't Andrew got it sorted now? Why did she constantly feel this need to unravel mysteries that were really nothing to do with her? Tallyforth used to complain of the same problem as an occupational hazard. Had she been too long in his company?

'Where is the boy now?'

'He's back at his mother's house now, I guess, till he comes before my governors or the courts send him down.'

'And meanwhile I've lost my pearl necklace and you need a top up,' said Donna, rising lumpily from the sofa and reaching for her sister's empty glass. 'Same again?'

FOUR

George Elliott had woken early, earlier than anyone else in fact, and so, rather than disturb her sister and brother-in-law, she had helped herself to a glass of orange juice and decided to have another look at the Castle remains. On her way out through the darkened hall, she'd stopped to borrow an old raincoat and picked up a couple of glossy leaflets about Bridgnorth lying on the timeworn oak settle that stood in the passageway beside the coats. At the heavy, studded front door she had paused again before leaving to take in what the first leaflet – a town trail guiding visitors around the key sites of the old town – had to say about East Castle Street where her sister lived. She read:

> 'The most interesting house in East Castle Street is the former Governor's House, now No18, the Apley Estate Offices, which is a brick building of circa 1633. The censuses of the nineteenth century show that this was a street inhabited mainly by wealthy or retired people. In 1861 a retired Indian colonel lived at No 17 (Old Castle House); a retired surgeon from the Indian Army lived at No 26; Henry Southwell, a carpet manufacturer employing a hundred people, lived at No 19; there were solicitors at Nos 18 and 15; a doctor at No 23; and one of Bridgnorth's first photographers at No 24.'

Pulling the door quietly behind her, she stepped out into the street where the early-morning birds were singing their eternal chorus of greeting and turned left towards the Castle ruins she had visited with Andrew the previous evening. It was only seven o'clock but the late April morning was still distinctly cool and she was glad of the borrowed raincoat. As she walked, she glanced at the elegant redbrick Georgian houses that she had recently read about and wondered about those distant inhabitants. Did the retired colonel from No 17 spend time reminiscing with the retired army surgeon from No 26 about their times in India? What sort of working conditions did Henry Southwell from No 19 provide for his carpet makers? Did the doctor at No 23 have to deal with industrial injuries from breaking carpet looms? Did the photographer hide underneath a black cloth to take his shots?

Of one thing she was sure – the solicitors would never have been short of work, drawing up deeds, witnessing documents, acting on behalf of their wealthy clients, ensuring that the minutiae of the law were observed by all concerned, or, if not observed, then interpreted in such a way that they might seem to be observed.

Reaching the end of East Castle Street and coming face to face with the imposing classical-style facade of Thomas Telford's St Mary's church with its huge, honey-coloured, Tuscan pillars, George Elliott opted to turn left through the churchyard rather than right toward the Castle ruins as she had originally intended. Something, she knew not what, seemed to propel her that way. Was it the early-morning mist rising from the river, portending a warmer day than had been evident recently? Was it the statement she had read in one of the tourist leaflets about the view from Castle Walk, that she was now approaching, being described by Charles I while staying at the Governor's House as "the finest in my dominion"? Or was it some inexplicable tickle in her stomach hinting that something murky was afoot that way?

George Elliott pulled herself up short. That was too much like Tallyforth, too much like his crazy hunches that had led them off on wild goose chases so frequently in the past. No, she decided, as she stepped on to Castle Walk and saw the shroud of white mist that lay like a thin blanket above the River Severn, it was not that. It was just....she couldn't really say. She paused to lean over the iron railings. The view wasn't that good now and not just because of the mist. True, you could see the wooded hillside opposite with its sandstone peak and beneath the mist the chocolate-tinged river snaking off in both directions. She could imagine it must have been a striking spectacle once. But now, beneath the line of the opposite woodlands, an extensive housing estate climbed in tiers up the steep bank, providing homes for the growing population of Bridgnorth.

Anyway, she thought, Charles I must have had his head chopped off fairly soon after he'd come out with that statement, so he couldn't have seen many more views, could he? George Elliott allowed a slight smile to play across her face.

She had gone left on Castle Walk, passing behind the garden of the Lathams' house and above the quaint funicular Castle Hill Railway, whose cream and blue coaches were rattling down their first journey of the day, when she arrived at a yellow metallic sign guarding the fenced off entrance to some steps. The sign stated that Stoneway Steps were closed until further notice to allow for necessary repairs to be effected. She was about to turn away and head back into the town centre, when she heard a scrabbling sound and then a hand appeared above the chipboard fencing. Within seconds the hand was followed by a Burberry-capped head and then the lithe body of a teenage boy, dressed in a dark blue track suit and white training shoes.

'What're you doing?' George Elliott asked. 'I thought the Steps were closed.'

The boy grinned.

'Just taking a short cut. No harm done. It's quicker that way. Me and my mates been coming up that way for weeks now. This time of day no one notices or cares.'

'Just a minute. If these Steps are officially closed, you're breaking the law here, young man.'

'Come on, lady. I'm not hurting anybody. Just taking a short cut. Anyway, d'you really think the pigs are going to waste their time arresting kids for walking up some old steps? Get real, lady'

Something in his manner had already made her suspicious but now her hackles started to rise.

'Wait there,' she ordered, moving towards him now and holding out her warrant card.

'It's you that needs to get real, young man. I'm a police officer and what you're doing is against the law. What have you got in your pockets?'

Why had she asked that? she wondered many times afterwards. What subconscious urge had driven her? There had been no need. At that stage he was just a daft lad who'd had the misfortune to bump into a representative of Her Majesty's Constabulary. At that stage he was just another youth wearing the badges of a wannabe hard knock – the checked Burberry cap, the black Umbro tracksuit with its distinctive white stripe down the side, the white Reebok trainers. At that stage he was nobody and he would just have received a ticking off from Detective Inspector George Elliott of the Mercian Force into whom he had had the bad luck to bump.

'Nothing. Honest,' he protested, trying to move away from her. 'All I done was take a short cut. That's all. Honest.'

'What have you got in your pockets?'

'Just my things. Fags. Lighter. iPod. There's no law against them, is there?'

'Show me.' George Elliott held out her hand.

With a sigh of frustration, the boy wrenched the cigarette packet, zippo lighter and white iPod from his pocket and held them out.

'Nothing else?'

'No, honest. I told you.'

'Come here. Let me check.'

His instinctive reaction was to take a step back and look as if he intended to walk away. His face took on that look of injured innocence, so common in someone who has been stopped all too frequently by the forces of moral right.

'This is police harassment. I done nothing wrong. You can't do this. I've got nothing.'

'We'll see about that, won't we? Hold your arms out straight.'

George Elliott took a determined step towards him, reaching out her hands towards his body. She felt around his upper body with expert fingers, noting the boniness of his young shoulders but also the muscularity of his arms and the firmness of his chest and stomach.

'And what's this then?' she asked, pulling a grey-white rectangular object from where it had been tucked into the back of his track suit. 'This doesn't look very personal. Care to explain?'

'I found it. Don't know what it is.'

He looked down at his trainers and a thin sliver of spit dribbled from the left side of his mouth.

'Where?'

He cleared the spit from his mouth with a swipe of his left hand, then looked insolently at her.

'Okay, I found it down there.' He pointed back behind him. 'It's just some old box. I thought it might fetch something.'

'Where precisely?'

'There's some sort of a hole they've been digging. I just went to have a look and found that old tat.'

George Elliott inspected the object. It was more than just a piece of old tat. It had a rectangular box shape with intricate decorative carvings on the upper part and weighed heavier than it at first looked. She wiped it against her raincoat, disturbing fragments of soil that still clung to it, and looked closely at it again. She guessed that the casing was a bone-like substance and might be surrounding some kind of inner box but was loath to investigate further in case she damaged anything.

'Do you know this might be valuable?' she began, waving the object at him. 'Have you any idea what this might be worth?'

The boy's eyes cast down to his shoes again but he said nothing.

'Did you honestly think that this was just a piece of old tat, as you called it, that you could flog? Didn't you see the decorations? You'd better come to the police station with me. You've got some explaining to do.'

She reached for her mobile phone and dialled her sister's home number, holding the boy's sleeve lightly.

'Donna, morning. Sorry to surprise you but I woke early and came out for a walk. Something odd has happened and

I need to know where the local police station is. I've got this lad with me acting suspiciously. Can't explain over the phone. Can you or Andrew come and find me? I'm at the top of Stoneway Steps.'

She held the phone away from her and grimaced at her sister's swearing.

'Yeah, I know. I'm sorry. But if you could, that would be really helpful.'

She snapped the phone shut.

'You just stand nice and still,' she said to the check-capped youth who stood sullenly before her, shifting uneasily in his scuffed white trainers. 'We need to sort this out before I let you go. What's your name anyway?'

He hesitated, then gave her a defiant look.

'Ryan Blakeway.'

FIVE

To save time getting to the police station at the opposite side of town, Andrew Latham had reversed his cherry-red Ford Mondeo into the top of the cobbled Cartway, one of Bridgnorth's oldest streets and the only route at one time for wheeled vehicles to travel from the river side up to the town's centre. Spotting George Elliott and her charge in his distinctive checked cap and sullen look, he papped his horn and opened one rear door and the passenger door.

'I think you know this young man.' George Elliott settled into the front seat next to her brother-in-law. 'Didn't you mention his name to me last night?'

Andrew Latham glanced in his mirror, then spun round with alacrity.

'You!' he said, his face agape in astonishment. 'What's he been up to?'

George Elliott briefly explained what had happened.

'I should have guessed, shouldn't I? If anyone of your age was going to be involved in all this, it had to be you, didn't it, Ryan Blakeway? What the hell do you think you were playing at?' Andrew Latham glared at the adolescent behind him.

There was no reply from the back seat. Ryan Blakeway sat impassively, his head bowed, his eyes focused on some invisible speck on the right knee of his track suit bottoms.

'I mean, what on earth were you doing, Ryan? After all the trouble you've got yourself into lately, don't you think you might just have taken things easy for a while? Given yourself some breathing space, some time for reflection? This is just crazy.'

Still no response from the back seat. Except that the boy's right foot began to tap impatiently and nervously.

'Ryan! Ryan, look at me, for God's sake!' shouted Andrew Latham, his face beginning to redden in anger at the dumb insolence of this youngster he had so recently sought to help. 'What on earth were you doing down there? The Steps have been closed for weeks. You must have known that. Were you looking for something? Or just being bloody-minded again and breaking the law?'

There was a silence. George Elliott could feel the tension. Curiously, although she was the police officer and not her brother-in-law, this interrogation, if that's what it might be called, one-sided as it was up to now, reminded her more of the time she had been summoned before her headteacher at the school she and her sister had attended for allegedly stealing some other girl's bike. Even though another girl had eventually owned up, George still could feel that heat of shame that reddened her neck when the headteacher, the formidable Miss Hicks, had accused her. It was like that now.

'Just curious, that's all,' said Ryan Blakeway at last. 'A mate of mine said that they'd found some bones when they were digging up the ground to do the repair. I just wondered what it all looked like.'

'What was that?' interrupted George Elliott, confused by this new line. 'Bones? What about bones? Where?'

'Dunno. It was just a rumour. Thought I'd have a look.'

'Do you know anything about bones being found, Andrew?' George Elliott turned to look at her brother-in-law, whose face was still suffused with deep pink, despite the fact that the youngster was now responding.

'Never heard of anything like that,' he replied. 'Who told you that?'

He had swung round to face the youngster again, as had George Elliott. The car seats creaked as they adjusted positions. Outside the grey sky was just beginning to brighten as a weak sun forced its way through the cloud cover.

'Just someone at school. His father works for the Cliff Railway. Said it was all hush-hush, in case, you know....in case it was a body.'

'Jesus Christ!' expostulated Andrew Latham. 'So you heard a story that a body might have been found in the ground by Stoneway Steps and you decided to go and have a look to see what you could see. Is that right?'

'Yeah, sort of.' Ryan Blakeway pulled the peak of his baseball cap forward over his forehead. 'Though it wasn't as straightforward as that.'

'What d'you mean, Ryan?' asked George, deciding she needed to intervene at this stage to bring the temperature down a little.

'Well, my mates dared me to do it.'

'Why? I don't understand.'

'It's just a story,' he responded, scratching his left knee. 'They say there's a ghost on the Steps. An old lady, dressed in grey. Loads of people say they've seen her but I don't believe any of that crap.'

'What's that got to do with this morning's little escapade?' asked George.

This was getting more and more confused by the second. First, this man-child bumping into her at the top of the steps, who turned out to be the same Ryan Blakeway that Andrew had been telling her about the previous evening. Then some story about bones being found in the ground. And now a tale about a ghost. Boys daring each other was no new phenomenon. And it wasn't just boys either. She and Donna had spent time in their youth doing exactly the same, daring one another to go inside an old air-raid shelter or to leap across railway lines before a train approached.

'I think I can help,' interrupted Andrew Latham, whose face was now returning to its normal colour. 'Bridgnorth is an old town, George, as you well know. And it has its fair share of ghost stories, like any old town, I guess. This particular story concerns a lady who was buried in the grounds of the chapel halfway down the Stoneway Steps. Allegedly she died in a fire with her children in her arms and they say that she returns from time to time hunting for her children. I'm sure there was a tragedy of that sort at one time but, to tell the truth, most people just treat it with the scepticism it deserves. Have you ever seen a ghost? Do you believe in ghosts?'

'No to both questions. But I still don't understand. What's this story got to do with your illicit visit this morning?'

Ryan Blakeway, still sullen, still staring at his legs, continued.

'Well, we thought that, if they had found some bones and it was a body, it might have been her, the Lady in Grey. They're a bunch of tossers, my mates. Got no guts. So I said I'd go and have a butcher's to prove there was nothing to be scared of.'

'And?'

'Well, there wasn't. Isn't, I mean. I don't know about the bones. I couldn't see anything. Expect they've moved them somewhere. If there was any like. So I had a little feel around and found this box thing you've got.'

So it was genuinely pure chance that had led to his discovery of the strange carved box she still held in her hand. She glanced at it surreptitiously before turning back to him.

'And thought you'd not only prove to your mates that they were silly but you'd have the bonus of a little something you could flog, eh?' said George.

'Just my luck to bump into a copper, wasn't it?' he complained. 'Ninety-nine times out of a hundred, there'd have been no-one at the top of the Steps. And, even if there had been, it would have been some old git walking their dog. And I had the bad luck to meet you.'

'And even worse, Ryan Blakeway,' said Andrew Latham, turning to face the front now and engaging first gear, 'you had the misfortune to be apprehended by my sister-in-law, who just happens to be a Detective Inspector with the Mercia Police. I think it's time we took you down to the station. They'll know what to do with you.'

SIX

Donna Latham was billowing around the kitchen in a voluminous pink dressing gown when they returned from the police station. The powerful aroma of fried bacon wafted through the air, joined by the more subtle smells of coffee brewing and bread toasting.

'Thought we could all do with a good breakfast,' she announced as her husband and sister came through the door. 'Been a bit of a funny start to the day really, hasn't it? Sit down at the table. George, pour the coffee. I'll bring the bacon sandwiches over and then you can tell me all about it.'

The kitchen they were in was huge, with stained oak floorboards, a spacious old stripped pine table and oddly-assorted wooden chairs at its heart. The plain cream walls were filled with brassily colourful art nouveau prints, out of character with the old room but strangely appropriate, George thought.

She sat down and poured coffee, while her brother-in-law excused himself to visit the toilet.

'Well?' queried Donna, placing a steaming bacon sandwich in front of her sister. 'So you met the little toerag, eh? What did you think?'

George held her coffee mug with both hands in front of her face, half-closing her eyes as she savoured its nutty aroma.

'Hmm, interesting. He looks and talks just like anyone else of his age. In fact, he could pass as a model for a typical ASBO but there's something about him which I sensed but which he wasn't letting on.'

'Fill me in,' invited Donna. 'Remember I've only heard half the story. I know you caught him climbing over the chipboard at the top of the Steps. I know he'd liberated some box thing from a hole where the Council had been working on their repairs but what else?'

George Elliott sipped from her mug of coffee before replying.

'The local bobbies have given him a caution. Not much else they could do really. The box has been sent off to Shrewsbury Museum Service for examination. He claimed his mates had dared him to go there because of some half-cock story about some bones being found while they were digging which they thought could be something to do with the ghost.'

'The Lady in Grey? That one's been running ever since we've been here and I bet for decades beforehand. You ought to visit the Theatre. They dine out on that story.'

Donna Latham's chubby face creased in a well-used smile.

'I didn't know there was a theatre? Where?'

'You talking about the Theatre on the Steps?' interrupted Andrew Latham, joining them at the table now and reaching for his coffee. 'Halfway up and halfway down Stoneway Steps. It used to be a Congregationalist Chapel, then the local free churches merged, the building became redundant and the local luvvies bought it for next to nothing. I was at school at the time but my dad was involved. I remember he used to take me with him sometimes on Saturday mornings to see what they were doing. It was a mammoth enterprise and it took years before they started putting on plays. The highlight of the year, though, was the pantomime. I can remember going to see those.'

'Bunch of sad people dressing up, more like,' said Donna, pouring herself another cup of coffee. 'And he still insists on us going every year. Honest, it makes you weep. Come on, Andrew. Eat up.'

'Sorry, I still don't understand,' said George. 'What's the theatre got to do with the ghost?'

'They say,' replied Donna with heavy sarcasm, 'that she haunts the theatre. They've even had all-night vigils with the doors locked *et cetera, et cetera*. You can imagine, can't you, George? They go in there believing and any slight disturbance in the night convinces them, even though it was more likely a rat under the floorboards or a pigeon in the rafters.'

'And,' cut in Andrew again between bites of his sandwich, 'the Lady in Grey is one of the ghost stories the theatre people use every Halloween on their Ghost Walk through Bridgnorth.'

'You mean there's more than one ghost in this town?' George laughed, spitting breadcrumbs indelicately.

'I told you, this is an old town. All old towns have stories like this. A lot of them go back to the Civil War days. That's really when much of the sadness of this town occurred.'

Donna Latham adjusted her pink dressing gown, pulling it up to her knees, and winked at her sister, as she stood up and moved over to the work surface with the cafetière to refill it.

'Are you ready, George? You're going to get the full works now. The all-time history of Bridgnorth, as told by Andrew 'Schama' Latham.'

Andrew Latham laughed briefly at his wife's mocking description of him. He had for too many years had to put up with her banter.

'You remember I told you last night about the plan to blow up the Castle?'

'Lavington and his hole,' George laughed. 'How could I ever forget the Old Lavs' *raison d'être*?'

'Right, but what I didn't tell you was why the Parliamentarians were so keen to take Bridgnorth.'

'Weren't they just intent on taking down castles everywhere as representing all they were opposed to?'

Oh dear, she was thinking. I really should know more about the Civil War and Cromwell and Charles I and all that sort of thing but it had only been covered lightly at school and she'd never felt any need subsequently to read more. Until she got there that weekend it had never really featured in her life. To tell the truth, she was surprised that she had become so absorbed in this bit of history and, despite Donna's bad-mouthing of her husband's enthusiasm for the topic, had become genuinely interested. She shifted her body slightly away from her sister to give him her full attention.

'There's some truth in that but, in Bridgnorth's case, it's a bit more complicated. You see, Shropshire was an important area for Charles I when he began his disastrous campaigns against the parliament he had so outrageously ignored for so many years. It's a county that, certainly since the time of the Conqueror and probably before, has been very wealthy. It still is. You only have to drive a few miles out of Bridgnorth to see the large country estates and their manor houses still in occupation, despite centuries of reform. The nobs still own nearly everything'

'Get on with it, Andrew,' pleaded Donna. 'Save the Red Flag stuff for another day. George is familiar with all that.'

'Sorry,' he grinned. 'Anyway, as I was saying, Shropshire was an important area for the king. He recruited here, he raised money from the gentry here, he thought he could rely on this county for constant support. However, as Shakespeare said, "there is a tide in the affairs of men which, taken at the flood, leads on to fortune". Or, in Charles's case, to misfortune. After the Battle of Naseby in 1645, the king was all but finished, although some areas, including parts of Shropshire, continued to resist. The Parliamentarian troops had gradually got control of most of the county by the start of the following year but Bridgnorth remained the major Royalist stronghold. In fact, Charles himself was here twice in late1645, staying at the Governor's House just up the road from here.'

'Was that when he said about "the finest view in my dominion"?

'God, I'd forgotten how quick you catch on to things, George,' replied Andrew, looking sharply across at his sister-in-law. 'It may well have been then but who knows? I don't know why the tourist people make such a big fuss of it. He probably said the same sort of thing all over the country.'

'So, how did Bridgnorth finally get captured? And why was this important?' asked George, seeking to shift a recalcitrant scrap of bacon that had lodged itself between two teeth.

'Apparently all the bigwigs of the county had assembled in Bridgnorth after they'd been chased out of their strongholds elsewhere, so it was the final important battle for the Parliamentarians. A troop of soldiers was sent from Shrewsbury to take the town, there was some kind of battle in the grounds of St Leonard's church at the other end of town, then the Royalist troops withdrew within the Castle walls, burning most of the town on their way. That's where many of the ghost stories arose. Folk were burned out of their homes, loads of them died, and those that survived had to live in home-made tents or in sandstone caves. For some strange reason the town still wants to be remembered for supporting the king, despite the cruel things that his soldiers did to the ordinary people.'

'Yes, yes, we know about the oppression of the poor, Andrew,' interrupted Donna impatiently, tapping her fingers on the table. 'Get on with it, for God's sake.'

'Okay, so I can see there might have been reasons for stories arising from that tragic sequence of events. And I know how it all ended, thanks to your Colonel Lavington. But you said that the Lady in Grey had died in a fire and been buried in the chapel. What's that got to do with the Civil War and the siege of Bridgnorth?'

Andrew Latham sighed and sipped from his coffee cup.

'Stories get confused over time, George. But what I told you about the Lady in Grey is correct. Clearly if she was buried at the chapel, she couldn't have been from Civil War times because there was no such thing as a Congregationalist chapel then. But stories and timescales get mixed up over the years. Maybe she was something to do with the Royalist soldiers' burning of the town. Maybe that's how she died.'

'I'd like to see this Theatre on the Steps,' said George. 'And have a look at where Blakeway found that box. If I arrange the latter, can you fix the theatre?'

'No problem,' answered Andrew Latham. 'Leave it with me.'

SEVEN

It had taken some time to locate someone at the County Council offices who was responsible for the renovation work on Stoneway Steps. It turned out that the rumour Ryan Blakeway had picked up about bones being found was accurate. A workman digging into the ground to get to the twisted roots of trees that had found their way into the structure of the wall on one side of the steps had come across bones. At first he had thought it was just irregular bones but then, as he dug, he had found more and more, so he had summoned the foreman. He had taken one look at the bones already found, scraped at the soft earth with his bare hands and realised that these were more than just odd bones and that these might be the remains of a body. At that point work had ceased, the site had been sealed, and the police had been informed.

This much George Elliott learned from her visit to Bridgnorth Police Station with Ryan Blakeway and her brother-in-law. The officer in charge, Police Constable Roger Walsh, after cautioning the youngster and sending him on his way with a flea in his ear and a warning about future conduct, had given her a full account.

'We sent for CID immediately, ma'am,' he had told her. 'You don't get anything like that normally in this town. We get more suicides than murders, to tell the truth. The bridge is a favourite place for jumpers and then there's the river of course. It's a quiet place, apart from the youngsters coming out of the pubs on Saturday nights. But that's the same everywhere nowadays, isn't it? A mate of mine used to work in Wolverhampton and there was much more bother there. I'm not racist but you do have to wonder about all that immigration and what it did to places like Wolverhampton. They have different habits, don't they, some of them? I know it's not politically correct to say so now, Inspector, but that Enoch Powell had a point, didn't he?'

George Elliott felt her face drain of its colour, not just in exasperation at the attitudes this man was portraying, which she knew were still sadly common enough in the police force, especially in largely-white communities like Bridgnorth, but at the mention of the name Enoch Powell. That was the name that Tallyforth had given her former lover, Inspector Larry Powell, the policeman from Wolverhampton she had met on a murder case they had been working on. The image of his powerful black body resting on snowy white sheets next to her caused a sharp shiver in her heart.

'I don't think your Chief Constable would be happy to hear you making remarks like that,' she said, seeking to control her face and at the same time drive out the image of Larry Powell from her mind. 'Whatever your friend's experiences were in Wolverhampton, you must accept that we live in a multicultural society and that all cultures have a contribution to make to our society.'

'Oh, I know that, ma'am, don't get me wrong,' Walsh had replied, backing off now. 'I was just saying things are generally much quieter in this town. That's all. So, when this bloke from the Council came to say they'd found what they thought was the remains of a body in the ground by Stoneway Steps, I had to send for outside help immediately. This was way beyond my experience, believe me.'

'And what did CID find?'

He told her how the forensics team had cleared all the soil away and how they could clearly see that what the workman had disturbed with his shovel had been a body. The bones, including the skull, were laid out clearly, except for the ones that workman had dug up already. They had taken a huge number of photographs from every possible angle. Then they had removed all the bones, bagged them all up and taken them off for further examination.

'And?'

'Nothing yet, ma'am. That was only a couple of days ago. CID gave instructions that the site was to be untouched until further notice, so the workmen haven't been down there since Wednesday. I can't tell them when they can start work again. They might have to dig further to see if there's anything else there. Who knows?'

George was ticking things off in her head – the sort of questions she would always pursue on a murder inquiry. Even though she knew this was not typical of a murder inquiry, she had a routine that had always helped in the past.

'Have their been any suspicious disappearances around here recently?'

Walsh looked straight back at her, aware she was testing him.

'Not that's been reported here, ma'am. I've been working at this station for the past fifteen years and I would have known. Besides I'm a local boy. Grew up in the town before I joined the force.'

'Forgive me asking, constable, but how old are you?'

'Forty-four, ma-am.'

And that was as much as she knew when she arrived at the top of the Stoneway Steps later that morning, where awaiting her was Norman Shaw, the District Surveyor. George Elliott had changed into black jeans and a denim bomber jacket in preparation for their visit. She noted his sharp, pinstripe suit worn underneath the luminous green jacket and the slight stoop in his posture. She guessed that he rarely strayed out of his office.

'Good morning, Inspector,' he began, his face frozen into a professional smile, 'you'll be needing one of these, I'm afraid. Health and Safety you know.'

She took the yellow plastic hat he handed to her and placed it on her head, flattening the spikes in her hair. Norman Shaw's silvery hair was likewise covered.

'Be careful, Inspector. The steps can be quite slippery at this time of year and with all the muck off the workmen's boots, you know....'

He unlocked the padlock securing the chipboard door and led her through. George Elliott followed him as he gingerly headed down the uneven steps curving downhill, until they came to a further recently-created chipboard gateway, where Norman Shaw indicated a ladder that that been placed against the wall.

'It's up there I'm afraid. Can you manage?'

She was about to say something but settled for a steely glance instead. Plenty time for harsh words later, if they were needed.

The scene when they reached the top of the retaining wall was unexceptional. There were the tools of the workmen – wheelbarrow, spades, forks, trowels and so forth. There were piles of chipped, weather-worn bricks and some new ones, ready for replacement. There was a small pile of dead vegetation and branches of trees. And there was a hole. Not a massive one, maybe the length of a small human being lying flat on the ground. Which presumably was the assumption that everyone was working on. Nothing in it now, of course, except for signs that someone had been digging into the side of the hole. That must have been the youngster, she thought. Searching for buried treasure. Typical, she thought. An adult wouldn't have thought of that. A boy might have. And that's why he'd got lucky. Until he climbed over the gateway in front of her a few hours earlier.

'Did you see the remains?' she asked Norman Shaw, as the two of them stood there in their yellow hard hats staring into the pit. 'Before they took them away, I mean?'

'Yes. My deputy came to see what was what when the foreman rang. It was he who concluded that there might be a body here. I came later to check out what he had said. The police were already here by then, of course. I had decided to alert them immediately.'

'And were you convinced they were human remains?'

Shaw's lips slanted downwards slightly and his eyes narrowed, as if such questioning of his interpretation was beneath his dignity.

'Oh yes, without a shadow of a doubt. I had wondered when I was first told. I thought it might have been an animal. These steps used to be known as Donkey Steps, you know, because they were one of the main routes up from the river and donkeys were used to carry goods up and down them. But when I saw the skull, there was no doubt in my mind. That was definitely a human being.'

She wondered why he might have thought a donkey could possibly have been buried above the wall but said nothing.

'It looks quite a small space. Would you say it was a small body? A child's maybe?'

The look of disdain re-appeared on his face and he smiled wanly in her direction.

'Could be, Inspector, could be indeed. But it's not my territory you know. You'll have to ask your colleagues who came to examine it and who took the remains away. They will give you a much better picture than I ever can. I'm a surveyor, Inspector, not a detective.'

Too true, George Elliott thought. Should never have expected a clear answer from a bureaucrat.

EIGHT

The Theatre on the Steps was quite a surprise, however. Donna Latham had offered to take her there because Andrew had been sent to find Tony Alexander, the chairman of the local Historical Society and part-time steward of the town's volunteer-run museum. George's brother-in-law had insisted that she could find out more precisely about the history of Bridgnorth Castle and its surrender in the Civil War and subsequent destruction.

'But you've already told her all she could possibly need to know,' Donna had wailed, as she pulled an old coat over her shoulders. 'For God's sake, Andrew, give the girl a break. She's not doing a bloody Open University degree you know. I'm sure you've bored her sufficiently already.'

In George Elliott's mind, however, was already forming a series of questions about those human remains that had been found in the renovation work. It was unlikely, she surmised, that they were recent. If anyone had gone missing in suspicious circumstances in Bridgnorth in the past few years, there would have been a record of it or, at the very least, local knowledge of it. That clodhopping local bobby had made it clear that he knew nothing of it. It was too unlikely and difficult a site for someone to have shipped in a body from outside. So, it was likely to be from some time in the past and maybe the distant past. Where was this site in relationship to the Castle Walls, for instance? Did the Stoneway Steps exist at the time of the Civil War?

The local history buff might provide useful clues, she had thought, so she'd agreed with her brother-in-law's plan.

They had to take the funicular railway down because of the steps closure and then walk back on the section of Stoneway Steps still open up to the Theatre, beyond which was another chipboard gateway preventing access to the upper reaches of the steps.

'I'm knackered,' puffed Donna Latham, pulling her clothing away from her plump body where exertion had caused it to stick. She was wearing multicoloured dungarees over a white blouse with a large red woollen scarf draped around the neck of her old overcoat. 'Every time I do this, I swear I'll never come up here again. And now I'm doing it. I must be mad. Give me a minute to catch my breath.'

George Elliott, slightly out of breath herself, though she was by far the slimmer and fitter of the two women, was grateful for the momentary pause to take in the large brick building that housed the Theatre on the Steps. There was nothing distinguished about the building itself, it was a functional oblong box, as no doubt its Non-conformist creators, who scorned elaboration, had wanted it to be. It must have taken some belief, she thought, to set about building on this spot with all materials having to be brought up those steep steps.

'Okay,' said Donna, giving her blouse one final flap, 'I don't think I'll need major surgery this time. Lead on, Macduff.'

George Elliott smiled and opened the wooden door into the theatre. It was heaving with activity. Andrew had warned her that there was a Youth Theatre that met there on Saturday mornings – some of the youngsters attended the Jack Mytton High School – but she hadn't expected as much. A gaggle of excitable young girls was standing around an electric piano where a bald-headed man was giving instructions on a song they had been rehearsing. A middle-aged woman with ginger hair was standing behind the bar pouring orange juice into paper cups while a kettle boiled steamily behind her. When they opened the door into the auditorium, they could hear and see another group of youngsters acting on the blackened boards of the stage, while on the back rows another cluster was donning ballet shoes ready for their turn.

'Well, hello there, can I help you?'

George Elliott looked round. Behind her was a tall man with thick black hair and a twirling handlebar moustache. His voice had the deep timbre of an ancient musical instrument.

'George, this is Gareth Wellbeloved,' said Donna. 'He runs the Theatre on the Steps. Gareth, this is my sister, Detective Inspector Elliott.'

'Charmed, I'm sure,' Gareth Wellbeloved said, sweeping his right arm theatrically across his chest and bowing. 'Welcome to our very special little theatre. How can I help you? I've not been breaking any laws lately, have I? Or am I to be arrested for acting with intent?'

He laughed aloud at his own pathetic joke, which he must have told hundreds of times. George Elliott smiled, more out of politeness than out of anything else. She had met his type before.

'You're very busy here. I'd no idea Bridgnorth was such a hotbed of thespian talent.'

'We aim to please. All the world's a stage *et cetera*, you know.' He smirked, a man who was obviously pleased with himself for reasons that no one else could quite see.

'Mr Wellbeloved, I wonder if you could tell me about your ghost,' George Elliott cut across his posturing. 'Have you ever seen her?'

'The Lady in Grey? Yes, many times. She stands over there, by the bar. And she never buys a drink. Quite harmless, mind you.' He grinned a well-rehearsed grin.

George and Donna looked to the curved wooden bar where he was pointing. There was naturally nothing to be seen.

'What's her story?' George asked.

'To tell the truth, I never believed a word of it,' he began. 'We get quite a few of these paranormal societies wanting to spend a night in here investigating and they all say they've seen her. But I personally never have. I'll tell you one tale though that had me half-believing. There was a bunch of people from the *Shropshire Review* and their friends who came here one night with video cameras and the lot. They swear that their cameras switched themselves on when there was no one near and switched off likewise. But what was really curious was the fact that they were all asked to sit in the

39

auditorium and to concentrate really hard, then write down a name. Eight out of ten of them wrote "Mary".'

'Yes, I can see that was a bit odd.'

'But that's not all. There's a headstone outside the back door of the theatre. It goes back to when this was a chapel and there was a graveyard out there. The name on that headstone is Mary. There's no way they could have known that because they were locked inside all night. They only found out when they rang me the next day and asked me if the name had any significance.'

The smirk on Gareth Wellbeloved's face was that of an accomplished raconteur, of someone who liked to startle others with extreme tales, as if somehow their telling enhanced him.

'Phew,' said Donna, applying lip salve to her lips. 'That's some coincidence, Gareth.'

'So the Lady in Grey is called Mary,' mused George. 'What about this business of her dying in a fire with her children in her arms?'

'Yes, I've heard all that too, though I don't know where it came from. I'm not an expert in these matters.'

George Elliott scratched her head and stifled a yawn. Where was all this leading? Was it of any significance at all? Why was she pursuing this matter?

'You don't by any chance know this boy Ryan Blakeway, do you?' she asked, chancing her luck.

Gareth Wellbeloved's face rapidly changed and the corners of his mouth turned down in a sneer, visible even beneath his outrageous moustache.

'Yes, I know him, the little so-and-so. He and his friends are forever banging on the door or shouting obscenities when we have a show on. That's his sister singing over there. She couldn't be more different. Lovely lass.'

He pointed at an attractive, auburn-haired fourteen-year-old who was fastening on her pink ballet shoes.

'Is that all you know of him?'

'I know the father's in the army but I don't know any more. As I say, the daughter's perfectly okay so why he's gone off the rails, heaven only knows. Why? Is he in trouble again?'

'Yes, you could say that. Anyway, if that's all you know of him.... Thank you.'

But Gareth Wellbeloved was not finished. His eyes lit up and his moustache bristled with theatrical excitement. He raised his right hand, pointing upwards with a bony index finger.

'Inspector, there's another ghost here too, you know.'

'Sorry?'

'Oh yes, if you believe in 'em, we got 'em,' Gareth Wellbeloved laughed and his black moustache puffed out from his upper lip. 'There is a man in a black coat and black hat. Stands up there on the balcony. One of our members says he saw him when he was on stage singing. And several people claim they've seen him from the steps trying to get in through the door of the theatre.'

'Wow,' said Donna, a great smile breaking out across her face. 'So we have Mary, Mary, Quite Contrary, the mysterious Lady in Grey and now we have the dashing Man in Black. The plot thickens.'

George Elliott looked at her sister and at Gareth Wellbeloved and realised they thought this whole thing was just a huge joke. She clenched her fists but decided not to say anything. There was more to all this than met the eye.

NINE

They found Tony Alexander enjoying a beer with Andrew Latham at the bar of the Railwayman's Arms, originally the Buffet Room of the Severn Valley Railway station and designed to look like a pub of fifty years ago. Tony Alexander looked and acted like one of those characters that people say have disappeared from modern life. Though not especially tall, his frame seemed large, especially when he greeted someone, clasping their right hand in his mighty paw and patting their shoulder simultaneously with his other hand. He wore cavalry twill trousers and a bulky brown turtleneck sweater, above which his silvery beard and sparkling eyes set off his large, egglike, bald head. George recognised him as the man who had proposed the toast to Lavington's Hole the previous evening.

'Ah, Inspector,' he started. 'What's your poison? The good thing about Saturdays is that the pubs stay open all day, so there's no need to rush.'

'What do you recommend?' George Elliott asked. It was four in the afternoon and she already felt she'd had a pretty full day.

'The Hobsons bitter is what I always have. Local brew. From Cleobury. Best beer around, if you ask my opinion.'

'Okay, I'll have a half of that. Thank you.'

George looked around the bar. Nowadays, thanks to a remarkable rescue operation after the Beeching cuts of the nineteen-sixties, the Severn Valley Railway was a highly successful private enterprise with steam trains running at weekends throughout the year between Bridgnorth and Kidderminster. Volunteers crowded to sign up for the opportunity of donning old railwaymen's heavy uniforms and waving red or green flags or blowing whistles.

The walls of the bar were adorned with railway memorabilia, including old station signs from around the country. Most of the customers were male, speaking in loud voices, many smoking unfiltered cigarettes. A good coal fire in the grate completed the sense of stepping back in time.

'And a pint for me, Tony, you old soak,' said Donna, entering the pub a few seconds after her sister. 'Expect dearest hubby's already had his quota, eh?'

Andrew Latham laughed ruefully.

'Only the one,' he replied. 'But now you mention it, I might just have another. This Hobsons is excellent. Here, Tony, let me get them.'

'Nonsense, what else am I supposed to use my pension for, if I can't spend it on some of you lot who are paying it. Sit yourselves down over there and I'll bring the beer over. Sure you won't have a pint, inspector?'

George Elliott declined. She had not decided whether or not to return to Birmingham that evening, so needed to keep her head clear, in case she needed to drive. She followed her sister and brother-in-law to a stained wooden table set below a glossy advertisement for holidays in sunny Paignton, featuring a young woman in a red and purple striped bathing costume waving an orange towel. It was all curiously incongruous with the world outside, even with Bridgnorth itself, but at the same time comforting in a strange way.

'Well, Inspector, so why are you so interested in Bridgnorth Castle and its fall?' asked Tony Alexander, placing the tray of drinks in the centre of the oblong table.

'Has Andrew explained?'

'Yes, I know all about the Blakeway boy. I taught his father.'

George Elliott pulled a querulous face at her brother-in-law.

'I ought to explain,' interrupted Andrew Latham. 'Tony was my predecessor as head of Jack Mytton. That's how I know him so well. That's how I knew where to find him on a Saturday afternoon.'

'Creature of habit, I'm afraid,' said Tony Alexander, reaching for his pint. 'Don't worry, Inspector, Andrew's told

43

me all about your little *contretemps* with Master Blakeway and, although I've never knowingly met the lad, from what I know of his father, his behaviour doesn't surprise me.'

'Was he a bad 'un too?'

He stroked his stubbly beard. His bright eyes twinkled behind the steel-framed glasses.

'Certainly was. Always in trouble. God knows how we managed to keep him in school for five years. When he decided to join the army, I thought it was the best thing for him. Give him a bit of discipline. Anchor him, know what I mean? I didn't know then he'd end up where he is now.'

'You mean in Iraq?'

Tony Alexander shook his head and took another gulp of his beer.

'Yes, but I mean waiting for the result of this Camp Breadbasket business they say he might have been involved in. I mean, you think, you hope they'll grow out of it, don't you? That's part of what we believe in education, isn't it? That we can draw them out, show them better ways, help them to better lives. But Tom Blakeway, God Almighty!'

There was a silence between them, though there was a steady hum of loud conversation elsewhere in the room and between the barman and his assistant as they wiped glasses. A train hissed into the station behind the bar, its engine grinding noisily to a halt and slowly dying.

'Were you surprised at the nature of the allegations?' George asked.

'I ought to say yes, that I was.' Tony Alexander's large face looked sad beyond belief. 'But I wasn't. He was sexually precocious at a very early age. One of my staff caught him simulating masturbation outside the girls' toilets once when he was only twelve. Another time he was found encouraging younger boys to get their penises out on the playing fields so he could take photos of them. He was always touching up the girls in the corridors. On several occasions he was suspected of creating filthy graffiti in the boys' toilets, though we could never prove it. So it was no surprise when, within six months of leaving school, he'd got one of his cousins pregnant. She was only thirteen and fortunately her mother realised early on what her daughter's state was and an abortion was arranged.'

'Nice piece of work,' said Donna. 'Whatever happened to the stocks?'

Tony Alexander looked at her, shook his head and turned towards George Elliott.

'Anyway, that's not what you came to talk about, was it, Inspector? You want to know more about the siege of Bridgnorth Castle, don't you? Finish your drink and come with me. I want to show you something. And you two. The exercise will do you good, Donna'

'Thanks a bunch,' replied Donna. 'If you're going up that hill, I'm going home. See you later, George.'

As Donna Latham billowed out of the front door of the Railwayman's Arms, George, Andrew Latham and Tony Alexander exited from the bar through the heavy door on to the station platform then made their way over the metal railway bridge through the smoke still rising from the recently-docked train to the far side and headed behind the station buildings and busy engine sheds up a grassy slope till they reached almost its high point.

'This is Panpudding Hill, Inspector,' said Tony Alexander, turning slightly out of breath from the climb and waving his long arms around. 'This is where the Parliamentarians camped themselves when they were besieging the Castle. You see?'

They were on top of a grassy mound, with the fields and hills of Shropshire behind them and the town of Bridgnorth, guarded by an impressive sandstone wall, in front of them. Tony Alexander pointed back across the valley to where the tower of St Mary's church stood proudly on the horizon and in front of it the leaning ruin of the keep of Bridgnorth Castle.

'You have to imagine what it all looked like, of course,' he continued. 'That wasn't the original church, of course. That's Telford's new one, built in the 1790s, when they feared the old one was going to collapse. Sadly there is no picture of Bridgnorth Castle as it was. No sketch, no painting, no drawing, no model. We have to guess what was there from the design of other castles of the same era.'

'What about those walls?' asked George, pointing to the massive sandstone wall facing them on the opposite side of the valley. 'Wouldn't they have been in place then?'

'Almost certainly not those walls, Inspector, because the Parliamentarians ordered the castle and the walls to be demolished. Though I suspect what we're seeing today is probably a lot of the original wall patched up at some later date. The Parliamentarians besieged the Castle for three weeks from here, firing their cannons across the valley and being fired at in return. There's a story about one cannoneer from the Royalist side who had a remarkable hit when his cannonball landed right in the bore of one of the guns over here, bursting it and killing the soldiers who were manning it.'

She looked and tried to imagine the noise, the crash and bang of those antique weapons, the clamour of shouting, the throngs of soldiers on the hillside behind them. It was almost impossible to think of such in its present tranquil existence.

'So how does Lavington's Hole fit into this?'

He told her how the siege had not been a success, how the Royalists had laid waste to the rest of the town by burning everything behind them as they bolted themselves behind the castle walls, purloining any food they could find to add to their existing stock of provisions, and how the thickness of the castle walls had made the castle virtually impregnable.

'So you'll realise that the task of winning here was rather thin. Until some bright spark, maybe Colonel Lavington himself, suggested digging a tunnel underneath the Castle. Come on, I'll show you where it is. We can talk while we're walking.'

They descended the hillside and headed down a track behind the railway sheds on to a busy road.

'Sandstone is very friable,' explained Tony Alexander as they walked. 'So it's relatively easy to enlarge some of the natural holes in it. There are records of people living in sandstone caves here from centuries back. Lavington would have noticed that there were probably houses back then built into the face of the sandstone outcrop on which the Castle sits. Look, here we are.'

They had reached the massive orange face of the sandstone cliff, in which George could see a number of cave entrances, all now closed off with metallic fencing. Landscaped paths led to each entrance and a signboard retold the story of the siege and its eventual end.

'When the Parliamentarians realised after three weeks or so that they were getting nowhere, they engaged Plan B. Lavington got his men digging in a line that would take them directly underneath the old St Mary's church where they knew the Royalists had their ammunition store. That's it.'

He pointed at one of the larger holes with its tall protective grill. All that could be seen behind it was black air.

'There's a cave there and from that they dug sixty-nine feet into the sandstone at an average of six feet a day, so that would have taken about eleven days. You can still see the pick marks. Hang on, someone's been tampering with this grill. It's been bent. That's dangerous. Kids could get in there and then who knows what could occur. I'd better contact the council.'

'I'll ring them, Tony,' said Andrew Latham, taking his mobile phone out of his jacket pocket and moving away to make his call.

'How did the siege all end?' George asked, while he did so.

As he answered her, Tony Alexander was pulling at the metal bars to test how loose they had become.

'The story is that the Royalists could hear the sound of picks and shovels directly beneath them and they panicked. The Governor, Sir Robert Howard, decided, in order to prevent a huge conflagration and destruction, to surrender and on 26th April 1646, on the communion table in St Mary's church, the articles of surrender were drawn up and signed. And that was the end of the Royalist command of Bridgnorth and of the king's controlling interest in Shropshire.'

'The same Sir Robert Howard whose pistol was on display in your museum until it was nicked by young Blakeway?'

'You know about that? Yes, the same one. I can show you the pistol if you like,' volunteered Tony Alexander. 'Interested?'

'Certainly,' George replied, though she didn't know why she was so interested. There was something about that body

47

that was puzzling her, that and the story about the ghosts. Was there any connection?

'There's someone on their way,' said Andrew, as he came back beside them. 'They want one of us to wait. Don't worry, George. Tony will stay and I'll take you back home. Yes?'

Still busy at the railings, Tony Alexander grunted acknowledgement. It was very curious. The grills had been there for years and had never been disturbed before.

TEN

The decision about returning to Birmingham or not was taken out of her hands. Before George Elliott had even got back to the Lathams' house in East Castle Street, she was met by an out-of-breath Police Constable Roger Walsh, who rounded the corner as Andrew Latham was putting his key in the front door.

'Ma'am, I've had forensics on the phone,' he said in between gulps. 'It was definitely a body. A young girl, they reckon, and she was shot in the head. They found a hole in her skull where the ball went through.'

'Any idea how long ago this took place?' George Elliott asked, feeling the excitement mount in her now, for this was more like her territory. 'Have they done any carbon dating on the bones? Surely they must have some notion?'

'Yes, ma'am.' His breathing had become more easy now and he lifted the helmet off his head to wipe the perspiration off his brow. 'They're pretty sure the body is at least three hundred years old, maybe more.'

'So that would place it in the seventeenth century,' Andrew mused aloud. 'That means Civil War times. That may well mean the time of the siege of Bridgnorth Castle.'

'Yes,' George cut across him. 'Thanks, Constable. Who was it that rang you?'

'Someone called Dr Clifford,' he replied.

'Jake Clifford? I know him. Good. Thanks again, Constable. Let me know when you learn anything about that object that young Blakeway dug up.'

'Ma-am.' Walsh turned away from the Lathams' front door and loped off along East Castle Street back to the police station.

49

They were greeted as they entered the house by the powerful smell of cooking, so headed to the kitchen where Donna Latham, pinny fastened around her ample body, was busy. Pots steamed on the Aga and the mouth-watering aroma of roasting meat oozed from its oven.

'I'm assuming you're staying tonight,' she said, as she bustled around the kitchen. 'We have people coming for dinner and you'll like them, I know.'

'Well, I wasn't going to stay, to be honest,' replied George Elliott. 'But your local bobby has just given me some news about the body that was found by the Steps. Seems likely it was a young girl killed in the Civil War period.'

'Walsh was here? Bridgnorth's answer to Sherlock Holmes?' said Donna tartly. 'Anyway there must have been hundreds of people killed back then, from what I understand. Not that I'm specially interested. Andrew and his pals are always trying to talk up this Civil War business, as if Cromwell himself was fighting here and Bridgnorth was the centre of the world.'

'You shouldn't mock it, Donna,' interjected her husband. 'Anyway George is interested, aren't you?'

George Elliott sighed, as she pulled off her bomber jacket. The news about the age of the body meant that it was only of historical interest now but she was still curious and there was a strange attraction to be had in seeking to solve an ancient mystery such as this. And the thought of her empty apartment was not enticing.

'Can't you two ever stop bickering?' Her eyes flashed briefly towards her sister. 'Yes, I am interested, as it happens, Donna. But not for the reasons Andrew thinks. It's that young girl I'm thinking of, the one whose body was found. With a hole in her head. I know it's three hundred years ago but that sounds like someone killed her to me. Young girls have never been combatants in warfare, or not until very recently. So why would she have been shot in the head? And who by? And who was she? I'm very curious.'

'It's a sure sign you're a copper,' said Donna, stirring a black pot on the Aga. 'Always suspicious. Always looking for solutions to things that may not even be criminal. Maybe she just got in the way of firing.'

George Elliott felt her neck redden, as she thought of arguing back with her sister, but then, with a massive effort of control, she kept her irritation in check. Donna might get pleasure from winding up her husband with her carping criticism but she wasn't going to have the same effect on her, however much she tried. Too many lost arguments from their shared childhood scarred the younger sister's memory.

'A hole in the head is not an accident, Donna. Can I use your phone? I need to speak to one of our forensic people about what he found when he examined the remains. And I'm still interested in that object that young Blakeway found. I think it may have been an ivory box. Maybe that holds some secrets that might help.'

'In the hallway,' said Andrew Latham, pointing George back out of the kitchen towards the front door. 'Help yourself.'

'And you are definitely staying?' enquired Donna, unfazed by her sister's put-down of her views.

'You can count on it.' George called back over her shoulder as she headed towards the hallway. 'I'm really intrigued by all this. And it's refreshing to be looking for solutions that are really academic. If we can find out who shot that girl and why, it's not going to change the world, is it? No-one's going down for it but it's what I do – solve crimes. I'm staying. Thanks.'

ELEVEN

The dinner guests were Alan and June Leadbeater. He was an estate agent in Bridgnorth, in practice on his own. There was a steady turnover of houses in the town and the surrounding district, as people sought to make a profit out of the burgeoning property market or to migrate from the urban areas of the Black Country and Birmingham. June Leadbeater was a lecturer in History at the University of Wolverhampton and also represented the Morfe ward on Bridgnorth Town Council.

They arrived at East Castle Street promptly at seven thirty and were greeted at the door by Andrew Latham, who had changed from the jeans and sweatshirt he'd been wearing all day into grey corduroy trousers and a rather fetching cinnamon sweater.

'June, Alan, how lovely to see you. Come on in,' he said, exchanging a light kiss on the cheek with June Leadbeater and shaking her husband's hand vigorously. 'Go through to the lounge. My sister-in-law is staying with us. I'm not sure if you've met her. Let me introduce you.'

By now they had doffed outdoor coats and been ushered into the lounge, where George Elliott, wearing a short green skirt and cream, low-cut blouse, was ensconced deep in an armchair. A small table beside the chair carried a large glass of white wine.

'This is my sister-in-law, George,' Andrew Latham pronounced, holding out an explanatory arm towards her as she stood. 'Or more properly Detective Inspector Georgina Elliott of the Mercian Police Force. But she's always George to us, aren't you? We don't stand on formality. Now, what will you have to drink? Red or white? G and T? Would you like a beer, Alan? I've got some excellent Hobsons bitter.'

'That would be first class,' replied Alan Leadbeater, a tall thin man with startling blue eyes and long greying hair that fell on to his shirt collar at the back. He was dressed entirely in black.

'White wine would be fine with me,' said his wife, an equally tall woman with bobbed black hair, a sharp nose and narrow, frameless glasses. She wore a green sweater and black trousers, tight to her thin bony body.

'Nothing much in a place like Bridgnorth to interest you, Inspector,' said the estate agent as he sat down. 'Very quiet, I'm afraid.'

'George, please. And I've heard about the town's quietness before. However, it wasn't always so, was it? I've been getting a guided tour this afternoon from your museum chap.'

'Tony Alexander? Good man,' said Alan Leadbeater, sitting down on the sofa. 'Thanks. Keeps the flag flying for the town. Where did he take you?'

Briefly she told them of the climb up Panpudding Hill and the subsequent visit to and exploration of Lavington's Hole and its neighbouring caves.

'Did you find it interesting?' asked June Leadbeater who had perched at the edge of the same floral-patterned sofa that her husband had sunk into.

'Absolutely. Even more interesting, though, was what we found.'

'Sorry?'

'George has discovered a murder,' explained Andrew Latham, re-entering the room with his guests' drinks. 'Tell them, George. Or is it not public knowledge yet?'

'I guess a three-hundred-year-old murder can't be classified according to our modern rules of law,' she laughed. 'Everyone will hear about it soon enough, I guess, so there's no harm in telling you about it.'

'I'm all agog,' smiled June Leadbeater, 'to think that we might get to know of something in town before the *Bridgnorth Journal's* ace newshounds have discovered it. Do tell.'

As they took their drinks from the tray that Andrew Latham placed on the table, George Elliott told them the full story about the discovery of bones, the sealing of the site and the subsequent finding, fully explained to her a little earlier by Jake Clifford, that a young girl who had been shot in the head had been buried there and that forensic examination suggested that the body dated back to the time of the Civil War. She also told them of the discovery of an object, possibly some kind of box, in the same hole where the bones had been found.

'How exciting!' said June Leadbeater. 'I'm absolutely fascinated by that period. It was the area I did my research in, you know.'

'The Civil War?' queried George.

'Yes, but I was more interested in the changes in people's thinking at that time. All those groups of Dissenters that sprang up – the Levellers, the Ranters, the Diggers. And the religious ferment of the time – absolutely fascinating. My doctorate was on Richard Baxter. He was a minister for a short period in Bridgnorth, you know. The house he lived in is in St Leonard's Close. The political and religious changes of the time were very significant and, even though we lost our opportunity to get rid of the monarchy for ever, the activities and the thinking of those people has had a profound effect on the way we live now.'

Before George could enquire further, her sister Donna appeared in the doorway, ovengloved hands outstretched towards them, her face even redder than usual.

'George, your policeman friend is at the door,' she said, gazing critically over her glasses, as if it was George's fault. 'And dinner is ready. So don't let him rabbit on for ages. June, Alan, would you mind bringing your glasses with you?'

As she led her two guests and her husband through to the dining room, George slipped past her to reach the front door where a red-faced Constable Walsh stood awaiting her.

Dinner began with *bruschetta pomodoro*, whose delicious crunchy toast and tomato topping kept mouths busy for several minutes, during which Andrew Latham poured out a bottle of Spanish *rioja*.

'These are lovely,' said Alan Leadbeater, his hand raised towards his mouth to prevent the possibility of crumbs landing on the table. 'Last time I had these was in Siena last year. Remember, darling? Sitting in the *campo*?'

'Mmm,' came the muffled reply.

'Glad you like them,' said Donna, who had removed her pinny to reveal a large blue denim shirt over white trousers. 'I've done pheasant for the main course. Hope you all like it. Bought them locally last year and froze them. Okay with everyone?'

Universal assent persuaded her to take the steaming casserole from the oven and place it on the table, where its powerful odour wafted heavenward. Beside it she placed a range of dishes containing roasted potatoes, purple cabbage, carrots and sprouts, whose distinctive smells added to the ambience.

'I'll serve the pheasant, if you don't mind,' she continued, 'then you can help yourselves to vegetables. Ah, my sister has deigned to honour us with her presence.'

All turned towards George as she returned.

'Everything all right?' asked Andrew.

'Think so. Walsh was just telling me there had been a fight down near the riverside early this evening.'

'The local youths kicking off early, eh?' said Donna, chuckling as she held out a large serving spoon in front of her. 'More success stories from my darling husband's school, I dare say. Why is Sherlock Walsh bothering you with that?'

'There's a boy been injured as a result. Apparently when they found him, he said something about Blakeway.'

'Not that toerag again!' expostulated Donna.

'What was the boy's name, the one who was hurt?' asked Andrew.

'His name is Richard More. Know him?'

Andrew's face had gone white and he clasped the table edges.

'Yes. In my sixth form. Oh dear.'

'You have some idea what it was all about?' asked George. 'Is there history?'

While he was nodding, Donna butted in.

'Can we just leave all that for now? Andrew, we have guests. Remember? Please, let's eat.'

As each took their turn to fill their plates with fare, there were murmurs of approval and congratulations to Donna, who finally sat down to her own plate.

'I'm intrigued by this young girl,' said June Leadbeater, after all had begun to eat. She was delicately chewing a thin morsel of pheasant. 'Where precisely were these remains found?'

'In the ground above the Stoneway Steps,' explained Andrew Latham. 'Between the theatre and the docking station for the Cliff Railway. I haven't seen the hole myself but George pointed out to me earlier where it is.'

'That would have been outside the castle walls then. My understanding is that there was a moat between the castle walls and the walls of the town itself. Presumably there would have been a bridge connecting the two,' said June Leadbeater, still chewing the same morsel. 'It seems odd now to think of the castle and the town separated like that but that's how the Anglo-Norman aristocracy managed things when they created towns like Bridgnorth.'

'What about access to the castle?' asked George, helping herself to more gravy. She had put the fight to the back of her mind now. Andrew would tell her later.

'Only through the Castle Barbican off the moat.'

'So how would people have got into the town if they were coming from the river side? Wouldn't there have been a lot of goods brought in by river?'

'Of course. The River Severn was a major thoroughfare for centuries,' said Alan Leadbeater placed his cutlery briefly on the sides of his plate. 'The Romans certainly used it for trade purposes. Even before the Industrial Revolution, there would have been regular traffic sailing down river and then being bowhauled back upstream.'

'And what Alan hasn't told you is that Stoneway Steps existed at least as far back as the early fifteenth century, as did the street we now call Cartway,' explained his wife.

'And the Steps gave access to the castle?' George took a thoughtful draught of wine.

'No, Stoneway Steps and Cartway converged at a gateway in the town walls known as Cowgate.'

'I've seen some real cows hanging around there,' interjected Donna. 'Usually with bags of chips in their hands!'

There was a faint frisson of polite laughter.

'Sorry, I don't quite get it,' said George, looking vaguely troubled as she rested her knife and fork on the plate in front of her. 'If the remains of this young girl were found next to Stoneway Steps, then they couldn't have had anything to do with the castle. Is that right?'

'Not necessarily,' answered June Leadbeater. 'The moat probably wasn't that wide, so the gap between the outer castle walls and the Steps need not have been very great.'

'What about someone shooting her then dumping her over the castle walls into the moat?' said Donna grinning. 'Sounds like a scene from a film, doesn't it? Isn't this exciting. Maybe we can get Scorsese or Spielberg to come and make a movie of it all!'

June Leadbeater looked over her glasses at her hostess with a half-smile.

'Actually that's not a bad interpretation. The idea of the body being thrown over the castle walls, I mean. Not your more lurid fantasies of Hollywood.'

'So she might have been something to do with the castle,' mused George. 'Interesting.'

'But why would anyone first of all shoot a young girl and then throw her body over the walls into the moat?' asked Andrew Latham who had been listening with increasing irritation to this fantasy that was being concocted under his sister-in-law's conducting. 'I know the Royalists were bastards but there has to be a motive.'

George Elliott chuckled.

'Exactly. That's what I think we might find difficult to discover after all this time. We can't exactly find any living witnesses, can we?'

'Oh, I don't know,' said Donna. 'Tony Alexander's pretty ancient, isn't he?'

There was laughter all round the table at this comment. Everyone knew Tony, everyone liked him and, if he'd been there, he would have joined in the laughter. He did seem to have been in Bridgnorth forever. And he was closing on his seventies now, if not quite three hundred and sixty years old.

TWELVE

'You were going to tell me about the history between young Blakeway and this More boy,' said George Elliott, settling herself into one of the Lathams' deep armchairs. She and her brother-in-law had preceded the others into the lounge. 'Have there been problems before?'

'The young man in question is one of our abler students. We've got high hopes of him getting to Cambridge next summer. His name's Richard More. His family believe they are descended from the family of one of the Mayflower Pilgrims,' replied Andrew.

'Sorry.' George Elliott stared at him in disbelief. 'What's all this got to do with young Blakeway?'

'This is a small community,' continued Andrew Latham. 'And memories are long. I don't know how true it is that Richard More is descended from the same More family whose children were placed on *The Mayflower* but it is quite likely. I happen to know the story. You see the original Richard More was the son of Katherine and Samuel More of Larden Hall in Shipton out on the road to Ludlow. He had two sisters and a brother. Katherine's marriage to Samuel, her cousin, was largely to do with ensuring that lands stayed within the More family. That sort of pre-arranged marriage worked for many people at the time but for Katherine it wasn't enough. Samuel somehow discovered that the four children she had borne were not his and, when his wife tried to sue him for divorce, he paid the pilgrims sailing on *The Mayflower* to take the children to America to save them from the stain of illegitimacy. Unfortunately Richard's three siblings died before they landed but Richard himself survived and lived into his eighties.'

'And?'

'Katherine More's lover, and therefore the father of those four unfortunate children, was a certain Jacob Blakeway.'

'So Ryan's related to him?' George gasped at the information.

'He thinks he is. There have been problems between the families in the past, I believe, but these two boys really do not get on very well at all.'

George Elliott was puzzled. All this ancient history that was buried in the town was coming to life again. First, the bones found by the Stoneway Steps and now this family feud dating back to the same period. And somehow Ryan Blakeway involved in all of it. She sat back in her armchair and brooded on these curiosities.

'I know you're interested in this young girl and her murder,' said Andrew Latham as the others joined them in the lounge. 'But I was curious about what June was saying about the dissenters of the Civil War period and how their thinking was responsible for much of what we take as normal in society nowadays.'

'Not politics again, Andrew,' groaned Donna, stretching out on the sofa. 'Can't we stick to the murder story? It's much more exciting.'

'I don't think there's much more we can speculate about that tonight,' said George. 'I need some time to look at things again tomorrow and then I really must get back to Birmingham. I've not done any shopping for next week and I'm low on all sorts of things. So go on, June, tell me more about these Levellers and Ranters and Diggers. And especially this Richard Baxter cove.'

'I recall that Tony Benn and Michael Foot were always citing the Levellers as being responsible for the birth of socialism, so they do matter,' said Andrew Latham, slipping his shoes off his feet as he relaxed into his chair.

'What did they believe in?'

George noticed out of the corner of her eye that her sister was making eyes again. She really was getting increasingly fed up with all this history.

'Remember that the Civil War was caused by Charles I's refusal to work with his Parliament but, when it ended in the late 1640s, many of those involved began to ask questions about the nature of sovereignty and about who Parliament was accountable to. Some argued that Parliament should be accountable to the people, because it was the people who put them there. The Levellers argued for Parliamentary elections every two years – can you imagine that?' explained June Leadbeater, peering with academic excitement through her glasses at her audience.

'Please God, no!' said Donna, as her sister laughed. 'I'd see even less of Andrew than I do now. As it is, he spends half his life sealing envelopes and canvassing for the local Labour bunch. And what a bloody waste of time that is! They'll never get anyone elected here in Bridgnorth. They're all in the pay of the Tories round here.'

June Leadbeater ignored her.

'That wasn't all. They also wanted a written constitution, which of course we still don't have. They wanted religious tolerance, so that all could worship as they chose.'

'Try telling that to the Muslims of Finsbury Park,' said Donna. No one looked at her or even acknowledged her words.

'They wanted equality for all people before the law. But the key thing, and the reason why Benn and Foot claim them as their forebears, is this notion that our rulers are accountable to the people of the land. That really was the beginning of the move towards the universal suffrage that we enjoy today.'

'And why we allowed unelected press barons like Murdoch to convince people to vote for a Thatcher government three times in the eighties, so they could make three million people unemployed,' spat Donna. 'It's all very well citing these glorious forebears of socialism. But what use were Benn and Foot then, when Tebbitt and Lawson and Thatcher were doing their wickedest?'

'I thought you didn't do politics.' George Elliott turned on her sister. 'Haven't you spent all evening telling Andrew off any time he gets near to the subject.'

Donna Latham sat up sharply, her face taking on its fighting look.

'I know. But it does really piss me off sometimes the way Andrew and his friends go on about socialism. Yes, I know we've got New Labour and Blair now and yes, they're certainly far better than that corrupt crew who were there before. But where was socialism when Thatcher came to power? Where was Benn, for example? Tearing the Labour party apart, not fighting for the glorious people.'

'But that's democracy,' said her husband. 'If you allow everyone to vote, you have to accept their decision. The people are sovereign.'

Donna was wound up fully by now, her face almost puce and her lips rehearsing words before she spoke them.

Alan Leadbeater, however, was buttoning his black jacket and inching forward in his seat.

'Very interesting. Still, it's late and I really think we should leave you people to your own devices. Thank you for a lovely meal, Donna, and for your usual generous hospitality. I hope June's enthusiasm for all things Civil War hasn't dominated the evening too much.'

'My fault, I expect,' said George Elliott, rising with the others to bid farewell. 'I've just become intrigued with the discovery of this body and I know so little about the period. We never studied it at my school and I did English at university, so it's fascinating for me. Helps me get some sense of all that was going on at the time.'

The Leadbeaters were ushered into the passageway by Andrew Latham, who found their outer coats and helped them on.

'Good luck with your investigations, George,' said Alan Leadbeater, as they turned in the doorway. 'From what you've told us, you don't seem to have much evidence to go on, so we'll both be very interested in what you discover, won't we, June?'

She smiled her agreement and they bade their final farewells before stepping out into the darkened street.

But there would soon be much more for George to think about.

THIRTEEN

The quiet Sunday George Elliott had planned did not turn out that way. She had bade her sister and brother-in-law goodbye by the middle of the morning, after Andrew Latham had insisted on taking her to see the imposing sandstone church of St Leonard, in whose grounds the early skirmishes in the siege of Bridgnorth had occurred.

'I may be back as soon as something is known about that object that young Blakeway found,' she had said. 'I don't want to give up on this. It is quite fascinating. But I have things to do at home and there are not likely to be any developments on a Sunday, are there?'

So she had travelled back to Birmingham, calling in at Sainsbury's to buy the necessities to maintain herself over the next week – food mainly but also a few household goods that had run out. The roads had been surprisingly busy but she had had no hold-ups and got back by midday.

Her apartment on the second floor of a modern three-storey block in Edgbaston was nothing out of the ordinary. Comfortably furnished, largely by IKEA, it required little by way of maintenance other than the once-a-week makeover effected by her regular woman from the Sweeping Beauties agency. She liked living close to the centre of the city, not just for work reasons, though it undoubtedly did help to be able to reach the Mercian Force headquarters in less than ten minutes, but also because, since its regeneration in the nineteen-eighties, Birmingham had become a swinging city with music bars, night clubs, and restaurants serving every kind of food you could imagine. On a Saturday night you could hardly move on Corporation Street it was so full of fun-loving young people determined to celebrate their weekend freedom and flaunting the latest fashionable outfits. Even when the weather was inclement and more mature people would have stayed indoors or, if deciding to venture out, donned raincoats or at the very least carried umbrellas, those young people thronged from one bar to another, from one fast-food joint to another, from one club to another in tee-shirts and skimpy dresses.

Of course, such boisterousness and such excitement generated its own share of difficulties, usually resulting from excesses of alcohol intake but occasionally turning into something nastier, the sort of case that George professionally as a young police officer might once have been called on to pursue. But that sort of thing was rare. Most calls upon police time were low-level, largely crowd control and dispersal or sorting out minor clashes between different groups of young people. So, George was able to enjoy the richness of city life when she chose to, especially the wide variety of restaurants. Or she could stay at home and, despite being less than a mile from the city centre, her street in the Edgbaston suburb was almost always peaceful and undisturbed. The greatest disturbance, to tell the truth, was the noise of dozens of cars revving up on a Monday morning to head for work.

When she got back home, George picked up some mail from Saturday's post, emptied her shopping bags and put everything in its appropriate place, then sat down while she waited for the coffee percolator to throb into action. She stretched out her legs, let her newly-styled blonde hair flop back on to the leather armchair, and looked around at her surroundings. Pictures on the wall, all reproductions of course, various trinkets she had bought somewhere or received as gifts, a photograph of her father placed on top of the TV set. It wasn't much to cling to, was it? she thought. Here she was, over forty now, still single, still in a temporary situation, as she put it. She was still waiting for Mr Right, even though she probably didn't believe there was such a person. Or ever had been, if she was honest. Was it her work? Was she just too involved professionally, too committed to police work? She wouldn't really admit to that. In fact, in recent years she'd worked really hard to separate her private and public faces, ensuring in particular that she took the leave she was entitled to and that, when an incident happened, say in some restaurant or club where she was enjoying her private life, she did not immediately leap out of her seat, brandishing her warrant. Others could do that work. So was it something about her? she wondered.

She sighed and picked up *The Independent* she'd bought at the supermarket. The front page, as usual she thought, was full of the latest news from Iraq – the government's continued attempt to justify the support that the Prime Minister had given the Bush administration for the original invasion, the decision to send more British troops out there because of the escalating violence, a suicide bomber in Tehran, car bombs in three other cities. When would it ever end? she asked herself. She was not particularly political in the sense of party-political. If pressed, she would admit to having voted Labour in the last three elections but that was more to do with the corruption and sleaze that had become so virulent in the previous Tory government. But, to tell the truth, professionally it made little difference to her which government was in power. None of them were able to eliminate crime and it was daft to even suppose they might. All that guff that Blair had said about being "tough on crime, tough on the causes of crime" meant little in her experience. There were bad people everywhere. You couldn't eliminate that, not even by rounding them all up, banging them in prison and throwing the keys away. It just wouldn't work.

She glanced again at the newspaper and started to read the report about further British troops being sent out to Iraq, when she came upon a mention of Camp Breadbasket. The columnist was using this case to illustrate his argument that sending more soldiers to Iraq would produce the greater possibility of abuses of prisoners by soldiers. Now, she knew from her time in the Mercian Force, that there were occasions when people suspected of particularly vicious crimes, the murder of a child for instance, might appear in court with unexplained bruising on their faces and arms. She knew that some officers were overzealous in their treatment of prisoners and, although it was reprehensible and something she would never herself partake in, she could understand how it happened. But Camp Breadbasket was where Ryan Blakeway's father had served. She remembered Andrew Latham's account and his suspicions that Blakeway Senior might well have been involved in the abuses. What exactly had happened? She remembered the photographs – an Iraqi prisoner tied up on the prongs of a forklift truck and another prisoner on the floor in a foetal position while a soldier in shorts and flip-flops stood on top of him.

George decided she wanted to know more. The events in Bridgnorth were still troubling her and, efficient and meticulous as she always was, thought the greater amount of evidence she had to consider, the more likely she would be to find the truth. The Blakeway boy had only been a sideshow really but she knew from the experience of working with Tallyforth that even sideshows in murder cases, even events that seemed completely unrelated, might end up having some bearing on matters.

She moved into the spare bedroom, switched on her computer and googled "Camp Breadbasket". Immediately she was taken to *The Guardian* archive, with articles from late February of that year, just a few months previous. She highlighted one article and clicked her mouse to reveal:

Four guilty, but questions remain

Defence says soldiers were sacrificed to shield superiors

Thursday February 24, 2005
The Guardian

> It has been more than 20 months since a roll of film containing horrific images of British soldiers abusing Iraqi prisoners was taken to a small processing shop in Tamworth, Staffordshire, by a somewhat naive squaddie.

Yes, thought George, she remembered now. The discovery was accidental. An off-duty soldier had taken his roll of film into an ordinary photographic processing shop for developing and the girl who had the duty of that work found the horrendous images that had subsequently led to the arrest and trial of four soldiers.

During that time, the army has been unable to find the men responsible for stripping the Iraqis and forcing them to 'put on a sex show' and perform simulated acts of oral and anal sex for the camera.

So what were these four soldiers being court-martialled for? she wondered. She read on.

After all the evidence it seemed the panel was no clearer as to what really happened on that morning, two weeks after the war in Iraq was officially declared over. They heard fusiliers claim they were not there, had been sleeping, or had not seen anything. Officers denied witnessing 20 Iraqi men being forced to run round with milk boxes on their heads while being beaten around the legs. A major described how he had destroyed his notes from the time because he had moved house weeks before the case began.

Surprise, surprise, George thought to herself. The code of misplaced loyalty – *omerta* they called it in Sicily – to one's fellows she had come across plenty of times in her career. Potential witnesses who claimed to have been asleep or absent from the scene at the time of a felony, or the "accidental" destruction of valuable evidence.

The crucial evidence that they did not hear was that of the Iraqi victims themselves, who the prosecution claimed could not be tracked down.

So where were these Iraqis? How hard had the British troops sought for them? And anyway, why did their evidence matter so much? The photographs were sufficiently damning, weren't they?

Two things the panel can be almost certain of is that had the abuse not been photographed, it would not have come to light, and that torture was more widespread across the British sector in Iraq than the army has previously admitted. They also found out that several senior officers – all of whom were accused of misbehaviour by the defence team – have since been promoted.

Now that was really rich – promotion for officers, court-martials for some of the squaddies. Typical. And yes, it happened in the police too. She thought again of her old boss Tallyforth who should have gone higher than Chief Inspector but never did because of his maverick ways. She hoped she had learned from that.

In spite of hearing serious allegations against senior officers, the panel was tasked only with deciding the fate of a fusilier, a lance corporal and a corporal. These three say that they have been served up as 'sacrificial lambs'.

It was hard to disagree with that conclusion. It did all look like a set-up, didn't it? Although there was no mention of a soldier called Blakeway, George could tell that the culture of silence would have protected any other soldiers involved. Her brother-in-law had informed her that Blakeway was at Camp Breadbasket and he had an unsavoury record and reputation, so it was easy to speculate on the likelihood of his involvement. But why was she so interested? What was driving her to look up this ancient history? All she could explain to herself was that her job made her morbidly fascinated with evil-doing and evil-doers. Something had stirred her in Bridgnorth. And that something was still stirring her.

FOURTEEN

The first disturbance to George's quiet Sunday at home came as she was still staring at the images on her computer screen that accompanied the article in *The Guardian*. The doorbell rang, startling her from her reverie.

When she opened the door to her apartment, she was even more surprised to see Larry Powell, in an open-necked shirt and grey flannels, looking decidedly downcast and humble.

'You?' she began. 'I thought we agreed.....'

'Sorry, George, I just had to talk to you. I just had to come round. I'd have rung but....'

His right foot took a step towards the threshold but lingered there, as if it were independent of its owner.

'But I'd have told you not to come, that's what you mean, isn't it?' she flared at him.

Larry Powell hung his head and moved his right leg back from the doorway.

'I suppose so. Can I come in?'

She clapped her hands against her sides in exasperation.

'What's the point, Larry? We went over it two hundred times last weekend. It wasn't working and....'

'Can we go inside to talk? It's really embarrassing out here.'

George looked around. There was no one in sight but there were footsteps coming up the stairs and the lift was whirring. One part of her wanted to just close the door on him but the other part knew she couldn't and it would be too humiliating to engage in an argument in public.

'Okay, come in. But you're not staying long. I have things to do, Larry. And there's no point your trying to persuade me to change my mind. I'm determined this time.'

He followed her into the kitchen where automatically she refilled and then switched on the coffee percolator where it stood on the black-tiled worktop.

'George,' he began, moving towards her with his arms outstretched as if to take hold of her.

'Wait a minute, Larry,' she protested, holding up her hands flat towards him. 'I agreed to talk. No more.'

Larry Powell's arms dropped by his side and he stopped half-way across the kitchen floor.

'George,' he tried another tack. 'We can make it work. I know we can. I can change. I've applied for a transfer to traffic division. We wouldn't see as much of each other professionally that way.'

'That's not the main problem'.

'But you said it was.'

'No, I said it wasn't helping, to be spending too much time together at work. But it wasn't just that.'

'What then?'

This was the moment she hadn't wanted to arrive. She had persuaded him to leave the previous weekend saying she needed space and time to think and had got him to agree to that, leaving him with the slight hope that she would change her mind when she knew she wouldn't. But it had been easier to let him down gradually than to be totally frank. And now she could not avoid it.

'I just don't love you,' she said, turning away from him so that she couldn't see the hurt that winced across his face.

'Why?'

There, she'd said it. And it wasn't too bad after all. Suddenly her words started to flow.

'I don't know. It just happens that way. You fall in love and it's magic. And then slowly it dies and then you're not in love any longer. Only you keep going in the hope that the magic will return. But it never does. Not in my experience anyway.'

By now the coffee percolator was bubbling away and she turned from him again to pour two cups of coffee. The bitter pungency wafted to her nostrils and she closed her eyes momentarily to savour it.

'So why didn't you say this before?'

'I didn't want to hurt you, Larry,' she said, passing him a steaming cup. 'You're a lovely man, Larry, and we've had some good times together but it's not enough any longer. I just wanted it to end painlessly, for both of us really.'

'And this is what you call painless?'

She could see that his eyes were glistening, as he fought to hold back his emotions. For a split second she thought of him in his tenderest moments but then she remembered the irritations – the way he whistled tunelessly when he was cooking, the shaving stubble he never cleaned from the washbasin, the phone calls from his ex-wife. Those most of all.

'You came round, Larry. I didn't ask you. We agreed last weekend to split. You took your stuff last Sunday. We've managed to avoid each other all week. I thought you understood. Surely you knew things weren't right?'

'Is there someone else?'

'No. No!'

'You sure?'

'Absolutely sure.'

'Tallyforth hasn't been back to see you, has he?'

'No! God help me! No! Look, Larry, I just need some space. I'm sorry it didn't work out. Like I said, the magic had gone and I just don't love you. Maybe it's me.'

'What d'you mean?'

She clasped her hands to her forehead. They had been here too many times before. Always his need for an explanation. Always his refusal to accept it.

'I mean, look at me. Larry. I'm over forty and I'm still single. I'll almost certainly never have children now and I still can't find a bloke that satisfies all my needs. So maybe it's me. Maybe I've set my sights too high. Maybe there isn't anyone who can match what I want. Maybe I'm just fated to drifting in and out of relationships.'

'D'you really think that, George? 'Cos if you do, I'm sorry for you.'

His dark eyes sought to hold hers but failed, as she turned away from him.

'Don't patronise me, Larry.'

'I'm not. I just think you're being unrealistic. Remember, I've been married once, you know. I thought we understood each other. Because of the work, I mean. My wife never understood that but you did. Or, at least, you said you did.'

George recalled the tearful ex-wife's phone calls again and braced herself to be firm.

'It wasn't that, Larry. We were both in the same work, so of course I understood. There's times when you've been enormously patient when I've been working all hours on some case. And I appreciated that. I couldn't have wished more support. But it's not enough. Larry. I need to be loved for myself. I need every waking hour to be thinking of that love. When we first got together, it was like that for me. I couldn't wait till I saw you next. You were my life, Larry. But that faded away some time ago. I kept going in the forlorn hope it would return but it didn't. And it won't. I know that now. I'm sorry, Larry. I really am. We were great together. But it just hasn't worked out in the end. I'm truly sorry.'

He sighed and placed his coffee cup on the work surface near the percolator.

'That's it then.' He tried again to catch her eye, hoping to rekindle something from their shared past. 'Can we go out for a meal occasionally? For old time's sake?'

'I want us to be friends. But I don't think going out is a good idea. And please don't turn up unexpectedly again, Larry. I'm not long back from my sister's in Bridgnorth and I promised myself a quiet day.'

'Sorry,' he said, standing to leave. 'I still love you, George.'

She glanced briefly at his face then away from him. Everything that had happened between them over the previous two years flew around in her mind but then it all went misty. She just wanted him out. She didn't want to listen to him any more.

'I know you think you do, Larry. But you'll see I was right when you've had time to think things through properly. Keep in touch, Larry. And don't go to traffic – it'll be the death of you. If I can handle working in the same department, you can. Give yourself time.'

As she closed the door on his retreating figure, George Elliott felt a slight pang of regret shiver through her body but she was adamant she was right. There was no going back.

FIFTEEN

The second disturbance to her day came a couple of hours later, once again from an unexpected visit.

'Hi sweetie! Only little old me,' chirped Steve Anthony, her long-time gay friend from Swansea University days, as she opened the door to her apartment. 'Just up in Brum Brum for the weekend. Thought I'd pop in and see you. And I've brought a little friend.'

George peered over his shoulder and saw a much younger man, dressed in combat trousers and a pink hooded sweatshirt with the legend PINK POWER picked out across his thin chest. His tightly-curled peroxide-blonde head was bowed so that at first she couldn't see his face, but then he looked up.

'Hi!' he said in a flat monotone.

'Who's this then, Stevie Wonder?' Her mouth puckered as she turned back to Steve Anthony and cocked a quizzical eye at him. 'Anyone I should know about?'

'Ooh no, it's nothing like that,' replied Steve, brushing past her and throwing himself on to the leather sofa. He was dressed in frayed denim jeans and white silk shirt. 'We met last night. At DV8 club. He stayed in my hotel last night because he had nowhere else to go. No, that was all. Honest! Ask him.'

George looked across at the young man who had by now also entered her apartment and arranged himself on the same sofa that Steve sat on, though in a less flamboyant manner. He was in his early twenties, she guessed, with a clear complexion and a somewhat sallow look. His eyes betrayed no emotion, but stared blankly back at her.

'When I found out who he was, I thought you might like to meet him,' continued Steve Anthony, idly lifting the book that was on the coffee table. 'Mmm, Hollingshurst, eh? You enjoying it? He's one of my favourites.'

'Yes, it's very good,' she replied, sitting down opposite them on an easy chair. 'So?'

'Don't you recognise the look?' Steve was teasing her as he replaced the book on the table. 'That troubled expression?'

'I don't know what on earth you're on about,' she said exasperatedly. 'Why should I want to meet this young man?'

Steve Anthony grinned, first at her and then at the youngster sitting at his side.

'Allow me to introduce,' he said, in mock courtly tone, extending his left arm with palm upturned. 'Detective Inspector Georgina Elliott, scion of the Mercian Police Force, crimebuster *extraordinaire* and my very best chum. And my new friend Miles, owner of the most hideous sweatshirt in the universe, prodigious dope-smoker and son of your old friend and colleague, Detective Chief Inspector Tallyforth'.

She gulped. Tallyforth's son? What on earth was he doing with Steve? Yes, she remembered several years ago that he had announced his gayness and the difficulty Tallyforth had had in dealing with all that. So much so that he'd even discussed those difficulties with Steve about whom he had been normally vitriolic. She hadn't heard about what had become of the boy since Tallyforth had retired eighteen months previously, ending a long professional relationship but also ending a tricky personal relationship which at times had been physically and emotionally very close and at other times had been racked with jealousy and anger.

'Your father and I worked together for many years,' she said, wondering how much she should say. 'Until he retired, of course. I haven't seen or heard from him since then.'

'I know,' said Miles Tallyforth, still with no expression on his face. 'You slept with him, didn't you?'

George was startled by the bluntness of his question, at which Steve Anthony chuckled.

'Let's just say they were partners in crime, shall we?' he said, patting Miles's knee. 'We don't need to dig all that ancient history up, do we? George is a very good friend of mine and I didn't bring you round here to engage in a slanging match. I merely thought you two should meet.'

George looked again at the young man's face and yes, she could now see some likenesses – the nose especially and the eyebrows. Then she looked away from him and back at Steve.

'So what are you doing up in Birmingham? And why didn't you come and stay with me?'

'You weren't here, sweetie. I only decided to come up yesterday morning to see the Bruckner concert at Symphony Hall and I rang but you weren't here, were you? So I booked into the Hotel du Vin for the night. Anyway, the good news is you're going to be seeing a lot more of me. I'm being transferred up here to head up the latest Home Office scheme to infiltrate the Muslim terrorist cells. *Salaam alaikum!*'

'When?'

'As of. The other reason I'm here this weekend, apart from the divine Bruckner of course, is to start apartment-hunting. I quite fancy one of those posh new penthouse apartments by the canal side in the Jewellery Quarter.'

'You must be earning to afford one of those'.

'All on The Firm, my darling. Her Maj pays well these days, you know. So anyway, how's tricks?'

George Elliott sank back in her armchair and kicked off her shoes. The great thing about Steve was that she could be completely open with him about anything. There was no need for guardedness as there seemed to be in every other one of her relationships, both inside and outside of work.

'I split up with Larry. Last week. He's been round this morning, trying to persuade me to change my mind but I won't. It wasn't working, Steve. I talked to you about it at Christmas, remember? I tried, I really tried and I kept hoping it would be all right but it never was like it was to start with.'

'It never is, sweetie.' Steve Anthony fluttered his eyelashes. 'That's why I'm still on my own. And at forty-one, I'm beginning to prefer my own company anyway. At least, for permanent living. That doesn't prohibit the occasional sexual adventure, of course, or the little dalliance with such as my friend Miles here.'

George Elliott realised they had been ignoring Tallyforth's son for the past few minutes. She sat forward and turned towards him now.

'Tell me about yourself, Miles. What do you do for a living?'

'I'm still at uni.' His voice sustained the same truculent monotone he had adopted since entering her apartment. 'I worked in local government for two years after I left school, then I decided I wanted more education, so I did my A levels at the Tech.'

'The College of Knowledge,' laughed Steve.

'What are you studying?' asked George, ignoring his interruption.

'History. I'm in my last year but I'm hoping to get a First and do a Masters afterwards.'

'Bright boy!' said Steve. 'That'll show your father, won't it?'

'I'm not trying to show my father anything.' There was the slightest rise in tone as his voice bristled briefly. 'We get on great now. In fact, he's doing a degree at Birmingham Uni as well. He's in his second year and really enjoying it. Mind, he doesn't stay on the campus like I do. He drives in every day but he says he's really enjoying student life, even at his advanced age.'

'Your father's doing a degree?' gasped George Elliott, scarcely believing what she was hearing. Tallyforth, the arch sceptic, who believed that intuition and experience were all you needed to understand the world and its ways, signing up to do a degree. And not merely signing up, like a lot of retirees did, as she'd read, worried about losing their marbles too soon in the latter years of their lives, but actually now in his second year of it.

Miles Tallyforth's face had lit up as he spoke. George recognised that there must have been a considerable overcoming of prejudices and resistance on the part of both son and father. Well, yes, she knew the softer side of the father, just as she knew his bloody-mindedness.

'What course is he following?' she asked his son. Surely it wouldn't be criminology.

'He's doing History too. He's really enjoying it as well. You should get in touch and talk to him about it.'

George took a deep breath and sat back. This was unexpected news and the idea, floated by his son, that she should get in touch with Tallyforth again....well, that was preposterous. Or was it?

But before she could think any further, Steve Anthony leapt to his feet.

'Come on, dearest Miles, I promised to drive you back to your pit on the campus. What some people will do for a ride on a Triumph Bonneville! Sweetie, we must get together soon. I might need your advice about my new place. I'll give you a bell. *Ciao*!'

And, with a semi-reluctant Miles Tallyforth tagging behind him, he was gone, leaving George to contemplate the import of all that had been said on the past half an hour, as she absent-mindedly filled the washing machine and placed two empty cups in the sink.

SIXTEEN

Monday morning broke fresh as a daisy and George Elliott dressed for work in a smart tailored suit that showed off her body well without suggesting tartiness. After a hurried breakfast of grapefruit, toast and coffee, she headed down the stairs in her apartment block to reach her car, pausing to collect, though not to open and read, her mail. She liked the smooth lines of the olive-green MG sports car that she had treated herself to after her previous year's performance review had upped her monthly take-home pay considerably. She liked the feeling of power that its two-litre engine gave her when she pressed the accelerator pedal. Driving this car was a real pleasure, she thought to herself, as she manoeuvred her way through the usual early morning Birmingham traffic to reach the Mercian Police Force headquarters.

There was a message on her desk as she entered her office. It was from Assistant Chief Constable Clarke, asking her to see him as soon as she arrived. Curious, she thought. 'Nobby' Clarke wasn't her boss any longer. Since he'd been promoted to Assistant Chief Constable, he no longer had regular operational responsibilities, so she rarely came into contact with him any longer. When he'd been Chief Superintendent, there had been recurring clashes between Tallyforth and him, she recalled, when she inevitably felt the after-effects as Tallyforth poured out all his anger about the way he was being held in check by unfeeling and ill-considered protocol to the detriment of crimebusting, as he saw it. She had always respected Nobby Clarke, not only for his precision and meticulousness, which she did truly admire and aspire to matching in her own police work, but also because he was clearly a man who knew and understood the politics of policing and who it was best never to cross for that very reason.

'You wanted to see me, sir,' she said, presenting herself at his desk in his glassy eyrie on the top floor of the building, overlooking what he saw as the jungle of the city.

'Yes, Elliott,' he began, turning his gimlet eyes on her. Expensive aftershave lotion wafted through the cool air of the room. The starched white shirt and immaculate black tie fitted perfectly on this martinet-like figure who faced her. She had always been slightly frightened by that figure, so different from Tallyforth in looks and style and approach. 'I hear you've been visiting Bridgnorth.'

She gulped, like a fish suddenly taken from its water. What on earth was her visit to her sister and brother-in-law to do with him? And how did he know anyway?

'Sir.'

'Lovely spot,' he mused, delicately balancing a silver paper knife between the index fingers of each hand. 'Used to go there a lot at one time. Keen fisherman, you know. Excellent barbel and salmon. Especially when the Severn was in spate.'

She had never had him down for a fisherman. He didn't seem the sort, though, come to think of it, he was known for spending large amounts of his time sitting at his desk staring into space, apparently doing nothing. Maybe the angling was just another take on the same theme.

'Sir.'

'I see you're a little surprised, Elliott,' he continued, still balancing the paper knife between his fingers. 'Excellent pubs, too, as I recall. Black Horse, Black Boy, Bell and Talbot. First-class. My brother was one of the founder members of the Severn Valley Railway you know. Lived in Bridgnorth then, so I used to visit and do a spot of angling while I was there and we always enjoyed a refreshing pint or two in the evenings. Do you know the town well?'

'My sister lives there,' George Elliott explained, flustered now at the direction this conversation was heading. Had he summoned her here to talk about the pubs in Bridgnorth? Surely not. 'Only been there a few years. Her husband was born and brought up there. Andrew's the head of a secondary school in the area.'

'So I understand,' said Assistant Chief Constable Albert Nobby Clarke, placing the paper knife back on the desk and leaning forward now to stare at her even more intently. 'And I hear you've been digging into a bit of history, if you'll excuse the pun.'

What on earth.....? Where had he found all this....? Of course, Jake Clifford of the forensics team. She'd told him her reasons for being in Bridgnorth and for being interested in the remains that had been dug up on the Stoneway Steps. But why was Nobby Clarke talking to Jake Clifford?

'Expect you're wondering how I know all about your movements, Elliott.'

'Jake Clifford, sir?' she said, offering him her explanation.

'Correct, Elliott. The good Dr Clifford. We meet socially on occasions. I'm curious, however, why you should be so interested in this person that died, as I understand it, some three hundred and sixty years ago. I trust this was just a passing curiosity on your weekend off and not something you intend to pursue. There's plenty of serious crime in the area without your having to go hunting antique mysteries, Elliott.'

'Sir, I was just curious. I had no plans to investigate further.'

She knew she was lying but felt it best to go along with what Clarke was saying. There would be plenty of opportunity in evenings and weekends to follow up that story. After all, the girl had been dead a long time, so it wasn't a matter of urgency to try to find out why she'd been murdered. She caught herself up short thinking that – it was the first time she'd thought about the dead girl as a real person whose life had been taken violently. But that was surely what it was. You don't get a pistol shot in your head for fun, she thought.

'Good.' Sitting forward again now, ready to dismiss her as promptly as possible. 'I'm glad we understand each other. You're a good officer, Elliott, and I wouldn't want you to get caught up in something that was wasting police time and affecting your career.'

Was she hearing this right? This sounded like she was being threatened that, if she kept on looking into the murder of

81

that young girl, it might affect her career. How? Why? Was there something else going on here? Was there some sinister reason why Nobby Clarke was warning her off? Or was she just being paranoid? The trouble with being a police officer, she reflected, was that it made you suspicious of everything. Still, Clarke had gone to all this trouble to speak to her and to try to ensure that she spent no further time investigating the case of the body by the Stoneway Steps.

'No, sir.'

'That's all, Elliott.' He looked down at a paper on his desk. 'Keep up the good work.'

She was still puzzled as she left his office to return to her own desk, where a telephone message had been left for her.

SEVENTEEN

'Ma'am,' came the voice of Police Constable Roger Walsh from the Bridgnorth police station, after she dialled the number that had been left for her on the message. 'There's been some a development in the Stoneway Steps death case. There's been some news from the Shrewsbury Museum Service. And that fight I told you about – the boy is in hospital.'

She sighed. God, it was only two minutes ago that she'd acceded to Nobby Clarke's request that she make no further enquiries into this case. Now here was Walsh giving her some new information. Yes, of course, she'd asked him to keep her updated and yes, of course, there was no way that he could have known that she had been warned off the case or that she could only pursue it in her own time. He probably thought that big-time Detective Inspectors in Birmingham had nothing better to do than to pursue – what had Clarke called them? – antique mysteries. And Walsh kept insisting on telling her about this fight. She was above that sort of petty stuff, wasn't she? If it hadn't been for the involvement of that Blakeway boy, she would not have had the slightest interest in the minor fisticuffs of Saturday night in Bridgnorth.

'Go on then. But make it quick. I've got a full caseload this morning. The Lady on the Steps is not at the top of my list today, Constable.'

'Yes, ma'am, sorry to bother you,' came his fawning reply. 'But I thought you'd like to know. You did ask me to...'

'Yes, I know. Get on with it, man.' She knew she was taking her irritation at Clarke's intervention out on the Bridgnorth bobby but what the hell!

'It was a box, ma'am. Like you thought. And it is valuable. It's made of ivory. The carvings on the lid are most unusual apparently. The museum people have never seen anything like them. They're not sure what they are. They've had to contact the British Museum to check it out.'

'Okay,' she said, glancing at her in-tray and wondering what she would be putting top of her agenda that day. Certainly not some strange carvings on an old box, she thought. 'Is that all?'

'No, ma'am, there's something else.'

'Go on.'

'Like I said, ma'am, it was a box,' Walsh continued. 'They had some problems but eventually they found a hidden catch and got it open.'

'And it was full of treasure!' she said, smiling to herself. 'Go on, Constable. Make my day. There was a secret hoard of gold in there, yes?'

She was teasing him and he knew it but she was his superior officer.

'No ma'am, not gold exactly. Treasure of a different sort. A package of letters.'

'Letters! What d'you mean? What sort of letters? Who from?'

'Apparently they're all in old handwriting. And the writing's faded a bit but they can all be read. They're from someone called Henry Tolliver.'

'Who's he? Do we know?'

'No, ma'am. They're still examining the letters.'

'Who were they addressed to?'

'They don't know that either, ma'am, except that they appear to be to his girl-friend.'

'The girl who died? The Lady on the Steps?'

'I wouldn't know that, ma'am.'

No, you wouldn't, you great Shropshire clod, she thought, unkindly as she immediately recognised. Her mounting excitement at this discovery was making her quick mind intolerant of the slowness of Roger Walsh who was only, she had to admit, doing what she'd asked him to do. He couldn't be expected to know the significance of all this. Any more than she could probably, she reasoned. She needed to get sight of these letters and find out what was in them. Maybe they would give clues to why that young girl had been murdered.

'What about the boy in hospital, this Richard More? Is he badly injured?'

'It would seem so, ma'am. He was found inside what we call Lavington's Hole. It's a cave down by the river. He was semi-conscious when he was found. Somebody had forced the grill open and dragged him in there. He told us it was Blakeway that had done it.'

She would ring her brother-in-law later to check up on Blakeway but on the other matter she needed to take care. Clarke had warned her off spending time on this case, so she had to be sure that any further investigation was done in her own time. Or maybe she needed to seek help from someone else, someone not in the police force, someone with time on their hands and the necessary skills to...

At once she found her thoughts turning towards her old partner in crime, ex-Chief Inspector Tallyforth. Maybe his new-found interest in History might be useful. But no, she thought, there was too much history between them, too much that had passed and been bad, too much *angst*. She would wait till she was due some time off. Or maybe find another excuse for visiting Shropshire.

EIGHTEEN

As luck would have it, two hours later George Elliott had the perfect excuse to visit Shrewsbury. A prisoner had escaped from Shrewsbury Prison who was known to be a particularly dangerous specimen, having been sentenced to ten years for his part in a violent robbery at a Post Office in another part of Shropshire, as a result of which the elderly postmaster had subsequently suffered a heart attack and died. She remembered the case well and had had a part in bringing the felon and his mates to justice. It seemed that he had been in the process of being transferred from Shrewsbury to a more secure unit elsewhere in the country because of his continued violent behaviour inside, when the prison van that was transporting him got bogged down in heavy traffic in the middle of the county town and he had kicked open the rear door and leapt out before either of the warders could restrain him. A call to her office sought her help in building a profile of the criminal to help in his recapture, so she quickly downloaded what information was on file and headed down to the police car park and her MG.

By the time she had negotiated the ever-busy, slow-crawling M6 through the Midlands and the faster M54 to reach Shrewsbury, her journey had proved unnecessary. The escaped prisoner had been apprehended in the middle of the town's Pride Hill Shopping Centre by an off-duty prison warder who had recognised him as he ordered a cheeseburger in McDonald's and had grabbed his arms before he knew what was happening. Fortunately for him, two Community Police Officers were on hand to help pin him to the ground until reinforcements arrived to escort him back to the prison.

So George Elliott was able to redirect her energies and her time to the case that was intriguing her most. She found her way on foot to the Shrewsbury Museum and Art Gallery, housed in the timber-framed building that had once belonged to a wealthy merchant, where she had been told she would find Gilbert Phillips, the Museum Assistant who had discovered the letters hidden inside the ivory box.

'This is the most exciting find I've ever been involved in,' said Phillips, a man in his early thirties whose thick black spectacles and equally black frizzy hair gave him the look of a startled rabbit. They were standing in his file-filled office, to which she had been shown. 'All we usually get here are things that Aunt Sally has left in her will and people who've been watching the *Antiques Road Show* think might be worth a fortune and expect us to purchase it from them. But these letters I would say were priceless, Inspector. I understand you have some professional interest in them?'

'Indeed I do.' She tried to look calm and detached but her brain was already into overdrive. What would these letters reveal? Would they give clues as to the identity of the victim? Or of the murderer? In her head this was already a criminal investigation, even though the death had occurred well over three hundred years earlier. 'I have a very definite interest in them. I was the person who caught the young man that found the box in Bridgnorth and was planning to make off with it.'

'Really? I understood that it was found by workmen digging at the site,' said Phillips, straightening the large knot on his tie.

'Trust me, Mr Phillips. I was there,' said George Elliott, looking at him wryly. 'It was workmen who dug up the bones of the young girl who had been murdered but it was a youth who discovered the ivory box. And, if I hadn't been fortunate enough to bump into him, you might not now be looking at these letters. Speaking of which, can I see them?'

He had not offered her a seat so she pulled a plastic chair across from the side of the room and sat opposite him. Gilbert Phillips's startled rabbit look took on an even clearer shape.

'I'm afraid you won't be able to handle them, Inspector. They are in a very delicate condition and, in the interests of scholarship, we are in the process of compiling a photographic record of each one so that they can be studied in full.' His lips curled slightly, as if he was taking delight in being thus obstructive. History mattered more than police business in this case. 'You will understand that, although there are many collections of letters from the period, it is rare indeed to find a collection such as this within Shropshire.'

George Elliott felt her temper rising. Interests of scholarship be blowed! A young girl had been murdered. Presumably these letters had something to do with her. Even more likely, according to what Walsh had told her, they were letters to her from some male. A boy friend? A betrothed? Maybe even, given the young age at which girls might have been married in those times, a husband? She was convinced these letters would hold clues to why she had been murdered.

'Mr Phillips, I have to see those letters.' The ferocious look in her eyes and the sharpness of her tone made it clear that she would not be denied. 'They are likely to provide crucial evidence in a murder enquiry. To withhold them from the police would be considered a criminal offence.'

Gilbert Phillips gulped and his frizzy black hair stood up even higher on his head. He turned briskly away from her, swivelling his head to address her as he did so.

'Inspector, I did not say you could not see the letters. What I said was that you could not handle them. They are in our climate-controlled room at the back of the building and, although in some cases the ink has faded slightly, they are all perfectly readable. Please follow me.'

They both rose and she followed him along a gloomy corridor to the room he had referred to, which he entered using a plastic card to unlock its door.

There were twelve letters in all, each on faded white paper that was tinged with brown at its edges and with occasional minor tears. They were written in a distinctive hand and each signed 'Henry Tolliver'. They had been laid out on a dark cloth beneath glass so that each could be read clearly, even though, as Gilbert Phillips had warned, in some cases the handwriting was faint.

Over the next hour George Elliott read each one in turn. They had been placed in sequence, with the dates at the head of each letter making clear what that sequence was. Before reading each in detail, she skimmed across those dates. January to April 1646. The later letters matching exactly that period when Bridgnorth Castle was besieged by the Parliamentary army, as Andrew Latham and Tony Alexander had explained to her a couple of days earlier. Might these letters throw some new light on that time?

She turned back to the first letter, headed 'Bridgnorth. January 2, 1646.'

'*Never such happiness have I yet known but when I am with you, those fleeting flying minutes that we steal from the night,*' she read. And she knew at once that this was a love letter, the sort of real love that she had spent her life looking for was there, laid bare in front of her eyes. As she read, the phrases came pouring out of this man's, this Henry Tolliver's, heart – '*I know your scented smell, I feel your lovely warmth*' and '*together we shall make an island, not apart from but in the midst of this world*' and '*your sweet kisses so inflame my mind*'.

George Elliott stood upright, reeling from the passion displayed in this first letter. Why had she never experienced love as deep as that? She thought again about her various lovers. Had any of them felt as passionately about her? Had she felt as passionately about them? Well, yes, with Larry at first it had been like that – the raging sexual passion that had driven them in those first weeks of their affair but that had faded, to be replaced first by an easy-going acceptance of and comfort in each other, before that too had faded to be replaced by irritations, minor scratchiness, dullness. Would this Henry Tolliver have experienced all that disillusionment too in time? Or would their love have been as enduring as he promised?

She read on through the letters. The second one, also from January of the same year, was more baffling with its references to people and places she knew little or nothing

89

about. Who was this William Pierpoint and where was this Tong Castle where Tolliver had been a tutor to Pierpoint's children? Tolliver had clearly been very attached to him and had accompanied him on a visit to the Parliament in London and to the raising of Parliament's standard in Shrewsbury[1]. But then at the start of the third letter[2] there was mention of the girl's father and the fact that Tolliver wanted to know who he was. Why had the girl kept this name from her lover? And anyway what was her name? It was all very mysterious.

She continued reading, feeling more and more baffled by the historical detail as she did so. She really had so little understanding of those tumultuous times. Had the king really been forced to flee from Parliament when its members would not accede to his wishes? And all that religious disputing! Did people really care so much about all that? It was hard to believe in this secular, almost atheistic twenty-first century.

But then the first mention of why she would not tell him who her father was. In that same letter where Tolliver explained the teachings of his Master Baxter[3], who had clearly been a considerable influence on Tolliver's thinking, was a reference to his lover's 'bower within the castle walls'. So she lived in Bridgnorth Castle. She was the daughter of one of the Royalist garrison, presumably one of the officers, for it was unlikely that the ordinary soldiers would have their families with them. Was this a Romeo and Juliet scenario? she wondered. It had all the bearings, didn't it? As she read, she began to realise that Tolliver was clearly a spy in the Parliamentary army used to infiltrate Royalist strongholds in order to find out their weak points. Was that how they had met? Had he been living under cover in Bridgnorth, maybe even visiting the castle itself, when he had chanced upon sight of her? In the heightened atmosphere of those troubled times, it was not impossible to imagine such a meeting and such a consequence.

---

1 See letter dated January 6 in Appendix.
2 See letter dated January 23 in Appendix.
3 See letter dated February 3 in Appendix.

And there it was, in the eighth letter[4]. Her father was the Governor of Bridgnorth Castle, Sir Robert Howard, the same man who had signed the surrender papers at the end of the siege when he believed that the Parliamentary soldiers were about to blow up the site of his ammunition dump in the church from their tunnel underneath Castle Hill and the same Robert Howard whose pistol had been found a few years previously under some floorboards in the Governor's House and been stolen from the Town Museum by young Ryan Blakeway only recently.

No wonder the girl didn't want to reveal who her father was to Henry Tolliver. It was Montagues and Capulets all over again, wasn't it? That she, the daughter of this powerful Royalist commander, should be consorting with a Parliamentarian soldier would have been a crime beyond forgiveness. Was that what had happened to her? Was that the reason why she had died? Was that why she had been shot in the head?

George Elliott read on in that same letter and was shocked by the scandal about this Sir Robert Howard and his wife Lady Purbeck. Could it really have been this same man in command of Bridgnorth Castle, who had once been imprisoned together with Lady Purbeck because of their adultery, and that later they married in secret? She scanned the remaining letters quickly, barely taking in the detail within them, except to note that this Lady Purbeck was the mother of the girl who Tolliver's final letter[5] revealed was called Venetta. The whole tale about Lavington's Hole and the surrender of the castle she knew already, of course, though she had to wonder if the information provided by Tolliver to Venetta had found its way to the Governor of the castle and helped to persuade him to capitulate.

She stood up after reading the last letter, arching her back to ease the slight ache developed from stooping over the glass casing where the letters had been temporarily housed.

---

4   See letter dated February 22 in Appendix
5   See letter dated April 20 in Appendix.

'So, Venetta,' she said aloud, more to herself than to Gilbert Phillips who was still at her side. 'You were discovered, I warrant. Your father suspected you were having an illicit liaison with a Parliamentary soldier and that was the reason for your death. Surely he didn't shoot you himself?'

'Quite.' Gilbert Phillips coughed discreetly. 'With respect, Inspector, we're not so much interested in her death as in these letters. They paint a most remarkable story of the siege of Bridgnorth from an insider's perspective. I'll lay odds that, when we study them more closely, we will come to an even better understanding of how this event shaped Shropshire's involvement in the Civil War.'

'Mr Phillips, you may be interested in the historical information in those letters.' George Elliott turned reluctantly away from the treasure trove of letters she had been reading, her brain racing with the wealth of information gleaned, much of it inexplicable to her at present, although she was determined to seek further help in understanding it all. 'I, however, am more interested in how she died and in who might have killed her. I will need copies of those letters immediately. How soon can that be done?'

'They have all now been photographed,' the museum assistant explained, smugly fingering the knot of his tie. 'And we are in the process of transcribing them from their original script.'

'No need.' She cut across his intransigence. 'I can read them as they are. Get me copies of the photographs please.'

'Inspector, I will need to ask my manager.'

'Just do it, Mr Phillips. I want those photographs and I want them immediately. Even better, send them to me as email attachments. Then I can print them off myself. Here's my email address.'

Gilbert Phillips took the card she proffered and, head bowed, moved out of the room to action her request, while she pondered how she was going to make sense of all these letters, given Nobby Clarke's warning to her.

NINETEEN

Ex-Detective Chief Inspector Tallyforth had let his hair grow down to and over his collar. He was lucky to have such abundant growth at his age, she surmised. Many men of similar age had taken to disguising their encroaching baldness by covering their heads with baseball caps or fedoras. The longer hair had the curious effect, however, of making him look more youthful from behind but slightly older from in front, where the contrast between the curling silver mane and the wrinkled face was more startling. He was wearing what he presumably considered was appropriate – denim jeans and a black corduroy jacket – though when she had walked through the campus, this was far from typical student dress in the twenty first century. Even on a Monday afternoon in April, the girls had bare bellies showing underneath their cropped tops while the boys mostly wore sweatshirts or hoodies.

She found him in the University Library, that grand classical building with its multiple floors and quite arcane organisation, as it seemed to her. She had in the end decided to phone him to ask for his help, reluctantly at first but then coming to realise that, given Clarke's warning, he was probably her best bet. She was letting this Bridgnorth business get in the way of her other work and, although she was deeply curious about it all, she needed to regain some perspective. Tallyforth, however, was a free agent so couldn't be prevented from pursuing enquiries that she would find problematic and he was studying History at the university so he would have easy access to some of the information that she needed in order to reach a better understanding of the background to the murder of the lady on the Stoneway Steps. There had been no reply when she rang his mobile number, so she had left a message and he had replied by text, suggesting she might find him in the library. At the Enquiry Desk, she had been given directions to the History section where he had said he was studying and, after several false turns, she had at last found him in an alcove surrounded by heaving shelves of books, his back towards her as he hunched over a table reading a thick, leather-bound tome.

'George,' he said, swinging round to face her after she had tapped him on the shoulder. 'How good to see you again. You're looking fantastic, if I may say so. I love the new hairstyle. Somebody must be making you very happy. Is it still Enoch?'

She decided not to answer this direct and barbed question. She knew him too well to get drawn into a squabble this quickly.

'Can we go somewhere a bit more private to talk?'

'Students' Union? It's hardly private but there's such a racket in there that no one can overhear anything you say. Come on. I'll treat you to a cappuccino and a muffin. Or are you dieting again?'

Cheeky sod, she thought to herself, though again she refused to rise to the bait, instead following him down the stairs and out of the Library building, across the grassy campus with its tall clock tower and through the every which way movement of young people towards the redbrick Students Union building.

'So, George, what's all this about? Haven't seen you for ages then you leave a message to say you're having trouble with Clarke and you need my help with some enquiries.' Tallyforth placed two coffees and a carefully-balanced plate with two chocolate muffins on it down on the table, pushing the detritus from its previous occupants to one side. 'As you will have gathered from my errant son, who told me he'd met you recently, I've decided it was time I did some studying at long last. I'm not quite the oldest student on campus – there is, I'm told, an eighty-one year old doing Geography somewhere or other – but I'm not far off it. I'm certainly older than most of the staff who are lecturing me but that's fine. And I have to say, it's been like a breath of fresh air coming here.'

She looked around at the crowded coffee bar and at the hundreds of students milling noisily about there. He was right about the noise – it was overwhelming. Everyone seemed to be shouting, a television was blaring in one corner, while a jukebox jangled in another. It didn't really seem his sort of place. He was a man of quiet spaces, up in the hills with his binoculars, striding through silent early-morning mists.

'What made you come?' George Elliott asked, sipping delicately from her white coffee cup. 'Never had you down for a student. Thought you'd take up some private security work or something of the sort.'

'George, give me credit,' he protested through a mouthful of muffin. 'Can you really see me poncing round John Lewis's in a Fancy Dan uniform?'

'I didn't mean that sort of thing and you know it.' The sparring was already starting, she realised. 'There must be companies that would want your expertise.'

'Boring, George. You know me. Routine is not my middle name. I couldn't have stood some nine-to-five job. Besides, I wanted to further my education. I didn't have your opportunities, you know. When I left school, you had to find a job, not go swanning off for three years drinking at the taxpayer's expense.'

Again she refused to rise. It was just like old times already, she thought.

'You're doing a History degree, aren't you?'

'Bingo.'

Right, time to get him on track. Just like the old days. Get him to focus. Together they could ..... No, that was wrong. For now she needed him to do some work for her, not the other way round. For now she was calling the shots. She was the investigating officer, not him.

'Are you at all interested in the Civil War?'

'Definitely. I didn't realise it until we came to that part of the course but we can't understand our modern world unless we understand what happened then.'

'Tell me.'

'George, that was when democracy really began to take root in this country.' Tallyforth's grey eyes began to glitter with excitement now. 'That was when ordinary people suddenly began to realise that they could have a say in how their country might be run. That's where the roots of our present democracy lie. That's also where all the world's great subsequent revolutions started – the French, the American, the Russian. They all took their spirit, their *animus* if you like, from what happened in Britain in the seventeenth century. They didn't all work out, of course, and the death of Communism was the latest failure. Have you read Fukuyama?'

'Who's he?'

'*End of History*. That's his book. His theory is that the death of Communism was the end of a historical argument and that democracy is inevitably the sole surviving way for societies to live by.'

'And that's why we and the Americans are bombing Iraq?' she asked, fleetingly aware as she said it of the stomach-wrenching images from Camp Breadbasket she had looked at the previous day and the suspicion that Ryan Blakeway's father was involved in those atrocities. 'Democracy at the end of a gun? Surely not.'

'You've become politicised since I last saw you, George,' he laughed. 'Been watching Channel Four News, have you? But you're right. He didn't foresee Al Qaida and the rise of Islamic fundamentalism.'

'Okay, I didn't want a history lesson,' she interrupted, annoyed with herself at being drawn into argument when she had promised herself not to. 'I just need some help. I went to stay with my sister in Bridgnorth over the weekend.

'Lovely spot. Always liked it there.'

'Yes, but I picked up on something while I was there that first of all intrigued me, then got me curious, and that now I'm determined to solve. Ever heard of a Sir Robert Howard from the Civil War period?'

He stirred his coffee and pondered.

'No.'

'He was the Governor of Bridgnorth Castle when it fell to the Parliamentary forces in 1646.'

A sudden thought entered his mind.

'Could be one of the Norfolk Howards, I suppose, but I've never heard of him, I'm afraid.'

'Look, there's a lot of things I don't understand from this period, particularly as it affected Shropshire and Bridgnorth in particular. I've got copies of a batch of letters from the time and I really need to know who these people were and what significance they had. I'm pretty sure that a murder was committed in Bridgnorth in April of 1646 of a young girl who was the daughter of this Sir Robert Howard and he may have been the murderer.'

She noted the pause, saw how his Adam's apple moved rapidly up and down a couple of times, could almost hear his brain ticking.

'George, remember, I'm retired from the Force, you know,' protested Tallyforth, but she knew he was hooked. She could tell from the sparkle of excitement in his eyes as he foresaw the joys of the pursuit. 'And why on earth does this matter to you? Aren't there enough crimes on the streets today?'

'I wouldn't ask, you know that, but Nobby Clarke's putting the frighteners on me for some reason and I can't spend as much time on this as I'd really like to. So will you help?' She allowed her eyes to plead with him, an old trick she knew would work.

'What's Clarke doing interfering with your work? He's Assistant Chief Constable now, isn't he? He doesn't have operational control over you, does he? The rules haven't changed, have they?'

'No, but he made it very clear to me that I should not be wasting my time on this case. I can't understand why it should bother him all that much. He said it was because it was history and I should be concentrating on current crime, but I think that was an excuse. It sounded like he was warning me off. Oh, by the way, how come Clarke and Clifford know each other socially?'

A whistle half-whispered from his pursed lips.

'Jake Clifford? Forensics?'

She nodded.

'Rolled up trouser brigade.'

'Sorry?'

'Rolled up trousers. Secret handshakes. Surely you know, George. Masons. Clarke and Clifford have been in the same Lodge for years.'

It was her turn to purse her lips in surprise. That had not occurred to her. In truth she had been slightly puzzled when Clarke said that he and Clifford met socially.

'Did you never get asked to join?'

'Oh yes, I was asked. Surest way to promotion in the Mercian Force. But I declined. I can't be doing without all that secrecy stuff. Besides, I've always believed people should be promoted on merit, not on whether they roll their trousers up at some secret ceremony or not.'

So that explained why he had never reached the higher ranks, she thought, not just because he was a maverick. But it still didn't make clear why she was warned off the Bridgnorth murder case. She reached into the clear plastic briefcase she had been carrying with her.

'These are photographs of all the letters that were found just this weekend in a hole in the ground where a few days earlier the remains of a girl's corpse were dug up. Clifford has confirmed that the bones date back about three hundred and sixty years, which puts us in Civil War times. You'll see from the letters that they belong to a girl called Venetta, who it seems was the daughter of Sir Robert Howard. It looks certain to me that it was her skeleton that was dug up. But I need to know more about the background to her death and who all these people are and particularly who this Henry Tolliver was. And I just don't have the time. Will you help?'

'It'll cost you.' Tallyforth grinned as he placed his now-empty cup back on its saucer. 'Have dinner with me tomorrow night and I'll see what I can find out. Okay?'

She hesitated for a moment, then thought about the current emptiness in her diary since the split from Larry Powell.

'Yes, but I'm paying. Adil's? Seven thirty?'

'Absolutely.' He grinned at her. 'Just like old times, eh George?'

Not bloody likely, she thought but smiled acknowledgement at him. She needed him now and needed to keep him sweet

TWENTY

She had only just left the university when there had been an urgent phone call for her on the mobile phone from her sister Donna in Bridgnorth.

She had hoped it was no more than a social call, even though that would have been unusual for her sister. But it wasn't, as she really knew all along. There had been another incident involving Ryan Blakeway. He had been sitting on a wall by the school gates but then had had fallen awkwardly and broken his arm. Andrew Latham had had to take him to hospital in Telford to have his arm seen to and he had wanted George to be told, as there was something she needed to know about the incident that he would prefer for Ryan Blakeway to tell her in person.

'Don't ask me why, George,' Donna had said and her voice had taken on its long-accustomed sigh. 'He just said it was important.'

So, chancing her arm once again and hoping that, since the call hadn't gone through the station switchboard, Nobby Clarke wouldn't know of her whereabouts, she headed out to the M54 to drive to Telford's Princess Royal hospital. Having found the A&E unit and explained who she was and the purpose of her visit, George Elliott was then taken into a cubicle where Ryan Blakeway, his right arm in white plaster up to the elbow, was sitting up on a hospital trolley on either side of which Andrew Latham and a middle-aged woman were sitting on tubular metal chairs. The antiseptic smell of hospitals pervaded everything.

'Geor...Inspector Elliott, thanks for coming,' said Andrew, getting up to greet her. 'This is Mrs Blakeway, Ryan's mum.

Mrs Blakeway, this is Detective Inspector Elliott, my sister-in-law. I asked her to come. I explained to you that Ryan's not in trouble but I do want Inspector Elliott to hear what he has to say about it all.'

Liz Blakeway, a small, dumpy woman in too-tight blue jeans and a vee-necked mauve sweater looked up briefly. Her frowning countenance told George that she was deeply troubled by what had happened to her son and that this wasn't the first time she had had these worries.

'So. Tell me what happened.'

'I should tell you that Ryan should not have been hanging around outside the school gates at all,' said Andrew Latham frowning. 'I warned him when I put him on temporary exclusion that he should keep well way from the school but, as usual, I'm afraid he took no notice. He was there when school finished and that's when the accident occurred.'

'And what exactly was this accident?' George Elliott turned her gaze directly on to the boy in the bed, making clear that she wanted his answer and not that of his headteacher.

'Nothing special,' Ryan Blakeway wriggled uncomfortably on the hard bed and forgot momentarily that he could not use his right arm to support himself as he did so. 'Ow!'

'So nothing special led to your broken arm?'

'Tell the inspector, Ryan,' cut in his mother, impatiently folding her arms in front of her.

'I was!' he protested. 'Give me chance!'

'Go on then. At your own pace, tell me what happened. I'm all ears.'

'I was looking for someone.' He wouldn't look at any of them directly, preferring to focus on the metal trolley on which he sat. 'This big kid from the sixth form. He lives near us but he's a boff, so we don't like him. He wants to go to university, the prat.'

'Richard More?' George Elliott chanced.

'Yeah, Pilgrim.'

'Pilgrim! What's all this Pilgrim business?' asked George, looking around in bewilderment at the other two adults.

'He's one of them Mores my dad told me all about. That bastard More who stole his children from our ancestor and

101

sent them to America,' said Ryan angrily from his bed. 'Just 'cos he was wealthier. It's the same story all over the world, isn't it? The rich control the courts, they control everything. If you've got money, you can do what you want.'

'Ryan, that's enough,' said his mother, reaching her arm out instinctively towards him, as she had done on so many occasions in the past. 'Your dad shouldn't have filled your head with all that business. It's ancient history now. There's no point in bringing it all back up again.'

'So presumably this Richard More who you were looking for knows all this story too?' interposed George Elliott, still puzzled at the relevance of all this.

'You bet he does, the boff. He's been lording it over me for years. Or at least trying to. He could do it when I was younger, 'cos he's two years older than me but, once I'd grown up, he couldn't.'

He tried to clench his fists but, of course, could only manage it with his left hand.

'So was that what your fight was about on Saturday night?' asked George Elliott.

'What fight?' The boy looked startled. 'I never fought no one.'

'Richard More was beaten in a fight on Saturday night and he said it was you. He's still in hospital as a result.'

'It wasn't me.' Ryan Blakeway's eyes blazed with hurt innocence but she couldn't tell if it was long-practised pretence.

Liz Blakeway looked across the bed at her, her eyes moist.

'Oh dear, I didn't know about that. Poor boy,' she said, clutching at her handbag.

'It wasn't me,' Ryan Blakeway repeated firmly. 'He's just trying to get me into trouble. He's done it before.'

'Ryan, I will not have this sort of feuding from pupils at my school,' said Andrew Latham, adopting his stern, brow-furrowed, headteacher mode. 'Once Richard More has recovered, I want to see you both in my office. We're going to sort this silly argument out once and for all. Mrs Blakeway, you're to come too. I'd like to have his father as well but I understand that isn't possible.'

102

'I can't come,' said Ryan Blakeway. 'I'm excluded.'

'I know and you will stay excluded until the governors' meeting but there's nothing that says I can't deal with you again while you are excluded. Inspector, Mrs Blakeway would like a word in private please.'

George Elliott followed Liz Blakeway and Andrew Latham out into the hospital corridor, where they had to stand back against the wall to avoid a bed containing a blanket-wrapped elderly man, stinking of death, that was being pushed along on the way to another ward.

'Andrew, what on earth has this got to do with anything? It's hard enough for me to find time to explore this business without you bringing me out here on some wild goose chase that's got nothing to do with anything.'

'Sorry, George, but there is a connection.' Andrew Latham scratched his left ear.

'Go on.'

'I'd better explain, Mr Latham,' said Liz Blakeway, her eyes clear now. 'It's about this old business. After the More children were sent off to America, nobody knows what happened to Katherine More or Jacob Blakeway. But the Blakeway family tells a different story. They reckon that Katherine and Jacob, who was little more than a labourer in fact, actually spent the rest of their lives together in relative poverty and that they had other children, one of whom became the ancestor of my husband.'

'I still don't get the connection'.

'Hang on, George, it will become clear in a moment,' smiled Andrew Latham, taking her arm and pulling her back to avoid another hospital bed moving along the corridor.

'I never had much time for school myself,' continued Liz Blakeway. 'I'm not from Bridgnorth, I'm from Shrewsbury. I didn't meet Ryan's dad till I was eighteen. He'd already joined up by then. Came to a club in Shrewsbury one night when he was on leave. And that's how it started. I knew he'd be away from home a lot, being in the army, but I thought I'd be okay. We lived in married quarters at Tern Hill at first but then Tom said he wanted our own place so we moved to Bridgnorth. His uncle had just died and his aunt was in a wheelchair, so she had to go into a Home. We bought their house for next to nothing. I didn't know anything about this family feuding business then. She was a nice old lady his aunt was. When Tom was away, I sometimes used to go and visit her. She had no children of her own. It was her that told me all about Jacob Blakeway and Katherine.'

George Elliott glanced impatiently at her watch. This was all very well but it was hardly adding anything to what she already knew. And that was of no real help to her in any case.

'She was the one who carried the family history in her head. She never had any proper schooling either. Worked on the farm all her life. Milkmaid mainly. Her husband did too. He was a farm labourer. But she knew all about Jacob and Katherine and their children. I used to wonder why it all mattered so much to her, then I realised. It was because she had the same name. As their daughter, I mean.'

'And what was that?' spat George Elliott, knowing that she was showing her impatience.

Liz Blakeway looked sideways at Andrew Latham, as if uncertain whether she should continue.

'Go on, Mrs Blakeway.' He smiled encouragement.

'It was Venetta.'

'What!'

'Now you know why I asked you to come over,' said Andrew Latham, a grim smile playing across his face.

TWENTY ONE

They were driving back to Bridgnorth from Telford in her MG. She had offered her brother-in-law a lift, since he had travelled to the hospital in the ambulance with Ryan Blakeway and because she needed to sort out some of this story that was now reeling inside her brain.

'George, I know you're going to ask how I know about those letters and what was in them, so I'd best explain that first of all. I told you this is a small community. Everyone knows everyone else's business. The cook at my school is Roger Walsh's wife, you know, the constable at Bridgnorth Police Station. I guess he must have told her about the letters in that box that young Blakeway found and, when I was talking to her this morning about the new healthy menus that we're being encouraged by the Local Education Authority to try out, she asked me if anything new had been found out about the person who wrote the letters. When I asked her what she meant, she told me that her husband had said they were from the Civil War time, written by someone called Henry Tolliver to someone called Venetta.'

'So how did you know about this Venetta business?" George Elliott asked, as she pulled out to overtake a slow-moving petrol tanker.

'Tony Alexander told me all about this feud between the Blakeways and the Mores that apparently went back centuries. I have to say that I hadn't seen any sign of it until today. Ryan Blakeway didn't start at Jack Mytton High. He only came here a year ago after he'd been excluded from another local school. And yes, he's been in trouble pretty much since he started, but there's never been any serious incidents involving Richard More. Or at least none that I'd heard of. Until this fight.'

'And Venetta Blakeway?'

'That was news to me too. As I said, Cissie Walsh mentioned the name Venetta to me this morning. When I was called out to the school gates this afternoon to deal with the incident, because it was Ryan Blakeway I decided to go with him to the hospital. One of my staff rang Mrs Blakeway and suggested she meet us there. When she arrived, she started asking him what he'd been doing on the school wall and he told her what he told you just now. He'd been looking for Richard More because they had had a disagreement and then he fell backwards. Mrs Blakeway started swearing at him then that she'd told him to forget about all that old stuff. So I asked her what she meant and she told me what she just told you, about this Venetta Blakeway that allegedly was the child of Jacob Blakeway and Katherine More nearly four hundred years ago.'

'And all this still has meaning around here?'

'I told you, George, even though the town's expanded in recent years, there's still a core of residents who go back centuries and these legends live on in some of them.'

She sighed to herself, slowing down now as they drove along parallel with the River Severn on the approach to Bridgnorth. Freshly-ploughed fields bridged the gap between river and road. A blackened tree stump was the roosting point for three cormorants.

'I just don't get it, Andrew. I've seen the letters and they make it quite clear that the recipient of them was called Venetta but she was the daughter of the Governor of Bridgnorth Castle, Sir Robert Howard. She wasn't called Blakeway at all.'

'Oh,' he said, looking slightly crestfallen. 'Sorry, I didn't know that. When Mrs Blakeway talked about this Venetta from way back in those Civil War times, I just sort of assumed that they were one and the same person. That's why I got Donna to ring you. I thought it was an important lead.'

'It is a bit of an unusual name, Andrew, I grant you that, but I can't quite see that there would be a connection. Maybe it was a more common name at the time. Anyway, when exactly are we talking about?'

'Well, we know that Richard More and his siblings sailed out of Southampton in August of 1620 and reached Plymouth in New England in November of the same year.'

'And how old was Richard More at that point?'

'Six.'

'And what about his mother, Katherine? What had happened to her? How had she allowed Samuel to take her children away from her and send them on this hazardous journey? Didn't she fight to keep them?'

'Oh yes, she fought all right. Samuel More had dragged both her and Jacob Blakeway through the courts, getting Jacob fined £400 for adultery with his wife and winning a divorce from Katherine which she disputed, presumably because she wanted to get some decent financial settlement for herself. And she did get him to provide information about what had happened to the children. She even got him to agree to pay her £300 by way of settlement for Larden Hall, which was her family's home.'

'When would all that have been?'

'The records about Katherine are silent after 1624.'

'So she might have gone off with Blakeway at that stage and had other children, including this Venetta? Who would have been maybe twenty at the time of the fall of Bridgnorth Castle?'

'Yes.'

'And it's likely, given her connections with the area, that they would have settled in the Bridgnorth area? Wouldn't there have been parish records, that sort of thing?'

'Remember, George, that lots of records got burned during the Civil War period, especially in Bridgnorth. It's not too surprising that there's little or nothing left from those days.'

'So, just for one moment, let's assume that the two Venettas are one and the same person, why would Tolliver have written that she was the daughter of Sir Robert Howard? Would she have been lying to impress him? Or maybe she was a ward of court? Didn't they have that sort of thing then? I'm sorry, Andrew. It's just preposterous. They can't be one and the same person. There must have been two Venettas.'

She had reached East Castle Street and pulled up just outside the Lathams' house.

'Fancy a cup of tea?' said Andrew Latham, as he opened the passenger door. 'Donna will be pleased to see you.'

'Okay, but just the one. I've had a busy day. I really need some shut-eye. In my own bed, before you ask. Thanks.'

She climbed out, locked the MG and followed her brother-in-law through the front door, glancing up the street as she did so and taking in the leaning greystone keep beyond St Mary's church at the end of the street. That was where all of this had begun, she thought. If only those stones could talk.

TWENTY TWO

When she did finally get back to Edgbaston, it was eight o'clock. She switched on her computer to check for emails. There was, surprisingly, one from Tallyforth. So, he'd mastered technology as well now, had he? The old Luddite for whom a mobile phone had been only used with great reluctance. Now here he was sending emails. The world was turning upside down.

She clicked her mouse to open it.

George,

Read the letters. Intriguing stuff. Have done a preliminary trawl in the Uni. Library and am attaching some basic information. See you tomorrow evening. Wear something nice.

T.

Sod him! She thought. Always something to irritate her. She opened the attachment.

SIR ROBERT HOWARD

Sir Robert Howard (1585-1653), the fifth son of 1st Earl of Suffolk, was a Royalist who inherited Clun Castle in Shropshire on the death of his brother Sir Charles Howard in 1622. He was imprisoned and excommunicated in 1625 for having his wicked way with Viscountess Frances Purbeck, Buckingham's sister-in-law. Amazingly, or so we might consider it nowadays (though remember that Jeffrey Archer is still a Lord!), despite this, he was MP for Bishop's Castle for six parliaments from 1624-40. He was voted compensation by the Long Parliament in 1640 but expelled for Royalism in 1642 and had his estates taken from him. Seems likely that he commanded a troop of dragoons during the Civil War and he was Governor of Bridgnorth Castle when it was forced to surrender in 1646 (guess you know that bit). Not clear what happened to him after that but in 1648 he married Catherine, daughter of Henry Nevill, Baron Abergavenny, by whom he had three sons. They lived in the 'Hall of the Forest' near Clun.

(Don't know what the equivalent of zipper was in those days, but he clearly couldn't keep his fastened! – T.)

FRANCES, VISCOUNTESS PURBECK

Frances, Lady Purbeck (1601-1645) was the daughter of Chief Justice Sir Edward Coke, who forcibly married her to Sir John Villiers. She must have been pretty strong-willed, because in 1621 she eloped and lived in adultery with Sir Robert Howard. For some time after this she called herself Mrs Wright and had an illegitimate son. For this she was sentenced for adultery by the High Commission Court to do penance in a white sheet at the Savoy church, though she escaped this sentence by doing a runner. The affair continued, however, and in 1635, the year after her father's death, she and Sir Robert Howard were both taken into custody and sent to different prisons, she to the Gatehouse and Sir Robert to the Fleet. Lady Purbeck escaped from prison disguised in men's clothes and fled to France. The government demanded that the French courts return her but whether she was given up or returned and submitted to her sentence is not known.

What is certain, however, is that some years afterwards she was in England cohabiting with Sir Robert Howard and was with him in the King's garrison at Oxford, where she died in 1645 and was buried in St Mary's church.

(Sounds a bit of a goer to me! Tolliver got all the story about her imprisonments right though – T.).

110

WILLIAM PIERPOINT

William Pierpoint (1608-1678), aka "Wise William", married Elizabeth Harris, daughter and heir of Sir Thomas Harris of Tong Castle. He was a celebrated politician of the Commonwealth period. He represented Great Wenlock in the Long Parliament, and exercised considerable influence in the House. During the early part of the Civil War he was one of the leaders of the peace party but after the breakdown of negotiations in the summer of 1643 and his appointment in February 1644 as a member of the Committee of Both Kingdoms, he became a vigorous supporter of the war. For some time he was looked upon as one of the leaders of the independent party but the trial of Charles I disgusted him and for several years he kept out of politics. He was on very good terms with Oliver Cromwell and on his death he backed the Government of his son Richard. He has been identified as the mysterious friend "as considerable and as wise a person as any was in England, who did not openly appear among Richard's adherents or counsellors; but privately advised him, and had a very honourable design of bringing the nation into freedom under this young man, who was so flexible to good counsels."

In the Convention Parliament of 1660 he was returned as member for Nottinghamshire but, when he was defeated in the following year, he never again sat in Parliament. In 1667 he was appointed one of the commissioners for the inspection of accounts.

(One of the great and the good – must have been a good influence on your Mr Tolliver – T.)

RICHARD BAXTER

Richard Baxter (1615-1691) was one of the foremost Puritans of his time. He lived his early life in Eaton Constantine, a little Shropshire village. His father was a reformed gambler who became a Puritan, which had a great influence upon the young Baxter. He eventually went to school in Wroxeter before moving to the Royal Court at Ludlow and then to the Royal Court in London. A courtier's life was not for him, however, and he moved back to Eaton Constantine where he decided on a career in the church.

In 1638 he was ordained and offered the position of headmaster at an endowed school in Dudley. In this town he befriended nonconformists. His own beliefs were unclear. He disliked wearing the surplice and opposed the cross in baptism, yet he saw nothing wrong with bishops and the liturgy. By 1640, while holding a position at Bridgnorth, he rejected the oath introduced by Archbishop Laud that sought to bind clergy to the hierarchical order of the church.

In 1641 he was invited to take up the position of lecturer in Kidderminster, where he rapidly transformed the parish into a godly community. In the Civil War, Baxter sided with the Parliamentary forces and joined various Parliamentary garrisons. After the Civil War he returned to Kidderminster and wrote a series of religious works. His politics upset many people. While generally agreeing with the idea of the Commonwealth, he disliked Cromwell and found himself supporting the restoration of the monarchy. He refused to sign the Act of Uniformity in 1662 and began preaching in meeting houses. In May 1685 he was tried by Judge Jeffreys, fined and imprisoned for over a year and a half.

Baxter is mainly remembered because he wrote so much. His works show the importance of religious thought in the minds of ordinary people, and provide an insight into the disputes of seventeenth century religion.

(Not my cup of tea, George, but you can see how he might have influenced Tolliver – T.)

There was a further run down on all the names mentioned in Tolliver's letters but they were not central to her concerns and she glanced through them cursorily, then clicked to close the document, switched the computer off and sat back. Okay, she thought, I've got a bit better picture of who some of these ghosts from the past were and I can see how their actions might have influenced Henry Tolliver. But there were still too many questions unanswered.

She reached for a notepad and began to write:

Howard – still a mystery. Did he live in the 'House of the Forest' with Frances Purbeck? Were there any children from his relationship with Frances Purbeck, other than this mysterious child called Wright? If not, who was this Venetta that Tolliver's letters were addressed to? Why was he made Governor of Bridgnorth Castle in 1646?

Lady Purbeck – if the girl to whom Tolliver's letters were addressed was really Venetta Blakeway, as was being suggested by Ryan Blakeway's mother, then what had she got to do with Robert Howard? But, if this Venetta was actually the daughter of Howard and Lady Purbeck, why were there no references to her in what Tallyforth had found out?

Pierpoint – that all sounded fine. He certainly had access to the great and the good of his times and, assuming Tolliver had been taken on as a tutor to Pierpoint's children (and there was no reason to disbelieve this), it was certainly possible that he would have taken Tolliver to London with him. All that checked out fine.

Baxter – yes, that checked out too. The influence on Tolliver made sense, if he had been schooled by him in Bridgnorth. And yes, that's why Tolliver knew Bridgnorth so well and was able to skulk around and not arouse suspicion when the siege was taking place. Quite likely he would have advised Lavington about the caves where he began his tunnelling under the castle.

The rest? – useful background information certainly but they weren't main players in the case now being investigated, though they were clearly central to that bigger plot which had led to the siege of Bridgnorth Castle and, presumably, to the death of this young woman, who may have been called Venetta Howard, Venetta Blakeway or even Venetta Wright.

That was the heart of the mystery. That and the identity of this Henry Tolliver.

Any why was Ryan Blakeway still so obsessed with Richard More?

TWENTY-THREE

It had been a quiet day at the Mercian Police Force's headquarters. George Elliott had been able to catch up on some much-needed filing and record-keeping. The only interruptions to her time had been from a phone enquiry relating to the prisoner who had escaped and then been re-arrested in Shrewsbury. She had taken the opportunity to speak directly to Jake Clifford from forensics – a risk, she knew, because of the Masonic relationship between him and Nobby Clarke but one she thought was worth taking. She had explained to him that she had been in Bridgnorth recently (which, of course, he knew) and had had a slight involvement in the case of the 'Body on the Steps', as the local press had decided to name it, and had wondered if, purely out of curiosity, she might see his report, although of course she had no professional interest in the matter. Clifford had prevaricated, as she had expected him to, but told her briefly over the phone that yes, it was the body of a young girl of somewhere between fifteen and twenty years of age and yes, all the indications were that she had been dead some three hundred and sixty years, though of course it was not possible to be too precise and yes, she had died as a result of a pistol wound to the forefront of her head.

All afternoon she had half-expected a call from Nobby Clarke but none had come, so maybe Clifford had been satisfied that her concern was no more than idle curiosity, or maybe Clarke had reasoned that his warning would be sufficient to keep her away from further inquiry. And Clarke was right – there was more than enough work to occupy her without delving into some 'antique mystery'.

Calling home to her apartment briefly after work in order to change into black jeans and navy sweater, she had then driven to Sparkbrook and parked the MG in a conspicuous roadside position before calling into the Asian-run off-licence to buy a bottle of Chardonnay, chilled in the cold cabinet. When she strode through the door of Adil's balti restaurant, she was deliberately ten minutes late. Had to get him on the back foot from the start.

Adil's lays claim to being the first balti house to open up in Birmingham and it certainly is one of the oldest. Situated within the now-famous Balti Triangle in Sparkbrook, it started serving its highly-spiced curries and huge naan breads in the nineteen-eighties, initially to the growing Kashmiri and Pakistani communities of the city but increasingly to the multifarious population of the city who had come to crave its exotic tastes and relative cheapness. By the time she arrived, it was already very busy, with only the occasional unoccupied table. The buzz of cheerful conversation and aromatic odours folded round her like a warm blanket

'Beer first?' Tallyforth half-stood from the bare wooden table where he had been waiting. 'Red Stripe?'

She smiled a greeting but declined his offer. Two glasses of Chardonnay was all she could allow herself, unless she wanted a taxi home. Which she had no intention of taking.

Tallyforth sat down heavily. He had smartened himself up from the previous day, when she had seen him in his *faux*-student outfit. Now he sported a smart cream shirt under his fashionably-faded blue denim jacket. And she quite liked the longer hair, she thought to herself. On some men of his age it could create a louche appearance but with him it gave an air of ancient nobility.

'You look good,' he said. 'Like your hair. How's things? Okay?'

She nodded, refusing to acknowledge his words other than cursorily.

'Can we order please? I've not eaten since this morning.'

'Watching the figure again, George?'

He couldn't resist, could he? But she had steeled herself.

'No, just busy.'

She pored over the card menu and jabbed her index finger at the chosen dish.

'I'm having the king prawn balti. And will you share some *aloo*?'

'Of course. I fancy the king prawn too.'

While they placed their order, she was aware that he kept glancing at her. No, she insisted to herself. There was no way. She should not have told him about finishing with Larry. Why wouldn't he just give up? Maybe this whole thing about involving him was a mistake. Maybe she should just stop it all now, forget about it all. Like Nobby Clarke had told her. But why? Why on earth would Clarke have been warning her off something like this, this 'ancient mystery'? His words still echoed around her brain.

'So, George, you got my email?'

'Thanks.' She tried being abrupt and businesslike. It was probably the best. He would know why. They had worked together long enough for each to know the other's whys and wherefores.

'Interesting stuff, wasn't it? I'm absolutely fascinated by the period. Obviously I knew about some of the major players in your Henry Tolliver's letters but not all. That William Pierpoint sounds an interesting character. And Richard Baxter. I'd heard of him but didn't know he had Bridgnorth connections though.'

'Yes, thank you. It was helpful to explain who those people were and how they interpenetrated this Tolliver fellow's life. But have you found anything about him?'

Tallyforth reached for the dish of poppadums that a broadly-smiling waiter had placed on the table between them and broke off a large piece which he then scooped chutney on to.

'No, not a jot. Afraid he's probably too insignificant to discover. From reading the letters he sounds as if he might have had some importance in the Parliamentary army in Shropshire. He was certainly at a number of the important places in the county where fisticuffs occurred. He may or may not have held any prominent position but, even if he

116

had, unless he was from some important family or other, his name would probably just have faded away into history.'

George Elliott too broke off some poppadum and nibbled on it. The tangy smell of warm curry and the sweet fragrance of coriander floated through the air behind her as an assortment of dishes was wheeled on a trolley to a table beyond them.

'What did you make of the letters?'

'Absolutely fascinating. This guy, this Henry Tolliver, has given me more insight into the Civil War period than I've ever had. It's all very well reading the classic textbooks of the period and even the more revisionist newer texts, but to hear about it from the horse's mouth – wow, that's something else!'

'I meant more about Tolliver and the girl, Venetta.' She tried not to sound impatient but her focus was on this poor unfortunate lass who had been killed, not on the broad sweep of history. Or History, as Tallyforth no doubt now thought of it.

He smiled, recognizing her old mannerisms, and snapped another piece of poppadum. At the same time the still-smiling waiter appeared at their table and placed before them the steamy black balti bowls, whose distinctively strong aromas climbed to their noses.

'There is absolutely no record of Sir Robert Howard and Lady Purbeck having a daughter at all, never mind one named Venetta. And his marriage that did produce children was well after 1646.'

'But she, I mean this Venetta, claimed that her mother was Lady Purbeck and that she lived in their home in the forest at Clun. Was this a tale of some sort? Was she making all this up? Could there have been some sort of mistake? Maybe, if what you found out is true, they were living together in Clun but out of wedlock. Maybe Venetta was illegitimate. Maybe that's why there's no record.'

Tallyforth sat back and looked across at her. A smile fluttered on his lips. She was doing everything he would have done. Asking every possible question, exploring every possible avenue, never letting go.

'I taught you well, George. That had crossed my mind too.'

'So, how do we find out?'

'About a possible illegitimate daughter? I don't know. I thought of contacting the Howard archivists in Norfolk but I can't see that they are likely to want to be interested in some new stain on their clan.'

'What about Clun? Might there be some records there?'

He spooned another mouthful of browny-pink king prawns into his mouth with a chunk of naan bread and considered.

'George, does this really matter to you? It's something that happened a long time ago whose significance is probably tiny. Do you really want to waste your time on it? Maybe Nobby Clarke was right in warning you off, whatever his reasons.'

For the first time that evening she felt her coolness deserting her, as she placed her balti dish flat on the table and looked defiantly at him.

'You always told me never to let go, didn't you? You always said that every mystery had a solution if only you looked hard enough to find it, didn't you?' she hissed at him.

He nodded, recoiling slightly at the new ferocity in her tone.

'Well, I'm not letting go. And there's something else that I hadn't told you before. The boy who found the letters has a great aunt who was also called Venetta. Coincidence? Maybe but I don't think so, especially when I found out more about his ancestors.'

And George Elliott proceeded to tell her old boss, her former lover, the person that she seemed inevitably intertwined with, all that she had heard about Ryan Blakeway and his mother and father, about Ryan and his rivalry with Richard 'Pilgrim' More, and about Jacob Blakeway, Katherine More and Samuel More and the children who had been placed on *The Mayflower* in 1620.

By the end of the meal, as they scraped the last segments of their curry from their dishes, Tallyforth was as intrigued and involved in the case as she was. And she knew it. He would visit the Shrewsbury Archives and Clun and Bridgnorth and anywhere else it seemed important to visit to find out more. It was a neat reversal of their previous roles, he thought, but he had never held much truck with status and position.

The job was worth doing for its own sake. Besides which, he might find something interesting abut his old adversary Nobby Clarke. Life had just got exciting again.

'But there's nothing personal in this,' George Elliott reminded him. 'I need your help but that's all there is to it. Agreed?'

He may have smiled his agreement, he may even have temporarily meant it but deep inside he knew there were ways in which they were bound to each other.

As she drove home, George was just thinking how relaxed she felt for the first time in several weeks when her mobile phone bleeped to tell her she had a message waiting. She pulled the MG into the side of the road outside her apartment block, switched on the interior light and clicked to open the message.

'George, Richard More has died in hospital. Sorry. Andrew.'

TWENTY-FOUR

The Shropshire Archives is on Castle Gates in Shrewsbury, between the bustling town centre with its buskers and shopping malls and the wide reaches of the River Severn that periodically rises spectacularly with torrents of water from the Welsh hills and threatens to enclose the town within its loop. Having found the building and made his way up the stairs to the reception area, Tallyforth was quickly instructed in the mysterious ways of the Archives and explained his needs to the patiently-helpful woman behind the desk. Her name, he saw from the plastic card she wore around her neck – a custom that was increasing in the country at large, he had noticed, as if people might need to check periodically who they were – was Fiona Lewis. She wore a long Paisley-patterned skirt and a green brocade blouse fastened to the neck. Her hair was blonde and spiky, just like George's, he caught himself thinking automatically, but she wore no make-up. He had time to take all this in because she was busy looking up some files for the information he was seeking – anything about Sir Robert Howard that he hadn't already come across, any references to children of the said Sir Robert Howard, and above all any mention of Venetta Howard/Purbeck/Villiers, or of Henry Tolliver, the biggest mystery of them all.

'I'm afraid there is very little.' Fiona Lewis looked up from where she had been poring over documents. 'There is a file for Sir Robert Howard, but I'm afraid it looks a little thin. I will order that for you if you would just complete this form. But there's nothing at all about the other two people you mentioned. You might try the church records.'

'Is that straightforward?'

Tallyforth completed the paper form in front of him and passed it back.

'Yes. I'll show you.'

She came from behind the counter and led him towards the opposite side of the room. He followed a step behind, noting the gentle swish of her skirt, as they passed people busy at tables or fingering volumes on shelves in an earnest silence. They were mostly people of his own age or older, indulging in the favourite pursuit of so many who had come to the latter years of their lives unscathed to discover the secrets of where they came from, always in the hope that one of their ancestors might have been a Norman baron, an Elizabethan adventurer or at the very least a compeer of Charles Darwin.

'This is the filing system for the church records.' Fiona Lewis waved his attention towards the wooden cabinet. 'It's all very straightforward really. The churches are all in alphabetical order, starting at this end. The non-conformists are at the opposite end but I don't believe you'll be looking among them. Once you've found the relevant church, you simply take the microfiche and slot it into one of our readers over there and scan through the period you are interested in.'

'So all I need to do is find the records for St George's in Clun and I'm away?'

She gave him a knowing smile.

'Many people make that mistake,' the *manqué* teacher in her explained. 'But you have to remember that the period you are interested in was a particularly turbulent time in our history. Records did get destroyed, so there are gaps. And it was not uncommon for people, especially prominent ones such as you are enquiring about, to use churches in larger habitations for the solemnization of vows. It's not impossible that there might be relevant records in the churches of Bishop's Castle, of Ludlow, or of Shrewsbury.'

'Sir Robert Howard was also Governor of Bridgnorth Castle when the Royalists surrendered in 1646,' Tallyforth explained. 'I still don't understand how he came to be there at the time but maybe he had earlier links with the town?'

'Exactly. Who knows? One has to be diligent in one's

researches, I'm afraid. From what I remember reading, the siege of Bridgnorth was the last battle between the two sides in Shropshire. Maybe all the important Royalists decided to fight together but I really don't know.'

Leaving her thin smile hovering in the air, she began to move away and abandon him to his search.

'What about illegitimacy?' he said, loud enough for an elderly white-haired woman sitting at a table beyond him to look up with a stare of fierce disapproval. 'Would there have been different ways of dealing with that?'

'That's possible too.' Fiona Lewis halted her stride and turned back to him. 'Maybe a smaller church nearby would have avoided suspicion. The rich and the powerful, you know.'

She gave him a swift smile and finally moved away but he knew exactly what she meant. He also knew that his search was going to be more complicated than he had thought.

The first record he tried, of St George's church in Clun, told him nothing new. There were no records of births from the 1620s or 1630s at all. The earliest records were from the 1660s after the Restoration. In vain he searched in the plastic microfiches of St Laurence's in Ludlow, of St John the Baptist's in Bishop's Castle and St Mary's in Shrewsbury but could find nothing that gave the name of anyone called Venetta from the period. The same was true of St Mary's in Bridgnorth and there were no records from St Leonard's in the same town because, of course he remembered that George had told him, the church was set on fire by an explosion of the ammunition stored there in the Civil War.

The file on Sir Robert Howard that Fiona Lewis brought across to the desk where he sat, was equally unhelpful, detailing his inheritance of the Barony of Clun, his time as MP for Bishop's Castle, his involvement on the king's side in the Civil War, his marriage to Catherine, daughter of Baron Abergavenny, and the birth of his three sons. There was no mention at all of Frances Purbeck or of the associated scandal. The file read as if it had been carefully prepared by the Howard family to stress only the positive and omit the dodgy bits.

The only other route was the smaller churches that the Archives woman had suggested but he did not know Shropshire well enough. He went back to her desk.

'You could try Newcastle-on-Clun.' Fiona Lewis pointed at the county map she had produced for him. 'It's very close by. But there are any number of small churches in that part of the county. You'll just have to try them all.'

Back at the desk Tallyforth looked at the map she had given him. She was right – there were lots of them. He had forgotten the impact of Christianity in its past manifestation and how it had been used by the aristocracy as part of their means of controlling the peasantry. It was no wonder that, once inflamed by Charles I's foolishness, ordinary people had wanted to burn down some of those churches. Where among all those villages of the south-western corner of Shropshire might Robert Howard and Frances Purbeck have had Venetta baptised? The church of St John the Evangelist in Newcastle-on-Clun was definitely a place to start but where else? In the valley of the River Clun there were Clunton, Clunbury, Clungunford – he remembered the names from Housman's *A Shropshire Lad* – and Aston-on-Clun. Around Bishop's Castle where Howard had been MP, there were Lydham, Cefn Einion, Churchtown, Colebatch and many other little hamlets. How many had churches? There were so many possibilities. And why did he assume that, if there had been other children, they would have had them baptised? Weren't there enough examples of the illegitimate offspring of the rich and powerful being left to fend for themselves without a proper naming ceremony or being given to the care of some elderly servant?

He tried them all from Newcastle-on-Clun onwards but without success. There was no record that even vaguely might have been construed as belonging to someone named Venetta. And it was an unusual name, so it would have stood out, even to his inexpert eye scanning these microfiche files from distant times.

Almost as an act of desperation he hunted in the general shelves and found the *Oxford Dictionary of National Biography* and there at last he came upon something that got him back on track, making the juices in his mouth flow under his tongue. The entry for Sir Robert Howard began, pulling no punches, by citing him as "adulterer and royalist adherent" and went on to repeat the tale he already knew about the affair with Frances Purbeck. In the middle of the piece about how she avoided her punishment at the Savoy, however, came the clincher:

> She evaded the penalties by escaping to France. When the storm was over she returned to England. On the allegation that she then lived with Howard at his house in Shropshire, and had other children with him, high commission proceedings were afterwards renewed.

Had other children with him? So, what George had surmised was also what others believed. That this fertile woman and this dandy with his pants around his ankles all the time had certainly produced further offspring. Venetta Howard/Purbeck/Villiers was at last coming into view but where to find her?

TWENTY-FIVE

'Social call, I hope, Tallyforth.' Detective Chief Superintendent Harry Gore, known everywhere by crooks and colleagues as 'Ruddy' because of his high colour, though the unknown sergeant who had once christened him thus had had an operatic pun in mind, held out his beefy hand. He was the type that, had he been born in Yorkshire, would have been referred to as bluff, more suited to walking the moors with a gundog at heel than policing the genteel borderlands. 'Been some time. What're you doing in this forsaken neck of the woods?'

He had stood up from behind the mahogany desk where he had been sitting when Tallyforth had been shown into his nondescript office on the third floor of the Mercian Force's western division headquarters. The room smelled of stale sweat and contained shelves of grey box files, a calendar featuring naked police officers tastefully photographed (all the rage after the success of the Women's Institute *Calendar Girls*), a small water cooler with a pile of plastic cups beside it, and slightly to the right of Gore on the desk a large computer screen

Tallyforth shook the proffered hand perfunctorily and smiled back at Gore. They had been contemporaries in the Mercian Force before his retirement and he still missed the camaraderie of their monthly get-togethers. They had been started by a well-meaning Chief Constable some years earlier as what he termed 'an information-sharing exercise', though in truth it was more in reaction to the then Home Secretary's plans to merge regional police forces after another incident where failure to share knowledge between different forces had led to public dismay and media demands for change. What Tallyforth enjoyed about these gatherings, that alternated between north, south, east, west and central Mercia, was the chance to metaphorically kick off his shoes and relax with his peers. Yes, information-sharing was central to their agenda each month but so was debate about common interests – the rise in identity fraud, the drop in the murder rate, the increased availability of guns in teenage gangs, the arrival of serious criminals from eastern Europe and so on. But, as important, certainly to Tallyforth and he suspected to many of his colleagues, was the fact that they could speak openly at such meetings. They did not have to appear all-knowing, as was so frequently the case in front of younger officers, nor did they have to be as circumspect as they usually had to be with their superiors, the Chief Constable and his Divisional Assistant Chiefs.

'Thought I'd look up an old chum,' Tallyforth answered, sitting down on the opposite side of Gore's paper-littered desk. 'How's things with you, Harry? You can't have long to go either, can you?'

'Ten months. Almost to the day. Can't wait, though a bit of me wonders what I'll do. I was never one for tending the chrysanthemums. What're you doing with yourself?'

'University. Started a History degree at Birmingham. Loving it. Best decision I ever made.'

'At your age?' Harry Gore's eyes performed a cartoon look of astonishment. 'Thought university was a place for youngsters. You always used to argue for the university of life as the best form of education. Changed your mind a bit, haven't you?'

Tallyforth stretched out his legs, crossing them at the ankle to reveal the criss-cross pattern of his socks emerging from his tan leather loafers.

'Yes, Harry. But there's no point in being an old curmudgeon if you can't change your spots occasionally. If you get my meaning. I'm really enjoying it. Especially studying the Civil War period. I never knew so much changed in such a short time.'

He went on to give a brief summation of the studies he had undertaken so far but quickly realized that Ruddy Gore's interest was superficial, as he saw that his eyes had settled into a fixed stare that indicated he was thinking of something else while giving the appearance of polite listening. You didn't get to be Chief Superintendent without developing that particular skill.

'That's part of the reason I'm in Shrewsbury,' Tallyforth explained, cutting his course description short. 'Been investigating a most interesting case involving the man who was the Governor of Bridgnorth Castle when it fell to the Parliamentarians. Fascinating.'

Gore shifted in his seat. Where was all this leading?

'This isn't just a social visit, is it, Tallyforth? You're after something, aren't you?'

'You know me too well, Harry.' Tallyforth grinned back at his old friend. 'Did you see that business about the young girl's bones they found on Stoneway Steps in Bridgnorth a few days ago?'

'I was briefed on it, of course, but it hardly comes under my jurisdiction dealing with a death from nearly four hundred years ago. We've enough to do keeping the peace here nowadays without having to dig up old bodies from that far back. The county must be full of them. Ever read that Edith Pargeter woman? Smashing book about the Battle of Shrewsbury. Henry the Fourth and Harry Hotspur. Thousands died there, you know. The bones are still there, under the earth just outside the town. Imagine investigating those.'

'Yes, I know,' Tallyforth insisted. 'But, Harry, did you know about the letters that were found with the bones? Letters from her lover. It seems that he believed the girl was the daughter of the Governor of the Castle, Sir Robert Howard.'

'I thought you were retired. What are you doing looking into all this.'

Tallyforth explained, a trifle reluctantly, that he was doing a favour for a former colleague.

'Not the lovely Sergeant Elliott? You used to have a bit of crush on her, didn't you?'

'She's DI now. And that was a long time ago, Harry.' No need to go down that particular avenue there and then, though the image that her name conjured up in his mind reminded him how seeing her had sparked off something in him.

And Tallyforth proceeded to give Ruddy Gore all that he had so far discovered about Venetta Howard/Purbeck/Villiers and Henry Tolliver, about the scandal involving Sir Robert Howard and Frances Purbeck, about the hunt for evidence that this girl Venetta was actually their daughter and the fact that his inquiries had so far yielded nothing other than remote and unproven possibilities. He also mentioned the fact that the love letters had been discovered by Ryan Blakeway, the son of a soldier serving in Iraq who might have been involved in the Camp Breadbasket case.

'Blakeway?' Harry Gore's eyes suddenly glinted, like pinpricks of white light in a setting sun. 'Tom Blakeway?'

'I think that was the name, yes. Know him?'

'You bet we know him. Definite trouble-maker. Had him arrested only last year for public disorder but he's been in trouble before. Whenever he gets home on leave, he's up to something. Usually fighting but he's been known for dealing drugs, for alleged rape and for firearms offences. Last time he was at the head of a bunch of so-called Telford supporters at the derby against the Shrews. We always have to double the force contingent for that match. There's a long history between the two clubs but it's mostly just ritual abuse-throwing and a bit of running gang-handed through the afternoon shoppers. On that occasion though this Blakeway character led his crew of bullet-headed thugs up from the riverside where we hadn't expected them – God knows how they got there. Anyway, they then went charging through the town centre and down Dogpole, pushing people as they passed and knocking people's bags to the ground, till they found a bunch of Shrewsbury lads waiting for them just by the English Bridge. Must have been pre-arranged, we think. Mobile phones most like.'

'Serious?'

'Not really. The boys in uniform got there pretty quickly and sorted them out. A few bloody noses. One or two cracked arms and bruised legs. That sort of thing. But Blakeway had a knife when he was grabbed. Said he wasn't going to use it. Only for self-defence. The usual excuses. Got off with community service. Which, of course, he didn't do because he was off to Iraq and his CO did some special pleading with the powers that be.'

'Not your sort of case, was it, Harry? Bit below you.'

'True, but we keep ourselves informed about potentials here as well, you know, Tallyforth.' Harry Gore smiled to himself. 'In my view, and that of some of my close colleagues, Tom Blakeway is an accident waiting to happen.'

'And the son?'

'Sorry, no knowledge. Though with a father like that, it wouldn't surprise me if he wasn't seriously dysfunctional.'

'He's involved in some trouble at school with another boy that seems to be the result of a family feud that's lasted centuries. Can you believe it?'

Gore tutted and scratched his left ear.

'Things tend to last over here, Tallyforth. You don't need to study history in Shropshire. We live with it day by day. If you'd lived and worked here as long as I have, you'd know that. It can be a bit of a bugger at times, when you have to scratch away at old sores to get at the truth, but it has its compensations too. We have a pretty good idea where to start looking when something happens. There's not that many incomers. It's mostly old stock here.'

Tallyforth nodded to himself. It was time to look a bit further afield and at the same time think about the Blakeway situation. George had hinted that it was probably unrelated and told him not to waste time on it but his sixth sense was nudging him, particularly after what Ruddy Gore had just told him, that maybe there was a crucial connection that they had all missed.

TWENTY-SIX

George Elliott had arranged to meet Steve Anthony for lunch. He was waiting for her outside the main entrance to the cavernous Symphony Hall complex in the heart of Birmingham. They cheek-kissed and she took his arm, as she had so frequently done ever since they had first got to know each other at university. He was the one man that she always felt totally safe with, the one she always confided in.

'Mind if we just go walkies?' he said, leading her towards the canal exit. 'I need some air after the morning I've had and you look a bit peaky too. Everything all right?'

'Fine. No, everything is distinctly not fine.' She grimaced agreement to his proposal.

In truth it had been an irritating morning for her. She had been desperate to go over to Bridgnorth to find out more about the death of the boy Richard More – a late night phone call to her brother-in-law had merely confirmed that he had died but no further details had been released by the hospital. But she had had to attend court giving evidence in a particularly nasty rape case and, although the proceedings had not yet been completed, she was anxious that the alleged rapist might get off. His victim – a Polish woman in her early thirties – had turned up in court wearing a lurid scarlet dress, cut low over her bosom and high at her knees. She hardly looked like an innocent victim and, even though George knew that the judge would warn the jury to base their findings on the evidence presented to them and to discount any personal emotions, she also knew the subliminal effect that the woman's attire might have on some of the jurors.

They crossed over the canal bridge outside the Symphony Hall building and turned left on the towpath, passing tables where besuited workers munched on sandwiches and swerving to avoid a jogger in black lycra shorts and white tee-shirt, his white iPod clipped firmly to his ears.

'I've brought a couple of apples.' Steve Anthony pointed at the orange plastic bag in his left hand. 'And some water. Will that do you? Good for the figure, sweetie.'

'Don't you start.'

'Sorry, only teasing. You look as radiant as the early morning dew.'

They walked on in companionable silence for a while, passing under the noisy traffic of Corporation Street and heading into the Gas Street basin where narrowboats were moored against the edge of the brown-black canal and where the glass and concrete facades of the new Birmingham towered alongside the industry-created waterways, reflecting themselves in the dank, still water.

'Well,' he said at last as they reached a wooden bench. 'Shall we?'

'Mm.' George Elliott sat down, splayed her legs out and folded her arms behind her spiky blonde hair.

'It's Tallyforth again, isn't it?'

'No! No! Really,' she protested. 'Well, not in the way you think. I have seen him again and he is helping me with something but that's all. Honest, Steve. Would I lie to you?'

'Not to me, but to yourself maybe, sweetiepie. What's he doing you for then?'

George Elliott sighed. In truth, she had enjoyed her evening out at Adil's more than she had expected. Tallyforth had been in one of his better moods – all charm and mildness, with none of the irritability she remembered from the past. They had parted amicably and there had been no pressure, no suggestion even, from him that the evening had had any purpose other than to involve him in the Body on the Steps enquiry.

'We went for a balti last night, that's all. He's making some enquiries on my behalf that I can't very easily do on my own. For reasons that....don't matter just yet. But there's an added complication. Before I tell you what's what, I need you to tell me about Camp Breadbasket.'

'Breadbasket!' Steve Anthony aborted his intended bite into the red apple he held. 'Why're you interested in that?'

'Tell me please.'

'The sordid details? The stripping of the prisoners, the sex acts and all that? Surely you saw about all that on the tellybox, didn't you?'

'No, I know all that. I mean, what was behind it all? Why did they think they could get away with such behaviour?'

'Following orders, they said. Their version of the truth is that their CO sent them out to round up Iraqis they suspected of stealing food from the camp and teach them a lesson by making them into beasts of burden. And that's presumably how some squaddies treat animals. Come on, Georgie, you know where they recruit from as well as I do. It's not exactly the Mastermind gene pool.'

Steve took a large bite from his apple and munched noisily.

'Yes, I know all that.' George was sipping from the plastic water bottle as she spoke. 'But even if they were obeying orders, even if that sort of behaviour is condoned in the highest ranks of the army, what has led them to think like that? I can't recall reading of this sort of thing in any of the other conflicts we've been involved in during the past fifty odd years, can you?'

A moorhen dipped its tiny black head into the water a few feet from where they sat.

'Georgie, it's why I'm here, my lovely, in big bad Brum. It's Crusade time again. Or that's what Her Maj's Government think. You've seen about Blair on his knees praying with Bush. You know they think they're fighting the forces of evil. Is it really any wonder that those they send out to fight on their behalf get contaminated with the same attitudes? And is it any wonder that the British Muslims think they have to be prepared to defend themselves? And maybe take action themselves?'

'You think there'll be terrorist attacks in the UK?'

'That's what the Sir Humphreys think. That's why I've been sent here to mingle with the community leaders and the imams and the like. Bonny, multi-culti Brum is just the sort of place where plotters might seek to bury themselves without being noticed. Anyway, what's your interest in the Breadbasket business?'

George chewed the last segment of her apple and washed it down with water, then started to tell him all about the Body on the Steps in Bridgnorth, the letters seemingly addressed to Venetta by her lover from the Parliamentary army, their discovery by Ryan Blakeway, the still not-understood feud between Blakeway and the older boy, Richard More, who had suddenly died, presumably as a result of the fight that Blakeway denied involvement in and Clarke's warning her off the whole matter.

'And Blakeway's poppa was at Breadbasket?' Steve Anthony asked when she had finished.

'Yes, it seems so, but there's been no mention of his name in the papers.'

'I can certainly find out if he was involved. But I'm not sure I can help with anything else. Are you sure that you're happy to let Tallyforth make these enquiries for you? Sure there's nothing more going on?'

'Absolutely,' she insisted, rising from the wooden bench and unconsciously smoothing her skirt around her slim backside. 'Steve, it's great to see you again but I have to get back to court and then to Shrewsbury about this boy's death. Give me a call when you get round to flat-hunting. I know someone who lives in the part of town you were talking about. I'll see what I can find out.'

Steve Anthony watched her swinging gait as she headed back down the canal towpath. If only, he thought, as he watched the perfectly-rounded spheres of her bottom. If only she were a boy. He didn't believe what she said about Tallyforth. Even if she believed it herself, he mused, she was in denial. There might yet be more tears.

He took a final swig from his nearly-empty water bottle.

TWENTY-SEVEN

The sleepy village of Clun sits on one of the historic drovers' roads that brought sheep and shepherds from the Welsh hillfarms into the markets of England and it was along this road a couple of days later that Tallyforth drove into the ancient settlement, following the line of the High Street with its stone cottages and sprinkling of shops and then across the ancient packhorse bridge. His first port of call was the Norman church of St George, where he hoped to find some record of Sir Robert Howard, who he had discovered had been the Lord of Clun Castle. After parking his Range Rover in the village car park beside the fast-flowing River Clun with the grey tower of the ruined castle beyond it, he walked slowly up Church Street to the attractively-styled lych-gate, like some kind of master carpenter's model of a Swiss chalet, and then along the tarmaced church driveway, sniffing the manure from the surrounding fields, hearing the insistent bleating of sheep and observing the ancient building with its curious double pyramid topping its squat tower.

Inside the gloomy, musk-smelling building he paused to take in the cold atmosphere, reflecting how this place had been central to the important moments of Clun people's lives for centuries. The church was surprisingly large, with its three rows of wooden pews, many of them holding colourful decorated kneeling cushions. Two lines of huge Norman pillars in stone the colour of honeycomb, with pointed arches between them, bore the weight of the nave. Above them the deep-stained wooden roof with its intricately woven beams and cross-braces added to the dark gloominess.

'Can I help you?'

Startled, Tallyforth spun round to see a big man in a black clergy shirt emerging from the vestry and approaching him with a practised smile.

'Simon Gardiner. Vicar of the parish, for my sins. Is there anything particular you're looking for?'

He was a large bear of a man, wearing yellow braces over his black shirt, as if his stomach could not be controlled otherwise. The smell of cologne mingled uncomfortably with that of stale underarm sweat. On his feet were a pair of green wellingtons. Tallyforth guessed he was somewhere between forty and fifty from the lines on his face and the greying of his hair that, like so many fat men's, was moist against his forehead.

'I'm here on a whim really,' he lied. 'I've been reading about events in the Civil War in Shropshire and came across reference to Sir Robert Howard being the Governor of Bridgnorth Castle when it was forced to surrender. He was Lord of the Manor here at the time, wasn't he?'

'Oh yes, absolutely.' Simon Gardiner's reedy voice, so unexpected from the grossness of his body, became enthusiastic now. 'Bit of a card was our Sir Robert in his day, believe me. You know about Lady Purbeck? There's a memorial to him in the Lady Chapel. Would you like to see? Please. This way. Excuse the wellies. Been tidying up the graveyard. Who'd be a vicar nowadays?'

Tallyforth followed as the Reverend Simon Gardiner clumped down the aisle of the church towards the aforesaid Lady Chapel, talking all the time over his shoulder. The wooden pews and the red-and-black tiled floor gave off the smell of ages past.

'The Lady Chapel used to be the vestry but, when it was decided to remove the old box pews and replace them with what you see now, someone had the bright notion of using the wood from those pews as panelling here to make it more holy-seeming, I suppose. It's lovely, isn't it? That's the memorial.'

By now they were inside the dark-wooded Lady Chapel and Gardiner was pointing at a bronze plaque set into stone high on the wall. Tallyforth strained his eyes to read what it said but the writing was too indistinct as three centuries of grime had worked their way into the metallic plate.

'I can't read it at all.'

'No, it's virtually indecipherable, isn't it? But all it says is that Sir Robert Howard was the Lord of the Manor of Clun and died in 1653 at the Hall of the Forest and that he had three sons, Henry, Edward and Robert.'

Tallyforth looked at the vicar, standing there in his wellingtons and braces, and wondered how much he should reveal about his main purpose in being in Clun.

'Did you say you knew about Lady Purbeck?' Simon Gardiner's thin voice interrupted his train of thought. 'It was quite a scandal. It was one of the first things I was told about when I was appointed here. Ernie Wright's our senior churchwarden and number one bellringer and a walking history of the village. If you want to know anything that's ever happened here since the Norman Conquest, Ernie can tell you. And probably before that, if you press him.'

'I know a little.' Tallyforth was still unsure how much he should reveal. Maybe this Ernie Wright character would be a better source. 'I know that there was an intrigue involving Robert Howard and Frances Purbeck. I know there was a child born as a result of that liaison and that they were both in trouble with the courts because of all this but I don't really know much more.'

Simon Gardiner turned to face him now, a look of glee on his round face as he began to retell the story of Edward Coke, his daughter Frances, her forced marriage to Sir John Villiers who became Viscount Purbeck, her tempestuous affair with Sir Robert Howard, the illegitimate child of that relationship, the imprisonment of Sir Robert, the intended penance of Frances and how she escaped her punishment by coming to live in the Hall of the Forest at Clun.

'Where is this Hall of the Forest? Does it still exist?' Tallyforth queried. Maybe there might be something to be discovered there.

'In the hills above Newcastle-on-Clun. But no, it's not there now.'

Tallyforth pondered this information. While the vicar recounted the tale, he was recalling Henry Tolliver's letter to his beloved Venetta on discovering that her father was this same Sir Robert Howard, *'a man who has disgraced the name he was given, who by his lascivious ways has so dishonoured the ancient line of nobility',* and her mother the same Frances Villiers, Viscountess Purbeck, *'Did she not think of the stain this adultery would bring upon your father's name? Did she not care for her children? And the stain they would carry through their lives?'* The power of Tolliver's words rang in his ears, as if he were standing beside him.

'Quite a story,' he said at last. 'It's hard to believe that a lovely old village like this should hold such a terrible scandal.'

'Yes, I know. Awful, isn't it? But its all part of life's rich tapestry. God will judge them, not us.'

Tallyforth shuffled his feet and stared again at the bronze plaque. Did these people really believe all this nonsense?

'I knew about the bastard child. Were there any others?'

Worth a shot, even if it gave him away a little.

'I really don't know about that.' Gardiner smiled wanly. 'I only know what old Ernie told me. He might know more. You should ask him. Would you like to meet him?'

'I don't want to put you to any trouble.'

'No trouble, trust me. He'll be in the pub at this time of day. He used to look after the graveyard but he's too old for that now. Which is why I.....' He pointed down at the green wellingtons. 'Come.'

He grabbed a navy blue fleece from a pew and ushered Tallyforth out of the gloomy church, through the churchyard, down the empty Church Road to cross the quaint stone packhorse bridge again, where they were forced to pause in one of its niches while a tractor passed noisily by them, and then up to the former market square where the White Horse Inn awaited them.

The pub was surprisingly busy for three in the afternoon. A group of three hikers in colourful anoraks and with their rucksacks stowed underneath their seats sat in one corner of the bar, two young men with paint-stained trousers and heavy brown working boots leaned against it, while an elderly white-haired man sat alone at another table staring at his three-quarter full pint of beer. There was a thrum of conversation and a smell of cheese and onion from the cobs displayed behind the bar.

'Ernie, this is....I'm sorry, I don't know your name.'

'Tallyforth.'

'This is Mr Tallyforth. He's been enquiring about Sir Robert Howard.'

The elderly man glanced up at them standing in front of his table. He was wearing an old tweed jacket over a collarless and greying white shirt. His eyes were soft with a film of water over them and blue veins stood out on his ancient neck.

'I've told him everything you told me but I just thought you might be able to answer more of his questions. Would you mind terribly? I have another appointment, you see.'

Ernie Wright grunted his acknowledgement. Simon Gardiner grasped Tallyforth's hand in his plump one and wished him God speed, then squeezed his hefty frame through the main doorway. Tallyforth moved to the bar, looked at the array of beer pumps and ordered a pint of Shropshire Gold. Seemed appropriate.

'So you've been talking to our vicar, have you?' Ernie Wright began as Tallyforth sat down opposite him on a hard wooden stool. His voice was cracked, as if there was phlegm on his lungs, and carried a light Shropshire burr. 'Bit of a rum cove, ain't he? Him and his yellow braces. Mind, I suppose we'm lucky to have one at all these days. Can't get vicars for love nor money, they says. Why you interested in old Howard then? Been dead a long time now.'

Tallyforth looked at the sallow face, with its rows of wrinkles like a ploughed field, and saw the twinkle in those watery blue eyes. Ernie Wright might be too old for looking after the churchyard but he wasn't so old that he'd lost his marbles. Or his wit.

'The vicar says you're a fund of knowledge about anything that's ever happened in Clun. I retired recently and I've just started doing a History degree at Birmingham University. I came across the story of Sir Robert Howard and Viscountess Purbeck and was intrigued by it. I just thought I'd follow it up a bit. That's why I came here.'

'Oh yes.'

'I'm curious about the offspring. I know there was this one illegitimate child, a boy I think, and I know Howard had three children from his later marriage. But it seems odd that he and Frances were apparently living together at this Hall of the Forest place for quite some time and there is no mention of any other children. Were there any?'

He'd said enough, he hoped, to convince the old man of the innocence of his inquiry, though, when he thought about it later, he wondered why he had engaged in this cloak and dagger stuff. For heaven's sake, it was nearly four hundred years ago. But then he remembered Nobby Clarke's attempt to warn George off. That was strange. Maybe there was some contemporary link. Maybe it was right to be circumspect.

'It's all a bit of a mystery, to tell you the God's honest truth.' Ernie Wright took a small slurp from his beer. 'Apparently after all the to-do in London, they settled down to a quiet life up in the forest and didn't have much to do with anyone. They'd have come to church of a Sunday, like everyone did, but they'd have had one of them enclosed box pews and come in the side entrance, I 'spect, so no one would see much of them. And remember, Clun was a tiny place then and all the ordinary folk would have worked in the fields. They wouldn't have known much about the goings on of the lords and ladies of the time.'

'Wouldn't they have been affected by the Civil War then?'

'I doubt much happened here. We'm still simple folk really.'

'So you don't think there were any more children?'

Ernie Wright stood a beermat on its edge and tapped it slowly on the table for what seemed like several minutes before replying. There was a yelp of laughter from the anoraked hikers and a black cat sidled through the bar space.

'Some say there was a daughter too,' he said at last, his eyes piercing Tallyforth's look. 'But the mother went back to look after her father, Sir Edward Coke as was, and maybe the daughter went with her.'

'Was she called Venetta by any chance?'

'I don't know that, sir. What I'm telling you is just gossip that was passed on over the centuries. It's probably nothing.'

But it was enough to put some oomph into the Range Rover as Tallyforth drove away from Clun.

TWENTY-EIGHT

By the time that George Elliott had extricated herself from the court case and taken the road to Bridgnorth, Chief Superintendent Ruddy Gore knew a lot more about Ryan Blakeway. The boy had been fetched from his home earlier in the day after confirmation from the pathology department at the Royal Shrewsbury Hospital that Richard More had died of complications arising from his head wounds. Immediately orders had gone out to Police Constable Roger Walsh in Bridgnorth to bring the boy into the police station for questioning. His mother had understandably insisted on going with him. On arriving at Bridgnorth, Walsh had briefed Gore more fully about the Saturday evening fight and about previous incidents involving Ryan Blakeway, including the theft of jewellery from the Lathams' home and the discovery of the cache of letters on the Stoneway Steps.

They met in Walsh's scruffy office, as he extricated two chairs from the mass of files and papers that bestrewed the room.

'Can you organise coffee for Inspector Elliott and myself, Walsh? Is that possible in this disorganised hell-hole? How on earth you manage to catch any criminals given this level of mess I do not know. It's George, isn't it? Don't mind if I call you that, do you?'

'Of course, Chief Superintendent.' George Elliott smiled ruefully as she sat down on the olive-green plastic chair avoiding the cracks. She remembered Tallyforth telling her about Ruddy Gore, his old sparring partner from way back when. Surprising to see him here on this matter – was there not someone of lesser rank who might have been more suited to this case?

'Oh, call me Harry. Everyone does.' Ruddy Gore took off his peaked cap and placed it atop a mound of papers. The red furrow across his brow marked where the cap had dug in. 'Gather you've had dealings with this youngster already, George. Was talking to your old boss earlier today. Before I knew anything of all this business.'

'You've seen Tallyforth?'

Why had he not told her he was visiting Gore? Or even that he had visited him? And where was he now? She had been ringing his mobile for ages without any success.

'Yes, called in this morning. Bit of a surprise him going to university, eh? Never would have put him down for that sort of thing. University of life and all that was what he always used to bang on about. Still maybe you can teach old dogs...'

She was aware from Tallyforth's reports of his encounters with Gore in the past that he had a bad habit of drifting into long rambling reminiscences but she was wound up like a coil about the tragic death of the boy Richard More and needed to get him to focus. Surely they should get on with their interrogation?

'I happened to be in Bridgnorth at the weekend and had dealings with young Blakeway,' she began and then filled him in on her knowledge of the boy and his family and the background to the feud that had existed between the two families, or more specifically between Ryan and Richard.

Gore leaned back on his plastic chair, causing it to creak with the strain of his weight, and thrummed the fingers of his right hand on the peak of his cap. Walsh briefly came into the office with two plastic cups of instant coffee and then left.

'Yes, Walsh has told me much of this feuding nonsense. Hard to believe it could have led to this though, isn't it?'

'I think we need to speak to Ryan, sir. My brother-in-law is head of the Jack Mytton High School in town and he has taken a particular interest in the boy. He believes that, although he is always getting into trouble, he is a boy of considerable ability. I have not seen anything of that myself but, maybe when he understands the severity of his current situation, he may reveal more. May I join you in the questioning, sir?'

'Of course, George. That was what I was intending. Tallyforth has told me in the past how much he respects your perspicacity. Shall we?'

Gore stood, gesturing George Elliott towards the door, and, after reclaiming his cap, followed her down the narrow corridor towards the interview room. Inside the buff-coloured room sitting behind a table were Ryan Blakeway, his mother Liz and Gareth Wellbeloved, the director from the Theatre on the Steps who was also a local solicitor whom Liz Blakeway had summoned. Opposite them sat Constable Roger Walsh, looking stern.

'May I stay?' Liz Blakeway asked, grasping her son's hand as it dangled from his plaster cast. 'I know what you think our Ryan's done but he needs me here now.'

'It's within your rights, Mrs Blakeway,' responded Ruddy Gore. 'And I'm glad that you have managed to get your solicitor here too. This is a very serious matter.'

'Thank you, sir.'

Ryan Blakeway gave his mother a surly glance, indicating that he was not intending to be as subservient as she was.

'Mr Wellbeloved, I understand you are here to advise this boy of his rights but I would like this interview to be as informal as possible. We need to establish the facts first of all before we start to apportion any blame. I would be grateful if you would let the boy speak as openly as he may, unless you have some objections to that?'

'No, indeed, Chief Superintendent,' replied Gareth Wellbeloved, his large moustache waving back across the table. It was ironic, he was thinking to himself, that the Blakeway family had engaged him in their business when it was this same youngster who was always causing trouble outside the theatre. 'We only want what's right, don't we?'

'Right, then let's make a start, shall we?' Gore once again removed his cap, intending this to indicate a certain informality, despite the fact that his sharply-pressed black trousers, pristine white shirt and neatly-fastened tie showed quite the opposite. 'Inspector Elliott, you know the boy a little, I think, so would you like to begin?'

George Elliott could see Ryan Blakeway wince every time the word 'boy' was used by Ruddy Gore and knew that it would not be easy to extract a complete story from him that made sense to them. But she had to attempt it.

'Ryan, you know that Richard More, the young man you refer to as Pilgrim, died last night?'

'Yes.' A sullen nod of the head. Constable Walsh had told his mother that he was wanted for questioning because of the death.

'We have now had a pathology report which tells us that Richard died as a result of complications arising from his head injuries. Do you know how he sustained those injuries?'

'No.'

'It seems likely that they resulted from a fight he had the other night.'

Liz Blakeway gasped and put her left hand up to cover her mouth.

'Would you like to tell us what happened last Saturday evening, Ryan?' continued George, in as soft a voice as she could, so seeking to disarm him.

Ryan Blakeway looked sideways at his mother, across the table at Ruddy Gore and then faced George Elliott.

'Pilgrim had been calling me all afternoon. I was helping on the market, like I do on Saturdays. My mate's mum has a stall that sells veges under the old town hall. It gets busy on Saturdays when all the yam-yams from Dudley and Wolverhampton come out so I give her a hand. She usually gives me a few quid. Anyway, like I said, Pilgrim kept coming past the stall and calling me.'

'What was he saying?'

'The usual. Loser. Wanker. Trashboy. That sort of stuff. Then he does that thing with his arms outstretched, like he's an aeroplane.'

'Sorry?'

'You know, Ryanair. Geddit? Anyway, I'd had enough and come four o'clock when we were packing up, I saw him coming past again and I told him I wanted to sort it all out between us.'

'Meaning?'

'Obvious, isn't it? I told him I'd see him down by Lavington's Hole at five. Nobody ever goes down there late afternoon, so it's quiet normally. And besides...'

'Besides what, Ryan?'

'I've found a way of getting inside. One of the metal bars is weak and you can move it and get through, if you're thin enough.'

Ruddy Gore shifted his large body uncomfortably on his seat.

'And then what happened?' continued George Elliott.

'Pilgrim thinks he's a tough nut but he's not. I got to the cave a bit late, about quarter past five, and waited outside for him but he never showed up. He's yellow, see. A big baby.'

'Ryan, the big baby is dead.'

'Yeah, well, I'm sorry but it wasn't me. Anyway, he shouldn't have been calling me all afternoon. If his ancestor hadn't took all those children away from their real father all them years ago and put them on that ship to America, none of this would have happened. Can you imagine taking four little children from their mother and father and putting them into the care of other people to sail across he seas? Could any of you have done that? Don't you think some justice had to be seen to be done? My dad told me that there's no justice in this world unless you make it for yourself.'

'And now he's dead, you think justice has been done, do you? Is that what you think, Ryan? You think that Richard More's death squares the circle, do you? Really, is that what you think?'

'It wasn't me. I didn't see him, so I couldn't have hit him, could I? It wasn't me. I've told you the truth. I don't know anything about it.'

Gareth Wellbeloved leaned forward and pulled at Ryan's free arm. The boy inclined towards him and nodded his head as the solicitor explained something to him. On his other side Liz Blakeway was still sitting with her hand to her mouth, her eyes agape with fright and astonishment.

'Inspector, I think we need a moment or two talk about this and we'll leave Mr Wellbeloved to advise his client,' said

Ruddy Gore, already out of his seat and replacing his peaked cap on his head.

In the corridor outside he turned towards George.

'George, this looks serious but we only have what the dead boy allegedly said about the person who hit him. And we can't get anything more from him, can we? What do you think? I think we might have to let him go for now.'

'Richard More's family aren't going to be as generous in their interpretation, sir.'

'Good point, George. Good point. But, as the boy says, justice must be seen to be done. Caution him and let him go home. He's hardly a threat to the public, is he? We'd better get forensics to do a full report into the cause of death, get Walsh to tell us exactly what the boy said when he was found and inspect the site where the fight took place.'

'Sir, if you're asking me to be involved with this, you'll have to square it with Assistant Chief Constable Clarke.'

'No, I'll get some of our boys on to it and keep you posted. You can get back to the big city. I'll get someone to let you know as soon as we've finished our enquiries. Old Nobby, eh? Yes, I'll contact him. Known him for years.'

History everywhere, she thought, as she prepared to return to the interview room to caution Ryan Blakeway.

TWENTY-NINE

All police leave had been cancelled for that Friday. The BNP was holding a march through the centre of Birmingham to celebrate St George's Day. It wasn't actually St George's Day – that was on the following Sunday when the official city celebrations, muted as they were nowadays and involving little more than troops of boy scouts marching behind a brass band, were held. The BNP had been trying unsuccessfully for several years to be allowed to participate in the official event but had always been denied, so their leadership had decided to organize their own rally and had been granted permission to do so on that Friday after the city council had tried to block it but been ordered by the High Court to allow it because of their interpretation of the Human Rights Act.

For George Elliott it was a change of duties for she was expected to watch the rally and be alert for any signs of trouble or any signs of known troublemakers, for inevitably the Birmingham Anti-Fascist Alliance had announced its intention to take over Victoria Square outside the Town Hall before the BNP marchers arrived there. She had not heard from Tallyforth since their meal together at Adil's on the Tuesday evening and thoughts of Henry Tolliver and Venetta and the Civil War had been pushed to the back of her mind temporarily, although she had received a phone call from her brother-in-law Andrew informing her that he had heard the terrible news about Richard More and about Ryan Blakeway's possible involvement. He had also mentioned that Tony Alexander had located the pistol once belonging to Sir Robert Howard and, if she had any time over the weekend and was still interested, she could call over and talk to him about it. She had made no commitment but promised to ring back later.

Nobby Clarke had taken operational control of police activity on the day of the march, deploying his troops to what he thought would be maximum effect. Victoria Square would be ring-fenced with barriers and uniformed officers from early morning to prevent the Anti-Fascist Alliance from controlling it. They were to be allowed to gather beyond its perimeter where they could wave their placards and shout whatever slogans they wanted but they were not to be allowed to meet the BNP marchers head on. Clarke had little sympathy for the BNP but was clear in his duty to uphold the right to free speech enshrined in law. Consequently, he had arranged that the route of their march would bring them into Victoria Square without their having to confront their opponents. Uniformed officers would walk along either side of the marchers to ensure there was no trouble. Non-uniformed officers, such as George Elliott, were to be placed strategically either along the route of the march or in discreet positions around Victoria Square, their chief task being to stay alert to potential flashpoints if any of the opposing parties were to break from their pre-arranged routes or stations.

George found herself high up in an office of the Town Hall itself with a bird's eye view of the whole of Victoria Square and of the march as it approached down Colmore Road. Arriving in her position early in the morning she had made herself as comfortable as she could by wheeling a leather-covered office chair from its desk position to the tall window. Having taken the precautionary step of bringing a large bottle of Malvern Water and a small bag of dried fruit with her, she had then settled herself in the chair with her police-issue binoculars to witness events as they unfolded.

The first arrivals were small groups of people with placards stating BRUM SAYS NO TO FASCISTS and SAY NO TO RACISM and SHOUT AGAINST FASCISM and suchlike. The usual suspects, she thought to herself. At first disgruntled at not being able to occupy Victoria Square, they had quickly sussed out the best positions for their placards, that is the positions that the media pack's cameras would focus on. They were gradually joined by others, some merely individuals who took up their seemingly accustomed places then later groups from different organizations in the city – the Sparkbrook Asian Community, Christians for Peace, the Socialist Workers' Party, West Bromwich Sikhs, Smethwick Rastafarians, the Birmingham United Mosques. Each group carried its own placard or flag, proclaiming their identity, and wore the uniform of that group. For the Sparkbrook Asians, it was casual everyday dress, for the Christians for Peace it was tee-shirts, jeans and sandals, for the Socialist Workers' Party it was black donkey jackets and denim jeans, for the West Bromwich Sikhs it was an array of brightly-coloured turbans, for the Smethwick Rastafarians it was their dreadlocks and multicoloured hats, for the Birmingham United Mosques it was *shalwar kameez* or *hijab*. By mid-morning a large assemblage of the concerned Birmingham citizenry was gathered there alternately chanting their slogans or standing around, expectantly.

Then there was a shout and, as George Elliott swivelled her binoculars, she could see the leaders of the BNP, marching six abreast as if in a military tattoo towards Victoria Square, preceded by a massive Union Jack being carried by four men, one at each corner, and two other men carrying aloft the white flag with the red cross of St George. The formulaic chants of the Anti-Fascist Alliance changed into angry shouts of abuse in an instant, as fists were waved, placards and flags were raised even higher and the line of yellow-jacketed police officers around the barrier stiffened. A terrified ginger cat appeared from nowhere and raced across the empty space behind the barriers, disappearing as mysteriously as it had arrived.

The office door behind George Elliott softly swished open and she barely had time to drop the binoculars on the cord round her neck to look around when a voice said:

'Big boys out to play again, sweetie.'

'Steve!' she had turned fully around now, her eyes dilating when she realized that it was none other than Steve Anthony who now stood grinning his toothy grin over her. 'What on earth are you doing here? How did you....?'

'Ways and means, darling. What you don't know never hurt you.'

'Come on, Steve. How did you find me?'

'If you must know, I persuaded my Sir Humphrey to get in touch with whoever was organizing the policing, which turned out to be you know who. Then I spoke to your Nobby Clarke fellow who told me exactly which high place you would be spending your time in. So here I am. I need to be watching this little show as well. Might as well do it with you, methinks. Any objections if I share your window?'

She laughed as he produced a neat pair of black binoculars from the pocket of his leather bomber jacket. It was good to have him there.

'Anyone special you're interested in?' she asked, resuming her position with glasses raised to her eyes.

'Ooh yes, you betcha. See that bunch behind that banner that says Birmingham United Mosques? See the one in the grey *shalwar kameez*, the one with the straggly beard? He's one of those preachers of hate that Her Maj's government dislikes so much but feels that we have to let him spout his stuff because of freedom of speech *et cetera, et cetera*. He's the sort that the *Daily Mail* gets frothy about. You know, he's corrupting the young by making them believe that Blair is the devil incarnate and that Britain wants to drive Islam off the planet. And, allegedly, we're daft enough to be supporting him, because he's scrounging benefits off the state. Ali Moussavi his name is, though the *Mail* with its usual subtlety calls him Ali Baba. But he's harmless. He's not one of those we're worried about. It's the quieter ones we have to watch, the ones who turn up at gatherings like this but don't actually do very much. See those three a few feet behind him? Not even shouting. Just looking around them. They're the type.'

'Of what?'

'That's it, sweetie pie, we don't know. The spooks keep telling us that there's going to be a spectacular in the UK but they don't know where or when. They just say they hear chatter. What that means I just don't know. But we have to be alert. We've become very unpopular since we joined in Bush's War on Terror. Even some of our friends in the Middle East and the sub-continent have turned against us. Think what that Breadbasket stuff has done for our reputation abroad.'

The leaders of the BNP march were approaching their goal by now, their bald heads glistening with sweat in the weak sunlight and their faces set in sour determination, as the crowd awaiting them increased the volume and vigour of its shouts. Arms were raised aloft in protest, clenched fists shaken angrily and leaflets were showered on the marchers who retained their grim expressions as they pressed forward through the police cordon and on to the steps of Victoria Square.

'Bloody hell! That's him. What's he doing here?'

George Elliott was almost toppling out of the window as she sought to confirm the sighting.

'Who, darling?'

'Blakeway. Ryan Blakeway. The boy I told you about. The one who's in trouble over the other lad's death in Bridgnorth.'

He was in the third row of marchers, once again wearing his Burberry cap but now in the black shirt and trousers favoured by his fellow-marchers. The white plaster on his right arm stood out in that sea of black. Beside him, and holding on to his other arm by the elbow, was an older man with a shaven head and tattoos bursting out of the arms of his black tee-shirt. The veins on his forehead stood out as he simmered with suppressed anger but the face was too similar to that of the boy beside him for there to be any mistake. It was Blakeway Senior. Tom Blakeway.

'And I'm pretty sure that's his father next to him.'

'The Breadbasket case?'

'The same.'

But before she could decide what to do about this identification, or even to pursue the thoughts that had started running like crazy hares in her brain, there was a sudden commotion and the ordered ranks of the BNP marchers split apart like segments of an orange. Someone from the mob chanting abuse had hurled a well-aimed plastic bottle at one of the leaders of the march and it had caught him on the bridge of the nose, knocking him to his knees. Other objects followed through the air – plastic cups, fruit and squashy vegetables, paper darts, a brown shoe, folded newspapers, even the placards that had been proudly proclaiming opposition to all that the BNP stood for. For a micro-second the black-shirted marchers fell back but then they turned, almost as one, their anger no longer having to be held in check, their inherent viciousness allowed full scope. They charged towards the mob, knocking over the red and white barriers placed there to protect them and sought to break through the police cordon beyond it, which had of course now been reinforced by those officers who had accompanied the march.

For several minutes there was pandemonium. Occasionally some of the black-shirted men would break through and start flailing at whoever was in front of them. Once or twice individuals from the Anti-Fascist Alliance gained entry to the inner circle of the Square and set about any thug they met. The whole scene was like a battle painted by Goya. And it was a battle between, as all involved saw it, the forces of good and the forces of evil, though each side saw itself as the former. A policeman was knocked to the ground and had to be rescued by his colleagues but gradually the police line was reinforced, as black minibuses parked nearby disgorged the reserve officers with their sinister shields and heavy batons that Nobby Clarke had kept for just such an emergency. Within twenty minutes – enough time for the carefully-placed cameras of the media to capture images that could be used to portray the Wild West lawlessness at the heart of the country's second city – order had been restored. A massive police presence had corralled the BNP marchers in the centre of the Square and forced the protesting mob further and further back down New Street and Waterloo Street. Arrests were made, seemingly at random, though George could see that both Blakeways had been led away, struggling violently but uselessly.

As she was about to put her glasses down again, she heard Steve Anthony exclaim.

'That one. I need to know about him. Can you get your people to find out? No harassment please. Just have his name and address taken then let him go.'

'Why him?' She had raised her binoculars back to her eyes to see where Steve was pointing.

A black-haired man in his mid-twenties, wearing faded denim jeans and a white cheesecloth shirt, was standing at the far edge of the Square beyond the line of police officers.

'He's doing nothing,' George said.

'Exactly. But he's watching everything. Why is he doing that? Why is he so interested in police deployment? Why is he looking up here?'

She gave him a quizzical look but radioed down to one of her colleagues in the Square with Steve's request and watched as the young man was questioned and then sent on his way.

'Thanks, sweetie. Must fly. Need to find out a bit about my dusky friend. Lots of love.'

THIRTY

'This country's going to the dogs. The blood's being poisoned by all these foreigners coming in here. There's too many of them. We're only a small island. We ain't got room for the thousands that come in here every year. They've got no skills to offer us or nothing. All they want is to scrounge off us. It's time to take a stand against them. You saw them out there today – all them black faces, them brown faces. Why don't they go back where they come from? They're always complaining that they don't get treated proper so why don't they just fuck off back where they come from? We don't want them. Bunch of useless tossers. Churchill wouldn't have allowed it. He'd be turning in his grave if he saw what's happening to this country now. Maggie tried to stop them but all those other wet bastards in her government stopped her, told her she couldn't do it. Why the fuck not? It's our country, not theirs.'

Tom Blakeway, eyes popping out of his angry red face, gripped his son's left arm tight with his free hand, the other arm being handcuffed to a uniformed police officer. They were standing inside the Town Hall, which had been turned into a temporary police station on Nobby Clarke's orders. The stately marble foyer of Joseph Chamberlain's proud city headquarters was filled with trestle tables behind which sat a number of police officers rapidly filling out charge sheets for those arrested in the fracas outside.

'Name?' The uniformed female officer did not look up.

'What are we being charged with? It's a free country, ain't it?'

'Name?'

154

Tom Blakeway stared belligerently at the dark-haired woman who was still refusing to make eye contact.

'Thomas Blakeway.'

'Address?'

Reluctantly he gave his home address and the other details she asked for, his anger cooling slightly now. He had been in this sort of situation too often before and knew he needed to keep his powder dry. He knew too that he had to do what he could to protect his son.

'My boy wasn't involved. He was just beside me. He done nothing.'

'Thomas Blakeway, you are being charged with assault of a police officer.'

'What about my boy?'

'I'll deal with him.' A voice came from behind them and, when they looked round, they saw a woman with blonde hair in black denim jeans and fashionable pinstripe jacket approaching them through the main door of the Town Hall. It was George Elliott.

'Ryan Blakeway, isn't it? And you must be his father.' She spoke brusquely, grasping the younger man by the elbow. 'Charge this man, officer. I'll deal with the boy. Come with me, Ryan.'

There was a brief struggle as Tom Blakeway sought to keep his son with him and had to be restrained by another police officer but finally the boy was separated from his father and was led away by George Elliott into an office off the main foyer, with his father shouting after him to wait outside afterwards.

Once inside the tiny paper-filled office where there was only one wooden chair and a small formica-topped table, George sat Ryan Blakeway down and glowered at him. He sat sullenly, his brow furrowed and his eyes full of spite. His Burberry cap had disappeared in the melee and there was a blood-red stain on his black tee-shirt where a tomato had caught him front on. He rested his plaster-encased right arm on the table.

'So, young man. I didn't expect to see you here. Your father's idea of a day out, was it?'

There was no response. His left foot tapped quietly and insistently on the wooden parquet floor. She waited, letting the echoing silence unnerve him.

'Or do you belong to this lot? I'm surprised. Aren't you in enough trouble already? Your headmaster said you were a bright boy. Didn't think you'd get mixed up with this rabble. He'd be surprised too, I shouldn't wonder.'

'Tosser.' The muttered word was barely audible.

'What?'

'Nothing.'

Again she let the silence sweep around him, as his foot tapped even more insistently now and she watched him attempt to clench his fists.

'Well? Are you a soldier of the British National Party? Or are you just here on holiday?'

'You lot will never understand.' He looked up at her now, his eyes blazing, his foot still. 'You lot should be doing proper police work, protecting people in their neighbourhoods and catching real criminals, not protecting all these Muslims and blacks. The police has gone soft. You're too busy being bloody social workers nowadays. You're not proper police any longer. No one's afraid of you any longer. You're too busy being politically correct. You're soft on proper criminals, they have too many rights. What about the victims? Don't they deserve proper support? Everyone knows that the ethnics do most of the crime in this country but most of them don't end up in prison because of the stupid Race Relations Laws that protect them. And even those who do get banged up get released after a couple of years. The BNP has plans to sort you lot out.'

'I'm so looking forward to that, Ryan.' George's lips curled sarcastically. 'Is it the next election when the BNP becomes the government? Or is it a bit further off?'

'If the election results weren't fiddled, we'd be in power now. Don't you worry. We're going to make sure it doesn't happen again. We're going to have candidates at every constituency next time round. And they'll check the votes are being counted properly. And we'll stop them postal voting cheats as well. We'll stop them Pakis from all that.'

He was getting more and more agitated, George could see, but she wanted him to go on a little further, if only to hear the full extent of the nonsense that was wallowing around like a mulligatawny soup in his brain.

'So that's your version of democracy, is it? That's what your father's fighting to bring about in Iraq, is it?'

He went silent again, surprised at this change of tack. His left foot resumed its tapping.

'My dad's a member of the British Armed Forces and proud of it. But we shouldn't be in Iraq. It's an unjust war. The BNP's been against it from the start. Iraq's never threatened Britain. We're only there to protect American oil interests.'

'So that's why some of your dad's mates think they can get away with degrading Iraqi prisoners, is it?'

'My dad wasn't involved. He told me that straight.'

'Not everyone might agree with you on that, Ryan.'

He started to speak but the decided against it, looking away from her and glaring at the shiny parquet blocks. There was no point in taking it any further, George decided. She had wanted to test out this supposed intelligence that her brother-in-law had seemed so surprised by and she now realised that much of it came from his association – or more probably from his father's association – with the BNP.

'Right, Ryan, you're free to go. But remember, you were cautioned yesterday over that Richard More business, which you claim you had nothing to do with, and you need to keep out of trouble. Your father will have been charged now so he should be waiting for you outside. And just one word of advice – if you have the brain that my brother-in-law thinks you've got, you'll see through all this BNP crap. You're just swallowing their propaganda. You're not thinking for yourself. And neither is your father. Much as you respect him because he's your father, you've got to make your own mind up on things. Only then will you be an adult. Think about it.'

THIRTY-ONE

After his visit to Clun, Tallyforth had driven to one of his favourite locations, Stiperstones – that last Shropshire rise before the endless hills of Wales lead off towards the Irish Sea. The A49 took him to Church Stretton then it was up the narrow Burway and over the grey expanse of the Long Mynd, down again to the tiny settlement of Bridges before the final thin uphill track. Leaving the Range Rover in the National Trust car park, he had taken the rising path through the bilberry bushes and the springy heather towards the first of the grey rocky outcrops that gave the hill its name. It was late afternoon by now and a thin mist was already drifting over the highest rocks as he approached, taking care that his ankles weren't turned by the treacherous stones underfoot. It was a place he had often come to. He loved high places in general, loved the exhilaration of climbing up to them and of the slight breathlessness caused by the increased exertion, loved the indescribable joy of standing on top and seeing down both sides as if it gave him power of some curious sort.

He had needed time to think about this mystery that George had inveigled him into and about George herself. They had worked together in the Mercian force for several years, brilliantly in his view and certainly with great success, as even Nobby Clarke had to admit, though he would do so reluctantly, not being someone who liked to give praise. They made a good team. Their strengths complemented each other – his intuitive feel and her dogged determination, like a fortunate amalgam of the hare and the tortoise. So he was sorry when, after his retirement, they had rarely seen each other. And it wasn't just because of their shared police work, was it? He had to admit that there had been a lot more between them. Their brief affair probably hadn't been such a good idea. Or rather the way he had handled it hadn't been too clever. He'd tried too hard but, if he was honest, and he really might as well be honest now, he told himself, it was the trying that was the problem. He'd wanted it all to be moonlight and roses and it could never last like that. She had been more down-to-earth, trying to get him to understand that reality was not like that. They couldn't just please themselves about how they lived and where they lived and what they did. There were their fellow-police officers for a start – they couldn't do lovey-dovey stuff in front of them. And then there were the families. Or more precisely his family. Or more exactly still his son Miles. Why wouldn't he bring him to visit? Why couldn't she meet him? He should have been stronger, Tallyforth rationalised to himself, should have forced Miles to meet George. But how could he? The boy was of an age where he could make his own choices, his own decisions. Hadn't he brought him up to be like that? He couldn't have forced him to do something against his will without losing his own sense of self-respect.

And then, when they did try once again to re-establish their relationship, she had decided she wanted a baby. Okay, he had understood all about the biological clock ticking inexorably but another child was not in his calculations, not in his life-plan. Even then he could see retirement a few years down the line and what use would he be then in his late fifties to a boy or girl approaching puberty? He had dismissed it as panicky female talk and would not even discuss it with her. Had he been wrong? She had said it was her choice and she would take responsibility for the child. She was younger than him. She would continue earning. But all he could see was himself endlessly washing nappies, doing the school run, managing the household budget, buying the school uniform. No way, José.

And then Larry Powell had come on the scene. Or Enoch, as Tallyforth always thought of him wryly, because he had been stationed in Wolverhampton when they had first met. Powell with his great black muscular body, his handsome features, his immaculate manners. The perfect mate, or so it had seemed. So where were the babies from that relationship? If she was so determined to be a mother, what better man could she find? Okay, he'd been married before but there were no children from that marriage as far as he knew. Was there something wrong with Powell? Tallyforth smiled again to himself. Wouldn't it be ironic, if Powell's sperm count wasn't strong enough to father sprogs?

But she had assured him it was all over between Powell and herself now, hadn't she? And did she really only get back in touch because of this Bridgnorth business? Surely she could have found some other way of resolving the matter. And why was she so anxious to resolve it anyway? It was scarcely headline stuff, was it? Not the sort of thing to advance your reputation or career, surely? So was she, even though she was giving the opposite signals, actually seeking something more from him? Was she really seeking to rekindle that old flame that he had thought long extinguished?

'Women!' He heard himself exclaiming out loud, as he picked his way through the late-afternoon mist on the cobbly quartzite path towards the Devil's Chair, that mysterious clump of stones that held so many mysteries and legends within its grasp. Its outline peeped out occasionally from the cloud cover and he could sense the awe with which it must have been regarded by superstitious folk in past years.

Tallyforth paused in his walk to sit on a rock beside the path. He looked back along he path he had walked and forced himself to reconsider the case she had asked him to investigate. There would be time to think of George again.

What the *Oxford Dictionary of National Biography* had indicated was that there was a real possibility of the girl whose bones had been dug up in Bridgnorth being the child of Robert Howard and Frances Purbeck. Ernie Wright, that old churchwarden from Clun, had suggested the same. If so, there was no reason to doubt the assertion in one of Tolliver's letters that she really was Venetta Howard, the daughter of the Governor of Bridgnorth Castle. Given that, then the relationship implied in the cache of letters between her and this Tolliver fellow was certainly very dangerous. She would have been following an extremely risky course in seeing him and it was very unlikely that no one knew about it. Was that how she came to her death? Had her father killed her on discovering her secret? Or had he ordered someone else to commit the foul deed? Or maybe Tolliver himself had done it. Maybe there had been some sort of death pact between them. But then, why weren't Tolliver's bones in the same place?

The other strand to the story that Tallyforth was finding difficult to comprehend, or rather difficult to link to the discovery of the bones and the letters, was this business of the Blakeways and the Mores. Not the current spat between two schoolboys that had led to the sad death of one but rather that older dispute that had led the four More children to be placed on *The Mayflower*. Was there really some connection between the two sets of events? Or was it just chance that brought them together? Was it merely a coincidence that the Blakeways had this aged aunt called Venetta?

He needed to get chapter and verse on the More story. George had told him that it had all occurred in the village of Shipton. Maybe there was someone or something there that might help.

He stood and retraced his route down the stony path back through the mist to reach the Range Rover. Enough for today. Shipton tomorrow.

THIRTY-TWO

The early dawn haze that had greeted George Elliott when she pulled back the curtains in her apartment on Saturday morning had been pierced by a sharp sun come midday. The pall that had hung over Birmingham had cleared and its nineteen-eighties skyscape sparkled as she had climbed into the MG and taken the road to Bridgnorth. Her sister-in-law Donna had rung the night before to invite her for lunch, prompted by her husband's concern about Ryan Blakeway and his explanation about Tony Alexander having gained access to the pistol believed to have belonged to Sir Robert Howard. Unsure as to whether viewing this pistol would add anything to her understanding of what had happened or not, George had accepted the invitation, as much as anything because she had felt frustrated all week by Nobby Clarke's prohibition of her pursuit of the 'antique mystery'. Besides she really wanted to quiz Andrew at greater length about the Blakeway family and this old story that had had such a tragic modern outcome. There had been no further news from Ruddy Gore and she hadn't heard from Tallyforth for some days. When she had rung his numbers, there had been no reply. Ditto with texting and emailing him. She felt irritated by his lack of contact, not for the first time in her life. He had always had the capacity to create massive frustration for her.

So, determined to spend her off-duty weekend in finally resolving the Body on the Steps case, with or without whatever Tallyforth might or might not have discovered, and to find out the latest news about Richard More's death, she had been pleased that the improved weather had meant she could let the soft top of the car slide back and allow the wind to blow through her hair. She had chosen the route through Quinton and Halesowen and on through Kidderminster because it was always likely to be less traffic-strewn but, while idling in a queue by traffic lights in the latter town, she glimpsed a statue of a man in preaching mode in the grounds of the church opposite the Ringway. She remembered what Tallyforth had found out about Baxter's time in Kidderminster and Tolliver's letters about his first teacher. Could this statue represent him? When the lights turned green, she managed to switch lanes and turn into the retail park, where she locked the MG and walked back into the church grounds to stare at the white marble statue that was indeed of the Puritan cleric Richard Baxter. The figure's right hand pointed up to the heavens, as if showing his listeners where they should be aspiring, while his left hand clasped a bible and his bearded visage gazed down at the imaginary flock gathered below. The inscription on the grey granite plinth read:

In a stormy and divided age he advocated unity and comprehension pointing the way to the everlasting rest.

Unity and comprehension. She certainly wished for the latter. Everything had become too complicated in this issue about the body of Venetta Howard, if that really was her name. Seeing Ryan Blakeway and his father at the BNP march the previous day had muddied the waters even more and she really did want to get to the bottom of all this as soon as she could. She could feel a surge of determination coursing through her bloodstream, the sort of surge that she knew from past experience could only come from some air-drawn realisation that matters were coming to a head. Even the reason for Nobby Clarke's interdiction had to become apparent soon, didn't it?

As for unity, what did that mean? Being united, but in what way? Or with whom? Her thoughts, unbidden, turned in a flash to Tallyforth and she remembered the tickle of pleasure that she had felt when she had returned to her apartment after their shared meal at Adil's. She had told herself that it was the fact they were back working together again that had caused this frisson of excitement, that she had missed the way they had complemented each other during past investigations. But had she been kidding herself? Had she really deep down been wanting more, been in fact missing him, all of him? Was that the sort of unity that somehow her inner being was seeking, even though her stern exterior face would not dare to convey even a hint of the merest possibility?

Back in the car and leaving Kidderminster far behind she was soon in the rolling pastures and lush woodlands of Shropshire, driving north on the old turnpike road parallel to the broad River Severn as it made its way south eventually to break out into the Bristol Channel. Approaching Bridgnorth, a passage from one of Tolliver's letters sprung into her mind:

> *"I did espy rising swiftly on a white horse down below me in the valley on the far side of the River Severn a cloaked horseman."*

And yes, Tolliver had apprehended that horseman and taken from him a coded letter from Charles I to his secretary Nicholas. The messenger had alighted from a ferry boat at ..... what was it called?[1] She pulled her foot back slightly on the accelerator pedal, as if slowing thus might help her recall, and, as she did so, a road sign bearing the legend Hampton Loade to her left loomed into her view and she remembered. Was it all true? Had this Tolliver fellow really apprehended the king's messenger in this way? Or was it all a fiction designed to impress his lady-friend, his Venetta?

Soon enough she was negotiating the roundabout at the bottom of the town by-pass and crossing the long-standing stone bridge over the Severn. She was glad to reach her sister's house in East Castle Street in Bridgnorth without any traffic problems.

'Terrible news about that boy who died and young Blakeway's apparent involvement in it, isn't it? Never liked the boy, as you know, but, if he did it…. Still, glad you could make it. I'm getting sick and tired of all this historical nonsense. Can't you knock some sense into these silly men

---

1   See letter dated January 28 in Appendix.

and their obsession with the past? The lawn needs mowing, the roses need deadheading, we're low on wine supplies and all my darling husband can talk about is this bleeding Body on the Steps mystery. Sort him out, will you, George?'

Donna Latham, dressed in a one-piece blue boiler suit that made her look like a RAF mechanic, reached forward to peck her sister on each cheek, at the same time seizing the leather holdall that her sister was carrying.

'I'll try, Donna, I'll try. That's all I can do. But it's got me enthralled as well, you know. And I have a feeling it's somehow or other connected to this lad's death.' She followed her sister into the hallway of their house. 'But d'you know I've been warned off it all by my superiors?'

'No, really?' Donna's eyes opened wide in feigned surprise. 'Why's that then? Surely they can't want you to be sorting out the modern-day villains instead, can they? How unreasonable of them!'

'I think there's more to it than that....'

'George, you're as batty as Andrew and his mate Tony. Oh, by the way, they said you were to meet them at the museum. It's apparently Tony's duty day so he's there all afternoon. D'you know where it is? It's dead easy. Just go right outside our house till you reach the High Street, then keep going past the old Market Hall till you reach Northgate. And don't be fooled. It's not one of the old gates to the town, it's a nineteenth century reconstruction. Go underneath Northgate and take the steps going up. You'll find my darling husband and his pal there. You'd better go straightaway. Good luck. I'll have some lunch ready for you when you get back but if you're not here by two, I'll scoff the bleeding lot.'

George Elliott allowed her sister to bully her out of the house and took the prescribed route along the High Street, passing on the opposite side to the Saturday market stalls selling their wares. There was a loud buzz of talk in the street, filled as it was with the town's citizens and the many visitors from the Black Country drawn by the busy street market. Then she was past it and approaching the gothic Northgate with its sandstone crenellations. Tony Alexander, his bald head glowing dully in the dim light of the museum, greeted her with his bear-paw handclasp as she came through the door. Behind him she could see Andrew Latham looking very grim.

'I'm not sure this is of great interest to you any longer, George.' Andrew Latham's handsome face wore the look of someone deeply troubled. He was blaming himself, in some way unknown to anyone else, for Ryan Blakeway's predicament and for the death of Richard More. 'After what's happened, I mean'

'No, I want to see it.'

'This is it,' said Tony Alexander, holding up the curiously-large wooden pistol with its shiny grey metallic workings. 'A genuine seventeenth century wheel-lock pistol. German probably. Just look at the craftsmanship. They don't make them like that any longer I'm afraid.'

'Not even replicas?' She cocked her right eyebrow at him.

'Sure, they make replicas but there's not the same individual craftsmanship in them, believe me.'

She took the gun off him and felt the smooth contours of dark wood and cold iron with her left hand, then raised it in front of her eye to take imaginary aim. She was surprised at its heaviness. She lowered it again and ran her fingers over the scratched 'RH' on its barrel. So, this was the pistol, believed to belong to Sir Robert Howard, that Ryan Blakeway with his mad ideas about the oppression of the people had stolen from the museum. And was this the pistol that ended Venetta Howard's young life? She took aim again. Could he really have killed his own daughter? Could he really have been so distressed at finding his daughter having an affair with a Parliamentary soldier? It was hard, if not impossible, to believe.

Carefully she handed the pistol back.

'What d'you think then? Could Howard have shot his daughter with this?'

'Assuming it was Sir Robert Howard's pistol, that is.' Tony Alexander's deep voice resonated in the museum. 'I don't know about that. Andrew has told me the story and I've even had a look at the Tolliver letters, courtesy of our opposite numbers in Shrewsbury. But I'm as mystified as Andrew and you are by the whole thing. If those letters are genuine – and I've no reason to suppose they are not – then they throw a whole new light on the siege of Bridgnorth and our understanding of what happened in those days. As a steward of the Bridgnorth Museum, I'm fascinated by it all but I have to rely on you and your colleagues to clarify the mystery fully, I'm afraid. I can't really speculate any more.'

'No, I can see that,' she said. 'Thank you anyway. It sort of mattered for me to have a sight of that pistol anyway. I'm truly grateful. Andrew, we're expected for lunch. Donna has issued her orders, I'm afraid. We need to look sharp.'

Andrew Latham smiled ruefully but nodded a joint thanks and goodbye to Tony Alexander and followed his sister-in-law down the Northgate steps.

'I have been to see Ryan Blakeway,' he said as they rejoined the busy High Street shoppers. 'He swears that he didn't meet Richard More and that it wasn't him who got into the fight.'

'I know, Andrew. But, if it wasn't him, who was it? Who else knew that Richard More would be down by that Lavington's Hole cave at that time?'

THIRTY-THREE

Tallyforth was sitting at a small wooden table outside the Café Express just beyond the black and white Market Hall on the High Street, a frothed cappuccino and a crumb-filled plate in front of him. He was scanning through a sheaf of papers, his eyes intent on seeking connections therein. His trip to the tiny hamlet of Shipton in Corvedale had been useful, if not entirely satisfactory in terms of solving the deep problem. He had marvelled at the magnificent Elizabethan Shipton Hall that stood next to the church of St James with its squat tower. Entering the grey church building through black metallic gates that bore a sign stating "This 11th Century church is always open. Visitors are most welcome", he had been confronted immediately by a brass plaque on the wall of the nave opposite the creaking main door commemorating the four children of the long-gone Larden Hall baptised therein – Elinor, Jasper, Richard and Mary More. As he had stood on the worn decorated tiles of the aisle of the tiny church, glancing briefly at the vaulted roof with its dark wooden beams and the military rows of wooden pews, he had noted that the plaque had been presented by the Massachusetts Society of Mayflower Descendants in 1996. He had purchased two thin pamphlets outlining the story of the More children. These had expanded upon what he already knew from George Elliott's explanation about the reason why these children were placed aboard *The Mayflower* in 1620.

Their father Samuel had married his cousin Katherine in this same St James's church in 1611. The marriage had been arranged, so it was presumed, in order to secure property within the More family, for Katherine was the heiress of

Larden Hall. Samuel spent much of his time at court in London but, as his children began to grow up, he noticed that there was a *"likeness and resemblance of most of the said children in their visages and lineaments of their bodies"* to a certain Jacob Blakeway, who was *"a fellow of mean parentage & condicion"*. He then divorced Katherine and took the children from her, claiming she was a dreadful mother who mistreated her children, and placed the four youngsters in the care of two of the elders set to sail across the Atlantic to the new world. Three of the children died on the voyage but Richard More survived to marry twice (and probably thrice, for there was a record of a Captain Richard More marrying in England) and move to live in Salem, where he was excommunicated from the church for *"gross unchastity with another mans wife"*.

Randy old devil, thought Tallyforth with a wry smile. Still that did explain the origin of the feud between the Mores and the Blakeways, even though it was hard to believe that its embers could still be glowing nearly four hundred years later. Despite what Ruddy Gore had said about history being all around them in Shropshire.

'Tallyforth! What are you doing here?'

His reading and reflection were suddenly interrupted. He looked up to see George Elliott's indignant face confronting him from the other side of the table where she stood, hands on hips, together with a tall dark-haired man.

'And why didn't you reply to my calls and my texts?'

'Hello, George. Didn't expect to see you here. I thought you'd be busy in Birmingham.' Tallyforth smiled at her. 'I'm doing what you asked – pursuing threads. Care to join me?'

'Chief Inspector Tallyforth is it?' asked the tall man at her side. 'I'm honoured to meet you. George has talked a lot about your time together in the Force. Andrew Latham. George's brother-in-law.'

Andrew Latham reached a long arm across the table to shake hands with Tallyforth.

'Mr Tallyforth now,' George interjected. 'Pensioner now, aren't we?'

Tallyforth gave a mock grimace before she continued.

'So, where have you been? And why haven't you been in touch?'

'Just a moment, George.' Andrew Latham took her arm. 'Remember, Donna's expecting us for lunch. Why doesn't Mr Tallyforth join us? I'm sure there'll be plenty. Donna rarely underprepares as you know. You two can catch up on everything then. All right?'

Never a person willing to take no for an answer, he helped Tallyforth from his seat and urged his two companions onwards, anxious that any further conversation they needed to have should occur in his home, not out there on the street. George Elliott's anger at Tallyforth, caused as much by the surprise of meeting him here as by her unreturned calls and texts, began to dissipate as they walked back the way she had come only a short while previously. She even stopped at the top of the cobbled Cartway to adjust their route so that she could point out the Stoneway Steps where the body had been discovered and where she had first bumped into Ryan Blakeway. She told him about the death of Richard More and about the younger boy's suspected involvement. The detour was brief, however, and they arrived at the Latham home just as the church clock was chiming two o'clock.

'Well, well, look what the cat brought in.' Donna Latham greeted the threesome as she swung open front door. 'You didn't tell me you were bringing your old flame, George. You wouldn't remember me, Mr Tallyforth, but I was at the regional meeting of the police liaison committees that you addressed some years back. George had told me such a lot about you and I was impressed, I don't mind telling you. Not that the local bloody liaison committee did any good. Just a load of middle-class folks moaning. I didn't last long.'

Tallyforth smoothed back his silvery hair with the fingers of his right hand and smiled wanly.

'Not planned, Donna,' explained George Elliott, pushing past her sister into the house. 'Met him on the High Street. Still don't know what he's doing here. Andrew insisted he come with us. Hope that's okay.'

'Of course it is, my lovelies. Plenty food for hungry folks. Come on in. Make yourself at home.'

She bustled off through the house to the kitchen, closely followed by her husband, leaving the other two to find their way to the front room.

'So?' She sat forward, elbows on knees and hands clasped beneath her chin.

'George, I'm sorry I haven't been in touch but I had a lot to do and there was no point contacting you until I'd sorted a lot of things out.' Tallyforth held out both his hands in a conciliatory gesture.

'So are you any the wiser about all this business?' she snorted.

He wanted to tell her he had solved the whole mystery, wanted her to appreciate his detective skills. He had hoped to have cleared everything up by now, not just because of his professional pride in getting the job done, but also because he really wanted to impress her. He really wanted, he realised as he looked at her trim figure in green blouse and short black skirt and the pert attention in her eyes as she waited for his explanation, he really wanted to be back with her. Yes, it had been a mistake previously but that was as much to do with the fact that they never had a break from each other. Living together and working together were too much. But now he was retired from the Mercian Force. Now he was a free spirit. And yes, if she wanted, he would offer help, advice, whatever, but they would not be treading on each other's toes all the time.

'I've been busy chasing up the loose ends,' he began, 'and I think I've got somewhere but I'm not all the way there yet. That's why I came to Bridgnorth this morning. There's a few things I need to establish in my mind but that can wait a little. It's really good to see you, George. Really good.'

And he started to tell her about his visit to Clun and the information, or rather intimation, from the churchwarden Ernie Wright that Robert Howard and Frances Purbeck might indeed have borne children in their time at the Hall of the Forest, although exhaustive searches in the Shropshire Archives had failed to turn up any reference to a Venetta baptised at that time. The confirmation of further children from *The Oxford Dictionary of National Biography* he also gave her, before going into exact detail about the story of Samuel and Katherine More and Jacob Blakeway, about the More children's journey on *The Mayflower* and about the life of the only survivor from them, the lascivious Richard More, after whom the recently-deceased boy had been named.

While he talked and waved his hands as if he were giving gifts away, George Elliott watched him carefully, gradually realising that she had always liked the softness of his full lips, the shine in his eyes, and the knotted brow that came when he was concentrating. She almost missed the entry into the sitting room of her sister, bearing a tray with plates of cheese, pork pie, piccalilli, mustard, cherry tomatoes and a crusty brown loaf of bread that she placed on the glass-topped coffee table between them.

'Eat,' came the instruction from the grinning red-cheeked face of Donna Latham.

'And drink.' Andrew Latham followed her into the room bearing four brown bottles of beer. 'Hobson's. The best. All right with everybody?'

Without waiting for answers, he began pouring the dark beer into long cool glasses and handing them around, while Donna simultaneously distributed willow-pattern plates.

'Excellent,' said Tallyforth. 'Haven't supped that for many a month. You're very kind. Here's to you both. I really didn't expect such hospitality. Cheers.'

As they raised their glasses, the telephone rang in the hallway.

THIRTY-FOUR

It was Tony Alexander calling Andrew Latham from the Northgate Museum. He had just been visited by the museum's curator who, after being told briefly about the police investigation and the possible involvement of the More-Blakeway vendetta, had pointed to the ancient turret clock that was one of their larger exhibits and explained that it was a relic of the old Larden Hall – the veritable home of the More family before the acrimony began. There was a press cutting that told more of the story and he wondered if Andrew and George would care to see it, in case it helped inform their enquiries.

After he had returned from taking the call and had given that information to the others munching on pork pie, cheese and bread, Donna made her husband sit down.

'Whatever it is, if it's waited this long, it can wait another half an hour, can't it? You're not rushing off now.'

Tallyforth, unused to her brusque manner, paused in his eating and glanced sideways at George Elliott, who shrugged her response.

'D'you think it's of any significance?' he said to none of them in particular, before biting a chunk of bread and chewing it thoughtfully.

'Who knows? You read the stuff about Shipton and the beginnings of the feud, didn't you? I thought Larden Hall was no longer there,' George answered.

Donna sighed noisily and obviously, as if to warn them off further discussion, then passed the tray of food around again.

'Ignore my wife,' butted in her husband. 'It's all done for effect. She just likes to be the centre of everything. I'm afraid all our historical interests leave her cold.'

173

'Too bloody true, matey,' said Donna, her face purpling with food and irritation. 'Too bloody true. But don't let me get in the way of your fun.'

She held her hands up to her shoulders, palms up in mock supplication.

'As far as I remember,' continued Tallyforth, watching Donna out of the corner of his eye carefully in case of further interruptions, 'the pamphlet said Larden Hall was demolished in the nineteen-sixties, I think. There was no mention of a clock though.'

They ate on in silence, though there was a certain tension in the air, as George, Tallyforth and Andrew Latham clearly wanted to go back to the museum as soon as possible, while Donna sought to restrain them by her heavy sighing and refusal to make eye contact. Tallyforth glanced again at George and saw she was merely nibbling on a piece of cheese, like a harvest mouse he thought, and he remembered affectionately the way she scrunched her nose up as she nibbled. Andrew meanwhile, having for once dared to try to silence his wife, had reverted to a cold and desperate munching, as if he knew to expect an argument when he eventually returned.

Eventually, an unspoken agreement was reached whereby, almost simultaneously, all four put down their plates, brushed stray crumbs from their clothing and drained the last drops from their glasses of beer.

'Go on then,' said Donna abruptly, though not as harshly as she might have given her previous objections. 'I know you have to go, you sleuths. Sorry to detain you. I hope whatever Tony has got for you is worth it.'

Excuses were offered, chairs pushed back, doors opened and the three were on their way, retracing their steps through the bustling market place and back to the museum, where Tony Alexander greeted them again.

'This is the clock from Larden Hall.' He waved them in the direction of a large wooden-framed contraption filled with ropes, pulleys, cogs and wheels. It was an amazing Heath-Robinson-type device. 'It's called a turret clock. It would have been housed in some kind of turret and didn't need

174

to be visible because it has no clock face and only struck the hour. This type of clock was invented back in the fourteenth century as a way of chiming the hour in monasteries to call the monks to their various duties. This one dates back to the seventeenth century probably, though it's possible it's older than that.'

They gathered around the strange machine, peering at its works in curiosity as Tony Alexander explained.

'And it came from Larden Hall?' Andrew Latham queried, looking up at his friend.

'Yes, it had been there for centuries, obviously, but, when Larden Hall was being demolished in nineteen sixty-nine, this was about to be thrown on a skip but someone spotted it, had it rescued and arranged for it to be given to the museum. And here it is, the pride of our collection.'

There was a crinkled piece of paper pinned to the frame that carried a picture of the turret clock beneath a headline that read "Clock link to adultery tale".

'But this is what you really called to tell us about?' Tallyforth straightened his back after bending to look more closely at the ingenious device. 'Is this about Samuel More and his wife and Jacob Blakeway?'

'Exactly,' said Tony Alexander, drawing their attention to a framed newspaper cutting, already mustard-yellow with age, with the same heading as the piece of paper attached to the turret clock. He handed it to them. 'You need to read this, I think.'

There was what is often called a pregnant silence as the three of them craned their necks to read the tiny print of an article from the *Shropshire Star* newspaper about the tale that linked to the clock.

'That's it!' expostulated Tallyforth suddenly, while the others were still reading. 'Look there, George. Half way down the page. There.'

He gesticulated feverishly at the section that had caught his attention.

'What?

'It was in the winter of nineteen fifty-eight to fifty-nine that Sir Jasper More of Linley, near Bishop's Castle, decided to

175

explore a trunk in his attic and found a document that blew the lid on the 17th century scandal which led to four More children from Shropshire being sent on *The Mayflower*,' he read aloud, almost gabbling in his excitement. 'Don't you see?'

'Sorry. See what?'

Tallyforth shook his head in exasperation.

'What is a document about the More family of Shipton doing in the possession of the More family of Linley?'

He paused, waiting for the cogs, not of the turret clock, but of the brains of his companions to click into place.

'You mean they must be related?' said Andrew Latham.

'Exactly. I've been looking in the wrong place, George. I told you I'd been to Clun and found nothing helpful. Likewise the Shropshire Archives, although the archivist woman did show me a map of the area around Clun and pointed out all the little villages that might have churches. There was one village, I can remember it now and I don't know why it didn't jump out and hit me at the time, it was called More and it's close to Linley where this Jasper More lived. The Mores of Linley and the Mores of Shipton have to be related. Why else would he have these old documents in a trunk? I'll take a bet with you now that Samuel More and Katherine More, who we know were cousins, were married to re-unite the Mores of the two parts of Shropshire.'

The excitement glowed in George Elliott's eyes now, as she took in what he was saying.

'All very well but what's that all got to do with Venetta Howard? Or whatever her name was?'

He took her hands in his and glared at her but it was not threatening, more of a desire to transfer his thoughts instantly to her without needing the medium of speech.

'George, remember that Robert Howard was MP for Bishop's Castle. Linley is just outside Bishop's Castle. He must have known the Mores of Linley. The aristocrats always stick together, don't they? When in trouble, they support each other. Always have done, always will do. If Howard and his floozy had children and needed them baptised secretly, where better to turn than to one of his fellow-aristos? I bet even the minister of the church was a More as well.'

'So, if this story about the Mores and the Blakeways only became public in the nineteen-fifties, how come that Ryan Blakeway has been conducting this feud with Richard More at school?' queried Andrew Latham, scratching his left ear meditatively and turning towards his friend. 'And what has it got to do with the poor boy's death?'

'Andrew, we don't know if that is connected or not,' interrupted George Elliott. 'I haven't heard any more from Chief Superintendent Gore about the causes of the boy's death. It might not have been as a result of a fight.'

'You know Shropshire, Andrew,' Tony Alexander answered. They were facing each other now, the newspaper article down at the museum steward's side. 'I warned you about this when you took over the school, remember. Matters don't die in Shropshire; they just go underground until such time as someone somewhere is ready to excavate them and force them into the open again. It's happened all my life.'

'Did it happen when you were the head?' asked George.

'The More-Blakeway business? No. Tom Blakeway was a pain in the arse but we didn't have any members of the More family in the school in my time. Glad I'm not involved in any of that matter. Tragic case.'

Tallyforth had taken George's arm and led her a little away from the other two. He was talking quietly but animatedly to her now.

'George, we have to get back to the Shropshire Archives to check out the church at More. I've got a strong feeling that I'm on to something here. If Howard did have this Venetta girl baptised there, then we have a solution to one part of the quandary, don't we? Any other ideas?'

'Go to the church itself? Or Linley? Presumably this Sir Jasper More would have had some posh house there. Might be worth a visit. But what about the boy's death? I need to get hold of Ruddy Gore.'

'Okay, you do that but I think these affairs are all linked together. We need to get out to Linley and More. When shall we go?'

She looked at him and realised he was back in command and she liked it, not because she was incapable of finding solutions for herself but because somehow this irritating man made her feel alive in ways that no-one else ever had done.

'Why not straight away?'

Tallyforth grinned his acknowledgement. Just like the old days, he thought. Just like the old days.

THIRTY-FIVE

Tallyforth's hunch about More had proved correct. They had reached the Shropshire Archives in Shrewsbury just in time to get access to the microfiche for St Peter's church in More. There they had indeed found the record for one Venetta Wright from 1627, the mother signing herself as Frances Wright and the father as Robert Wright. As Tallyforth said to George, Frances Purbeck had clearly liked the surname, since it was the name under which their first bastard child had also been baptised. Could it have been, he wondered, because she had always thought of herself as being in the right? And that she was making a point to those who sought to condemn her and her lover, the bold Sir Robert Howard?

'It has to be a possibility, doesn't it?' Tallyforth repeated his theory again to her as they left the county town behind them and headed south on the A488, busy with Saturday shopper traffic and trucks delivering goods to the towns and villages of the Marches. They were in the green MG, at her insistence – though she welcomed his taking command in one way, she wasn't prepared to cede complete control to him – and he had to shout because the hood was still down as the sun spilled over the greening countryside. They were heading towards the tiny hamlet of More.

'So Howard was her Mr Right?' George Elliott laughed as she said it. That sense she had felt earlier in the morning was proving correct. They were, she was confident, close to cracking the whole grisly story.

'And she must have been a right little goer.' He laughed too at his words and she gave him a wry smile, as if to suggest that this was maybe a bit too suggestive, but then she remembered their history and she gurgled with laughter herself.

The air was crisp and clean, except for the occasional whiff of diesel as they overtook a loaded truck or of acidic manure from some recently-ploughed field. The road sped them through the commuter villages of Pontesbury and Minsterley then out through the fields and meadows of rural Shropshire, becoming in places the border between England and Wales. The crags of Stiperstones loomed above them to the east as they drove.

'Funny but I was up there a couple of days ago,' Tallyforth shouted, pointing behind him as George negotiated a wide bend.

'Birdwatching again?'

'No, not this time,' he laughed, 'though I did see a couple of whitethroats hopping around in the bilberry bushes. No, I just needed somewhere to marshal my thoughts. You know me.'

'The man who thinks on hills?'

'Something like that.'

They were in a jovial mood. And why shouldn't they be? At last they had found that the Venetta who had been the recipient of her lover's letters was truly the daughter of Sir Robert Howard, the Governor of Bridgnorth Castle at the time of the Parliamentarian siege and the subsequent surrender, and Lady Frances Purbeck. There could be no question that she was the Venetta Wright who had been baptised in St James's church in More in 1627. She would have been nineteen when she died.

George cast her mind's eye back to when she was nineteen. She had just started her second year at Swansea and was sharing a house out in Sketty with two other girls from her English course and Steve Anthony. They were enjoying the experience of self-catering, having lived in a hall of residence for their first year, and had not yet reached the stage of student poverty where they were living off baked beans on toast. Steve had taken the lead in introducing them to experimental cooking, his potato and leek gratin already a firm favourite. She smiled to herself at the recollection of Steve in his embroidered pinny prancing around the tiny kitchen.

They had also discovered from the helpful Fiona Lewis in the Shropshire Archives that Sir Jasper More, the man who had found the documents about the four More children and their disputatious parents, had been MP for Ludlow for many years. The family home was Linley Hall and, although the present Hall was from the eighteenth century, one Shropshire authority had claimed that the Mores had lived on this piece of land since the Norman Conquest, the original More being a loyal follower of Duke William. Several Mores had been MPs before Sir Jasper – it seemed that running the world was in their blood, so the conjectured link with Sir Robert Howard made good sense.

They had left the main road by now and were travelling more slowly along a narrow, hedge-lined lane with green or ploughed fields either side of the car. The road swerved suddenly and George found she had almost completely circled the church without realising it, as they found themselves back where they had first entered the tiny hamlet, for the road neatly encircles the church building. They got out of the car and walked through ancient gravestones leaning perilously in the grass up the path to the church of St Peter with its squat Norman double-pyramid tower.

'Just like the one in Clun.' Tallyforth pointed at the tower. 'No wonder Howard felt at home here.'

'It's lovely, isn't it?' George Elliott was talking not just about the church tower but about the rural tranquillity of the place. As she let her eyes move around from where she stood on the high mound of the churchyard, she could see the brown timber and cream-painted plaster of the adjacent farmhouse and the sun glinting off the grey slate roofs of cottages.

'Probably been like this for centuries. Hard to believe places like this exist when you're stuck in Birmingham, isn't it?'

They pushed open the heavy wooden door and went inside, their footsteps echoing in the silent, white-washed building with its wooden trusses holding up the vaulted roof. Unlike many churches of its type, however, it was bright and airy thanks to its many high windows. A deep crimson carpet all the way up the nave gave warmth to the place.

'Look at this.' George led his gaze to the curiously-designed paving, rather like a mosaic, with its regular curved black shapes, like windmill blades, processing regularly on the white marbled background.

'It says here that the tessellated pavement is believed to be from a Roman villa, excavated in 1835.' Tallyforth was reading from a notice on the wall that gave a brief history of the church. 'If that's right, then the Romans must have been here even before the Mores!'

'And there's a More chapel up here in the north transept.' George was reading over his shoulder from the same notice.

They took a few steps on the plush red carpet, passing rows of wooden box-pews with their metal catches, then turned left into the equally-airy side chapel. Inside it beyond a black-and-white tiled floor they were confronted by a row of grey stone memorials to various members of the More family, in the centre of which was a white marble memorial to a certain Harriet More, wife of the rector in the mid-nineteenth century. On the right-hand wall was a list of books in the More Church Library, books donated by Richard More in 1680. Beside it there was a large engraved brass coat of arms in a wooden frame, depicting a stylized pelican inside a black cloud with two smaller pelicans above it.

'Presumably the More crest,' said Tallyforth gazing at it.

'So this is where you think it all began,' mused George. 'Where Venetta Howard was baptised as Venetta Wright. In this church.'

'That's my guess, George. Can you feel the past around you? I've started visiting some of these old churches as part of my History study. The more I do, the more I feel surrounded by the ghosts of the past. They crowd round you sometimes, you know.'

She cocked her eyebrows at him. Was this the same Tallyforth she had worked with for so many years? He'd never had time for church or churchy matters in those days. Although, when she came to think of it, he had always relied on gut instinct, on what he called his sixth sense, hadn't he? Was this the same thing?

'So any conclusions?'

'George, we came here to get a feel of this place. I know now that Venetta was baptised here. The ghosts of the past are telling me that. I can feel her calling out to me with every fibre of her being.'

This was getting a bit too much for George.

'Okay, so we now know who Venetta was, who her parents were and where she was secretly baptised. But we haven't got that much further, have we? We still know absolutely doodly squat about this Henry Tolliver. And how is Richard More's death connected to all this?'

Tallyforth gave his little smile and tapped his nose.

'I've got an idea about that.'

THIRTY-SIX

'Guv'nor in?'

'Sorry, you've come to the wrong place. The Governor's House is further down the road. That way. Can't miss it.' Donna Latham, still in her blue boiler suit, pointed in the direction.

'No, the guv'nor. Mr Latham. I want to talk to him.'

The figure to whom she had opened the door after his repeated rapping on it was a bullet-headed man in blue jeans and a white sleeveless tee-shirt over his muscle-bound chest. Blue tattoos covered his exposed arms and sprouted out of the top of the tee-shirt below his neck.

'Tom Blakeway. Ryan's dad. I want to speak to Mr Latham.'

She raised the glasses from the silver chain around her neck and peered closely at him, the slight curl in her lips revealing her instant distaste. The rancid stink of tobacco every time he opened his mouth was an affront to her nose.

'Sorry,' she said at last. 'Do you have an appointment with my husband? Is there something I should know about?'

'Just tell him I'm here, will you, lady? No offence but I've only got three days leave. I'm back with the regiment Monday morning and I want to see Latham, sorry Mr Latham, now and sort things out.'

Donna gave him her fiercest stare, for she was not a person easily intimidated, certainly not in the fortress of her own home in the safe environment of rural Bridgnorth. She had little or no idea what he was talking about, though of course she knew about Ryan Blakeway and had, against her own better judgement and certainly her own liking, entertained the boy in their home in the past. That had been a mistake, as she had clearly forecast to her husband before he insisted on his silly plan. She was not easily going to yield to the implied threats of this tattooed ape on her doorstep.

'I'm very sorry,' she replied, choosing her words carefully and speaking them slowly to give herself, and she hoped him, the illusion of control. 'You can't just turn up at my house and demand to see my husband. There are proper ways of doing things and you know that perfectly well. If it's a private matter, you should write to my husband. If it's a school matter, as I assume it is, you should contact the school. In fact, if you were on leave, you should have done so yesterday.'

'Couldn't, could I? It was the march.' Tom Blakeway's eyes bulged with rancour as the thought of the BNP march and its unfortunate outcome flooded through his brain.

'March? What march? I thought you said you were on leave. How could you be marching?' She looked down over the top of her glasses at him, hoping to frazzle him with her stare but he was not a man to be frazzled lightly, if at all.

'Begging your pardon, ma'am, but that's my business. Look, I know I'm out of order here but I need to see Mr Latham. Will you please tell him I'm here and I need to talk to him about this business between my son and the More boy at school?'

Although he wasn't exactly wheedling, for he was not a man who ever wheedled either, his tone had modulated somewhat and Donna was almost on the point of agreeing to his request when the decision was taken out of her hands.

'Hello, who's this? Oh, Mr Blakeway, what are you doing here?' Andrew Latham's tall figure had swung into view behind his wife. He had been upstairs in his study when he heard the loud rapping on the door and, when he had realized his wife was still talking to whoever it was there, had descended from the second floor to investigate.

'Mr Latham, I was just apologising to your missus here. I know this isn't the right time or place but I've got to go back to camp and I need to talk to you about this business between my Ryan and Richard More. Can you give me five minutes? That's all I need.'

Andrew Latham looked at Tom Blakeway in his bovver-boy outfit and then at his indignant wife, who was making it obvious she did not approve of any of this. Ah well, he thought, if this was a way of getting to the heart of this long-time feud, then maybe it was worth putting up with Donna's guaranteed subsequent nagging.

'Very well. Five minutes. But that's all. I have work to do and I can't spare more time.' He was lying and he knew it, for he was actually doing *The Guardian* crossword in his study but neither his wife nor Blakeway knew that.

He ushered Tom Blakeway past his wife and into the front room, showing him to the floral-patterned sofa, and sat himself down on the wrinkly leather armchair. Donna headed back into the kitchen, shaking her head in despair and disbelief. What a softie her husband was. Always and forever. But then, she had known that when she married him.

'Well?'

'Mr Latham, my missus tells me she's been blabbing to you about this old feuding business between the Mores and the Blakeways, is that right?'

Blakeway sat bolt upright, his hands clasped to his knees and his legs apart. He stared directly at Andrew Latham, his gaze unblinking and determined. Although there was an air of menace that clung to him, this was more because of his physique and his attire than anything else. His voice was that of the misunderstood squaddie everywhere, insisting on giving his version of events and insistent that there could be no other.

'Yes, your wife did tell me all about that. Naturally, I knew a little beforehand about the More children on *The Mayflower* but I hadn't realized that you were related to the Blakeway of the period. It was your aunt who knew about it all, wasn't it?'

'Aunt Netty, yes it was her. My grandfather told me about it when I was a boy but I just thought it was one of those boring stories that old folk rabbit on with. Never gave it much thought, tell the truth. Till Aunt Netty told the missus and she told me. I got the whole story then and it made my blood boil. I'd joined up by then and I could see what was what. All them poncy officers who'd been to public school bossing us about when they couldn't tell their elbow from their arsehole. 'Scuse my French. If the boys hadn't got together to sort things out properly, we'd have been wiped out in Iraq.'

Andrew Latham shifted his weight on to his right buttock and crossed his legs.

'So? What's the point of this visit then? I know all about that and I know that's the reason the police believe your Ryan was in a fight with Richard More, which has led to his unfortunate death. Is there something else I should know?'

'Yes.'

There was a silence. Tom Blakeway, still in his upright pose, looked down at the Persian carpet that lay on the wooden floor in front of him, seeming as if to gather himself for something monumental. His breathing became quicker and then finally he looked up again and across at Andrew Latham.

'Ryan didn't do it.'

Andrew Latham sat upright himself, uncrossing his legs and leaning forward as if to speak but he truly did not know what to say.

'It's true. Ryan didn't do it.'

'So who did?'

'Guv'nor, my Ryan's a good boy and he's a bright boy. I couldn't believe it when my missus told me you'd had him stay in your home. None of my teachers would ever have done anything like that for me. That Alexander the Great had a real down on me at school. I hated it. And him.'

'It was a mistake. I should never have done it. He stole some of my wife's jewellery.'

'I know and I'm sorry. But you got it back, didn't you?'

'Yes, eventually.'

'Just give him another chance, guv'nor. You know how bright he is. I know I've filled his head full of this feud between the Blakeways and the Mores and I've probably said a lot of other things out of order but I don't want him growing up a softie. But if the kid's got brains as well, like you seem to think, then I want him to have the chances I never had.'

Andrew Latham looked across at him, noticing that the hard edge to his voice had softened and that the angry furrows on his brow had melted away now. Could this man, the scourge of everything he had ever touched, or so it seemed from what everyone had said, have a genuinely caring nature buried away inside him? Was there really hope for everyone, as he had always in his optimistically wildest moments tried to believe?

'What do you want from me?'

Tom Blakeway's hands moved from his knees and clasped together, the upright stance sagged minutely but noticeably.

'Give the boy a chance, guv'nor. Tell the police it wasn't him. You've taken his side before. He needs someone to take his side now. Let him back into school and just give him a chance, will you?'

'As far as school goes, it's up to the governors, I'm afraid.' Andrew Latham gave the tame excuse that generations of headteachers have used to give themselves thinking time. But he knew already that he was going to accede to the other man's wish. Wasn't this why he had made a career in teaching, to change the world by offering opportunities to those who had never known them? No one in their right mind would become a teacher, and certainly not a headteacher, unless they had a streak of idealism, a belief in a better world for the youngsters in their charge. 'As regards the matter involving the police, I believe the matter is out of my hands. I'll see what I can do but I can't promise anything.'

'Tea, anyone?' Donna appeared suddenly at the door with a silver tray on which stood a white teapot, cups, saucers and a plate of digestive biscuits.

'Mr Blakeway was just leaving.'

'Oh, what a shame! I thought you two chaps might like a little refreshment while you were having your little chat. Oh well, never mind. I'll have a cup anyway. Andrew?'

Tom Blakeway stood and marched towards the front door.

'Thank you, guv'nor. Thanks for your time. Appreciate it.'

Andrew Latham followed him, opening the heavy wooden door to allow the other man to step outside then closing it on his retreating figure.

'Well?' Donna stood at the doorway with her tray of tea things, her face full of unspoken irritation.

'Sorry about that. I'll take mine upstairs. I've work to do. I'll tell you later.'

And she would tell him later too.

THIRTY-SEVEN

'Fancy a drink, George?'

They were approaching an old, magnolia-painted hostelry called The Feathers in the village of Brockton on Wenlock Edge. It had been after five o'clock when they finally left More, detouring briefly past the stately Georgian manor house that was Linley Hall, home of Sir Jasper and all the other Mores before and since him. As George Elliott drove easterly through Shropshire under his direction, with the soft top back on now as the early evening began to cool, Tallyforth had reminded her that the newspaper article they had read earlier in the Bridgnorth Museum had stated that Jacob Blakeway *'a fellow of mean parentage and condition'* came from a place called Brockton. He had taken the trouble, when she had stopped to fill up with petrol on their way to Shrewsbury earlier in the afternoon, to look up Brockton on the AA map in her car and noticed how close it was to Shipton. He had made a mental note then that they really ought to visit this village to ascertain whether there was any local knowledge of the Blakeway family.

'What? Here?' She changed down through the gears as she answered, for the inn was on a crossroads.

'Looks like an old place. Maybe someone here can help us.'

Expertly she steered the MG into the car park behind The Feathers and they got out, passing through a courtyard with tables and metal seats to enter the inn through a glass door at the rear. Inside they found a small trestle table by a window and Tallyforth went to the bar to order drinks and make enquiries. He returned with two pints of copper-brown beer and placed them on the table.

'This is the stuff to put hairs on your chest, metaphorically speaking of course, George. Shropshire Gold. Had some the other day in Clun. Very tasty. Cheers.' He raised the barrelled glass to his lips and took a deep draught.

'Well?' George was impatient to know if his enquiries had produced anything before she drank herself.

He returned his glass to the table and leaned towards her.

'All in good time. This place has a bit of a reputation for its food apparently. They're expecting a full house later and the chef's busy preparing stuff. He'll be able to spare us some time in about ten minutes. He owns the place and knows everyone in the village, I'm told. Comes from round here originally, went off to catering college, got a job in Raymond Blanc's kitchen, then came back to the village. Nice place, eh?'

They looked around them. It was still only just after six o'clock and there were a mere handful of customers, all male and all elderly, sitting in the bar area with their pints.

'Looks like the locals at this time of night,' said Tallyforth. 'Wonder if any of them can help. Shall we go over?'

Without waiting for an answer, Tallyforth pushed himself up from his chair, seized his beer in his right hand and headed across the room. George Elliott had no option but to follow him.

'Mind if we join you chaps?'

There was a muttered agreement from the four old men sitting there, one of whom had a foul-smelling brier pipe gripped between his teeth and another of whom had a black and white sheepdog nestling under his legs. The other two were virtually identical in looks, with sharp noses, deep-set grey eyes, hollow cheeks and white hair. The only distinguishing difference was that one twin had his hair parted on the right, the other on the left.

'This is Inspector Elliott of the Mercian Police Force.' Tallyforth indicated George with a casual flip of his left hand as she sat down next to him and opposite the four men. 'Nothing to worry about but we wondered if you could help us.'

'We'm peace-loving folks round here,' said one of the twins. 'We never has no trouble here, in't that right, Ben?'

191

His brother nodded agreement, as did the other two men.

'No, I'm sure that's absolutely right,' George Elliott cut in, anxious to ensure they didn't see her as some hard-bitten cop trying to stir things up in the country. 'Allow me to explain. Did you read about the discovery of the bones on the Stoneway Steps in Bridgnorth?'

'The Body on the Steps? Course we did. We've talked about nothing else since last weekend, have we? 'Cept, of course, the Wolves match. Lost again, didn't they?' said the twin called Ben.

They all laughed and the sheepdog twisted itself round differently under its owner's legs.

'Well, you probably don't know that the bones were of a young girl, maybe twenty years old, and they date back to the time of the Civil War. We believe her name was Venetta Wright but she was in fact the daughter of Sir Robert Howard who was the Governor of Bridgnorth Castle at the time.'

'Oh yes,' said the dog-owner. 'Why wasn't she called Howard then?'

'Long story.' George Elliott sighed, but decided not to go into any detail. 'Illegitimate child. But we're fairly confident that it was her.'

'And we also think that there's a connection with a certain Jacob Blakeway who came from Brockton back then,' added Tallyforth, leaning into the conversation. 'He got into trouble by having a long affair with the lass from Larden Hall in Shipton. D'you know the place?'

'Yes, was took down back in the nineteen sixties. I watched the demolition. Hadn't been lived in for years and they say the timbers were sold to some American who was going to build his own mansion,' said Fred, the dog-owner. 'You were there too, Jim. Remember?'

'I do that,' replied Jim, who took his pipe briefly out of his mouth.

'Ever heard of this Blakeway fellow?' continued Tallyforth.

George Elliott gave him a questioning look but said nothing. What was he up to?

The man with the pipe and the man with the dog looked at each other, while the twins almost simultaneously lifted their beer glasses to their mouths. There was a studied silence. The dog gave a light croak as it slept. A young couple entered the pub from the car park.

'No?' queried Tallyforth, looking from face to face.

'Better ask Bill and Ben here,' said Fred.

The two brothers looked at each other and nodded, as if to say they were ready to fill in the gaps. Then they both lifted their beer glasses in unison and supped long and deep.

'We'm called Blakeway,' said the twin with the right-side hair parting at last, who was the Bill referred to. He put his glass back on the table. 'Our kin's lived in this village since Adam were a lad.'

George Elliott could feel her breath catch at the back of her throat.

'Are you related to Tom Blakeway?' she asked.

'Our cousin's boy. In the army now. Gets hisself into a bit of bother atimes. All right though really. Ain't seen him for years, mind,' said Ben Blakeway. 'You after him for summat?'

'No. Another long story. Too long. Let's just say we've had dealings with him recently. Nothing to bother you with,' replied George and she took a long swig of her beer.

'So had you heard of this Jacob Blakeway?' Tallyforth persisted.

'Fathered them children as went to America, din't he? That's the one, innit? Everybody round here knows the story. Everyone who comes from here like. None of them posh incomers know nothing mind. There's only a few families left in the village now. Some took ship to America, some emigrated to Australia, New Zealand. A lot died in the Great War.' Bill Blakeway stared mistily at his beer, thinking back.

'Did this Jacob Blakeway father any more children then?'

'Well, of course he did. How else would we be here now? Him and Katherine – her was from Larden Hall originally but she lost all that – they had three more children. There was Venetta, Henry and Jacob junior. Three on them. We'm both descended from them.'

'You know a lot about your ancestors.' George re-entered the conversation. She couldn't go back beyond her grandparents. Was this something to do with Shropshire,

this long memory? Were they all like this? And that name –
Venetta. So there were two of them.

'Have to in our family, don't you, Ben? Drummed into us
dead early like. They reckoned Katherine had royal blood,
didn't they, Ben? Said she was related to King Malcolm of
Scotland somehow way back. Don't know if it was true or
not but it's kept being told in our family ever since. Never
done us no good, though, has it? We'm still here living in
Brockton. We ain't got no castle, have we Ben?'

The twins both threw their heads back in simultaneous
gushing laughter. It was clearly a joke against themselves
they enjoyed telling. Their two elderly compatriots, who
had heard the story many times before, smiled indulgently.

'I see you've been getting acquainted with the Brockton
Historical Society then,' said a man in chef's white coat and
checkerboard trousers who had suddenly appeared by their
table. 'I'm Brian Garside. They said you'd been asking after
me for some local knowledge but I think you've found it,
haven't you? What these guys don't know about Brockton
is, believe me, not worth knowing. Fred here used to be
headmaster of the school, Jim's been churchwarden at St
Peter's up the road in Easthope for God knows how many
centuries and the terrible twins – well, what can I say? Have
they told you they're related to royalty?'

Tallyforth and George Elliott nodded, while Fred and Jim
groaned in mock anguish at hearing the tale yet again. Fred's
dog woke up and its head scanned around the room before
it settled back to quiet snoozing.

'Sorry, I can see you have. Look. I'm really sorry but I'm
expecting a busy evening. I've had a cancellation. You two
wouldn't like the table, would you? I could catch up with
you later if you like.'

Tallyforth looked at George Elliott, who returned his look
then smiled.

'Why not? Thank you,' she said.

'Great, I'll get the girls to set one up for you for what?
Seven thirty? Okay?'

They nodded agreement and he spun on his heel to return
to his kitchen.

'So are you both descended from Jacob junior or from Henry Blakeway?' asked Tallyforth.

'Oh Jacob junior, definitely,' answered Ben Blakeway. 'He was the one with his father's seed, warn't he, Bill? Besides Venetta never married and neither did Henry, so the story goes.'

George noticed that the Blakeway twins' glasses were standing empty.

'More beer, gents?'

'That's kind of you, Inspector,' said Fred, who had not been included in the invitation but had decided to include himself and his friend Jim. 'They know what we have at the bar. Just tell them it's for us. You're a proper lady. Thank you.'

George Elliott gave them a rueful glance but went to the bar to order more drinks, returning immediately when the young girl behind the bar offered to bring the beer over.

'How come this Henry never married then? Must have been very unusual in his day, mustn't it?' asked Tallyforth, still interrogating the twins.

'They say he'd lost the love of his life.' Bill Blakeway replied as he reached for the beer that the barmaid was balancing on a tray before them, while his brother and George Elliott removed the other glasses. 'In the wars, they say.'

'I could show you his gravestone up in the churchyard,' said Ben. 'You know the one I mean, don't you, Jim? I showed it you.'

'Not tonight you won't. It's nearly dark already,' Jim said.

Tallyforth looked at his watch and out of the window. True, it was getting gloomy but maybe, if they drove quickly, they might be able to see it.

'Besides, it dunna tell you nothing,' said Bill. 'Just 1623 to 1675 and his name. Henry Oliver Blakeway.'

George Elliott sat back so quickly she almost upset the table on which all the beer glasses sat. Henry Oliver. Henry Tolliver. Surely not. But they were so alike, there had to be a connection. But why would he call himself Tolliver instead of Blakeway? What was that all about? She looked across at Tallyforth who was smiling contentedly to himself.

'Did you know…?'

'No, but I had sort of guessed.' Tallyforth tried not to sound triumphant, especially now they had become so much closer again. He didn't want her going off on a rant at him for not saying anything earlier. He had to be careful. 'I knew that people in the Civil War period used pseudonyms to protect themselves against future recriminations. We know this Tolliver fellow had worked as a spy under cover in Bridgnorth and in Shrewsbury from his letters to Venetta, so it would have been sensible for him to change his name regularly. Who knows if he was Henry Tolliver in Shrewsbury or only in Bridgnorth? And whether he called himself Tolliver when he was tutoring the Pierpoint children at Tong. But he certainly would not have wanted to be found out by Howard's men. Do you know what profession this Henry Blakeway had?'

Tallyforth's last remark was addressed to the elderly twins sitting opposite him.

'They say he were a schoolmaster,' answered Bill Blakeway. 'If it's true, he were the only one in our family what ever had any brains, that's for sure, ain't it, Ben?'

Ben Blakeway nodded and laughed.

'And I can vouch for that too.' Fred, the ex-headmaster of the village school, smiled.

'Bingo!' said Tallyforth as he reached across to take George Elliott's hand and squeeze it affectionately. 'I think we have solved your little 'antique mystery', haven't we? And all before dinner. I'm famished. Shall we find our table and order? I think we're entitled to a decent bottle of plonk for our efforts, don't you, George? Gentlemen, many thanks.'

George Elliott made no effort to detach herself, as he led her by the hand to the other end of the room where the barmaid had indicated their table was. It was just like old times. It was better than old times. A warm glow spread through her body, even before the wine arrived.

THIRTY-EIGHT

The stone flagstones of the floor had been mopped clean and the wooden tables polished. The cream curtains had been tied back and some windows opened on to their latches. But still there was the latent smell of stale tobacco and beer hanging lightly in the air.

'It's ironic that young Blakeway found the letters his distant forebear wrote, isn't it?' George Elliott was in reflective mood. 'What we'll never know is whether Howard killed his daughter or not. I've seen Clifford's report on the wound in her skull and he's quite clear, even after all this time, that the ball fired from the pistol would probably have penetrated her eye and exited through the back of the skull. He reckoned it would have been fired from less than six feet away. Whoever fired it must have had her standing terrified right in front of him. Could you imagine taking a pistol to your son Miles?'

She held her cup of black coffee half way to her mouth meditatively. They had just polished off a bacon, fried tomato and scrambled egg breakfast and Tallyforth was spreading marmalade on a thickly-cut slice of toast. The bar of The Feathers was empty apart from themselves and the occasional appearance of Brian Garside with breakfast items. There had been a certain inevitability about their decision, after dinner and after wine and brandy, to stay the night at the hostelry. A celebration of many things had definitely been in order, they had simultaneously thought.

'Certainly not. Although I did have some problems when he came out a few years ago, as you know. But no, it would never have crossed my mind to go to such extremes.'

She watched him as he munched his toast. His jaw still moved from side to side in that metronomic way he had of breaking up hard food. She grinned lightly to herself. Old memories stirred. No, he was too much of a softie to ever think of threatening his own.

'So Clifford reckoned that whoever did it would have been only a few feet away from our Venetta, did he? Has he seen the gun?' he continued.

'No, but I have. Well, I think I have. Didn't I tell you? They have a muzzle-loading pistol from exactly that period on loan in the Bridgnorth Museum with the initials 'RH' scratched into its stock. Apparently it was found under the floorboards of the Governor's House in town some years ago.'

'And you've seen it?' Tallyforth looked up from where he was buttering another piece of toast. 'You think that was the weapon that killed Venetta?'

'It makes sense, doesn't it? Remember Tolliver's last letters when he thought Howard had been on the Stoneway Steps looking for his daughter? And then when she didn't turn up for their last trysting, as he called it? Doesn't that all suggest that his suspicions were correct, that their affair had been discovered and that Venetta had been locked up to prevent her seeing him again?'

'And you think that he shot his own daughter with that same gun you saw in the museum?'

'Why else would he have hidden it under the floorboards of the Governor's House? Doesn't that suggest guilt to you? It could never be any use to him, could it? Let's assume that he placed it there when the surrender to the Parliamentarians was about to take place. He would never be back in that house again, would he? But he knew that Henry Tolliver, or rather Henry Oliver Blakeway as we now know him to be, would get the soldiers to scour the property for the murder weapon once he found that his beloved Venetta had been shot. What more natural than to hide it and brazen things out? We know from his affair with Frances Purbeck that he was no stranger to duplicitous behaviour, was he?'

Their conversation was interrupted by the arrival of Brian Garside, in jeans and open-neck shirt, at their table.

'Everything all right with you two? More toast? Coffee? Anything else?'

They looked at each other and simultaneously shook their heads.

'Your room all right last night?'

'Perfect,' said Tallyforth, reaching across to take George Elliott's hand. 'Just perfect.'

'It's very atmospheric. I love all the old beams and everything. You've made a really good job of it,' George added, smiling back at Tallyforth and squeezing his hand in return.

'Okay, just give me a shout when you're ready to leave and you can settle up for everything then.'

As Brian Garside disappeared again, George Elliott's mobile phone rang loudly through the empty bar.

'Yes?'

Tallyforth watched as she listened to whoever was speaking, nodding occasionally and looking grim but saying little apart from 'Yes' several times. As she clicked the phone off and placed it on the table, he saw that her face had gone white and her eyes had deadened.

'Everything all right?'

'That was Ruddy Gore. Blakeway's confessed. He's been charged with manslaughter.'

'The boy? Good grief!'

She looked across at him, her eyes almost frozen at the news she had just received and that she was having difficulty comprehending properly.

'No, his father. Tom Blakeway.'

'The father? How come? I didn't know he was around.'

'Apparently all that Richard More had been able to say was "Blakeway" and everyone, including me I admit, assumed he meant Ryan. But it was the father he meant. Tom Blakeway had come home from his barracks on the bus, had been out drinking in the Black Horse on the other side of the river and saw Richard More standing outside the cave. So he pushed him inside, warned him against picking arguments with Ryan and punched him. The boy bashed his head as he fell and that caused a cerebral haemorrhage. That's what he died of.'

'Bloody hell! So how come Ryan Blakeway didn't see him?'

'More must have been inside that Lavington's Hole. It's pitch black in there. I guess the boy was knocked out. He must have been in there as I went past with Andrew later on. We saw the metal grille had been tampered with. God, Tallyforth, maybe if we'd got to him sooner, he might be alive now.'

'George, don't blame yourself. It's over.'

'Yes, it certainly is for that poor boy.'

'And for the feuding, I think. So, George, are you happy? Everything resolved?'

She smiled grimly back at him. It had been a strange week. It was difficult to remember that it had only been just a week ago that she had come, unwittingly, across Ryan Blakeway climbing over the barrier at the top of Stoneway Steps with his hidden treasure tucked into the back of his track suit bottoms.

'Yes, I think so. In my mind at least. I guess Tom Blakeway will be charged with manslaughter, though it will be difficult to prove. If his word can be given any credence, it just seems like a tragic accident. But he's confessed to hitting the boy, so he is responsible. I don't know what the historians will make of the other matter but I'm satisfied that Sir Robert Howard, Governor of Bridgnorth Castle and Baron of Clun, murdered his daughter Venetta because he had discovered her affair with the Parliamentarian soldier and spy known to her as Henry Tolliver but to us as Henry Oliver Blakeway. And the pistol he used to murder her is the one he subsequently hid under the floorboards of the Governor's House. And yes, that curious family feud that dates back to those times has reached its tragic conclusion too. So, yes, I'm content.'

'Good. And us?'

She paused momentarily and smiled at him.

'Content too.'

She drained her coffee cup and was about to get up from the table when another thought struck her. There was something else, something they had forgotten about in the excitement of discovering the truth about Venetta and Henry.

'What's Clarke's interest in all this then? I still don't understand why he warned me off.'

'I have a theory about that, George.' Tallyforth withdrew his hand from hers and took the napkin off his lap. 'I worked under Nobby Clarke for many years. As I told you he is a mason. But he's also a leading light in the Catholic church in Birmingham. Very few people know this because the Catholic hierarchy has always looked askance at freemasonry but Clarke loves secret societies. It's where he gets his kicks. And where he gets his information too. I always wondered how he knew so much about everything and then I found out.'

'So? What's his being a Catholic got to do with this business?'

'George, just remember we're talking about the Howards, England's leading Catholic family. Their titular head is the Duke of Norfolk who, as Earl Marshal, has the task of arranging state funerals and coronations. They are that important. And Nobby Clarke would have known all that. I'm not saying that anyone leaned on him, because it's unlikely they would have known all that we've now found out but he would have pretty quickly worked out the possible consequences of besmirching one of their kin.'

'Good grief! D'you really think so?'

'Yes, absolutely. Trust me, I know the way his mind works.'

'So when he finds out what we've uncovered, there'll be trouble, will there?'

'Time to worry about that later. Come on, let's go. I have to get back to my car in Bridgnorth and I've got a tutorial at the university this afternoon. So you, dearest George, will have to manage Clarke on your own. I'm going back to my History.'

He laughed as he pushed his chair back and ushered her towards the staircase.

'You bastard!'

APPENDIX

I am grateful to the Salopian Museum for permission to reproduce this collection of letters. The originals may be viewed in the Museum itself, under special licence.

THE TOLLIVER LETTERS

Bridgnorth. January 2. 1646

Most dear and loving heart,

Never such happiness have I yet known but when I am with you, those fleeting flying minutes that we steal from the night. Your sweet and tender hand I now caress in mine as I write you this, in thoughts of you forever bound. Your gentle laughter gurgling forth like a mountain stream I think I hear afresh at the river's side. Your sparkling eyes, so quick to espy all that moves, so alert to mirror my very thoughts, flash inside my weary head and I am undone again. I know your scented smell, I feel your lovely warmth, I sense your tiny fingers clasped in mine. I would that we could be together forever and not torn asunder by this cruel war.

Oh, my princess of the night, together we shall make an island, not apart from but in the midst of this world it is our misfortune to dwell in, where we shall love one another and you shall paint and sew while I shall read my learned books and sing. We shall look the doubting Thomases in the eye and tell them that our love is greater than all heretofore and we shall gain strength from the hatred of those that deign not to honour our love. If your father do not confirm his love for you at first, because of what I am, I am very confident a little time will make all well again and his affection to you as dear and hearty as ever. If you had failed in anything of duty or love to him it had been some just case of exception, but in going the way your conscience tells you to be right, I hope he hath more goodness and religion to continue in displeasure with you for it.

Outside my tent, a sheet of snow covers the world, wherein all voices are swallowed and the noisy oaths of soldiers are made gentle and time disappears. I am all stillness, relishing these moments stolen from the busy round of day and loving the feel of this pause. Of you I dream and trust your heart is filled with my love as mine with yours is. Your sweet kisses so inflame my mind that I cannot but think of the last even we met in the shadows of the Bailey wall. Oh! When will we be together again? The day is too long I fear to keep me in its thrall. I can hardly forbear these hours I must endure until our next tryst.

I pray you will be safe until then and rest your ever-loving soldier in God's faith,

Henry Tolliver

Bridgnorth. January 6. 1646

Dearest heart,

You ask what sort of a man was my master, William Pierpoint, and I must needs to tell you that he is the sweetest and the wisest man that ever I have known in my short life. He did take me under his wing as soon as I commenced to be in his household at Tong Castle where I was appointed as tutor to his children at the behest of Master Baxter who did teach me from the scriptures at Bridgnorth. Master Pierpoint was the Member for Great Wenlock at that time and was much involved with the doings of the Parliament, so oft times he was away from home and did leave me in the charge of his sweet wife Elizabeth whose father had Tong Castle before times for she was his only child and thereby his heir.

I did teach his children reading and writing and some Latin, as I was instructed by my master, and betimes I also read to them from the Scriptures, for such was the way that Master Baxter had taught me to do himself. If I may make so bold to say thus, I was not greatly taxed in this work but rather gave much of my time to reading in Master Pierpoint's fine library which his wife did allow me to frequent each afternoon while she was visiting with the children. There I did study the ancient books of learning and lore and did steep myself within the writings of

205

the Puritans whose beliefs met much favour with my humble mind. Therein did I read of the glorious history of our nation and how the dark night of Papacy had descended on it again in those days before the Puritan brethren sought to build a new dawn for the Gospel of Our Lord. I read of the corruptions that were retained in the church and of the superstitions that still bedevilled so many of my fellows, so that they were bitterly incensed by little and everywhere stirred up thoughts of envy and persecution. Mistress Elizabeth did tell me, when I asked the meaning of that instruction of Archbishop Laud for the tables on which we took our communion to be placed at the east end of the church and thus taken from the main body where they had ever been, she did tell me that this was so to make a barrier between the priest and his flock and that thus the people, rejected by the priests, would give over the study of righteousness and commit themselves and their salvation to be managed by the priests themselves.

Master Pierpoint did one time allow me to accompany him to London for the Parliament when the Earl of Strafford, that was the King's favourite and erstwhile his Lord Lieutenant in Ireland where he did rule with a fierce and many say a cruel whip, was accused of high treason by those who later were to become the leaders of the Parliamentary forces, especially the honourable gentleman Master Pym. When we did ride to Parliament that day in my master's coach, I was surprised that so many of the common citizens had foregathered in Westminster to petition the Lords for justice against this Strafford. I being a mere countryman and never having seen so many people gathered together before in my life was struck with terror, but that Master Pierpoint did calm me saying I had no need of fear for they were seeking to persuade their lords and masters to hearken to them and that this was a better thing than taking up arms. Justice! Justice! – I heard them call as we rode through them. Master Pierpoint did tell me that these citizens blamed the Earl of Strafford because their trade was failing and they could scarce feed their families.

And then some several days after, for we had stayed that time in London where Master Pierpoint was much exercised on his business and where I had leisure to explore the busy streets and see the wondrous houses and palaces, we were together on Tower Hill when the traitor Strafford was brought from the Tower to the scaffold. Here, as they fastened his hands behind him and set him before the scaffold, one of the host that had foregathered around the scaffold to witness the execution and who they called Freeborn John did call out to the crowd of citizens, telling them that he was a mighty traitor but that the King was hiding behind his cloak. The traitor himself then spoke forth to the people:

- I am come here to satisfy you with my head; but that I much fear the reformation which has begun in blood will not prove so fortunate to the kingdom as you expect and I wish.

Then he did deliver his head to the block and it was severed from his body with one blow from the axeman who was his executioner.

My master did not know and no more did I that the war we are now engaged on was to break out soon after that. Master Pierpoint was still striving to sway his fellows in that Parliament that all could be resolved peaceably, if they could but find the words to persuade the King to listen to the demands of his people and see their sad plight. But it was not to be so.

I was with Master Pierpoint but less than two years and then, when the King raised his standard in Nottingham, my master did come out for Parliament and stood up in Shrewsbury, I standing beside him, to read Parliament's call to arms. As he spoke, he was rudely interrupted by one gentleman, a supporter of the King, as so many of the Shropshire gentry were, who pulled at my master's cloak and did seek to tear the declaration from my master's hand. Whereupon Sir Francis Ottley, who was later appointed the Governor in that town and who was widely perceived to be a secret papist, escorted by a drummer and waving a thick wooden staff, forced his way through the throng and was just as threatening of my master. Methought there was to be a wrestling there and I prepared myself to come to the aid of my master, for he was not a strong man, but then the mayor ordered all to go home on threat of punishment for inciting a riot.

My master was not easily taken away from that throng by me but did at last listen to my remonstrations and begged me that I should take up arms on the Parliament's side as being the only way to cure the King of his arrogance and make him perceive the sad plight of his people.

My dearest one, I was young and innocent of the world's ways then but have now seen much wickedness in my life. Four weary years have I had in this bloody war, until I saw you and your lovely face that so brightens my dark visage with your smiles. And soon, I pray, this war will end and you and I can be together beyond this civil strife that has torn our blessed nation apart.

Dream sweet dreams, my love, until we meet again.

Henry Tolliver

Bridgnorth. January 11. 1646.

My only love,

You upbraided me yestere'en for that I was boastful and taking airs from when our army did capture the seat of Shrewsbury but only trust me, my love. I was not wont to be overweening for I trow that very few men – some say but ten or eleven – died when the town fell. It was a work of wonder that so few should perish but it was because of the artful scheme for taking the town that was devised.

I had been for some time since living within the town's walls about my feigned business, working as a draper's assistant to carry my master's wares wheresoe'er he chose to send me. Which post did give me chance and fortune whereof to learn the disposing of the King's soldiers in the castle, for they were forever in need of new cloth, being returned from battle with torn and scathed clothing. There I did see one day many troops of soldiers marching forth from the castle, all heavy with pikes and swords and muskets, summoned, so I heard tell by those whose gossip comes from hearing such things at the tables or in the bedchambers of their lords and masters, by Prince Maurice to help him to relieve the siege of Chester.

The plain folk of Shrewsbury were much incensed at this state of affairs, for the King's soldiers had taken with them much of the town's store of provisions, besides their horses and fodder and bait, leaving them in a poor state. There was much anger in the ale-houses that evening that I did witness and, despite the support that had heretofore gone to the King's favour, it seemed certain to me that people's minds were turning towards our side and, when I durst to advance such notions among those folk, they did not gainsay me as once they surely would have but instead did hearken to my words.

Straightway I did send a messenger post-haste to my fellows in Wem, which had but one year since been defended from the King's soldiers and where the Parliamentary Committee was then installed, to tell them that perchance now was the time to strike. I was not alone for there were other fellows of like persuasion living in Shrewsbury at that time, of whom one was a minister and another was a soldier in the King's troop. The minister it was who rode with the message those few miles to Wem, stating that now, when Shrewsbury was but thinly guarded with many troops away in Cheshire and the common folk in uproar, was the hour ripe for our Parliamentary army to strike.

Accordingly, I did send a plan that there should be some men who could enter the grounds of the castle by cutting down with saws some of the wooden palisade beside the River Severn. This was far from where the few sentries would be keeping watch, one of whose number was the aforesaid King's trooper who was to so distract his fellows by what means he could, so allowing passage for the soldiers who would then climb past the broken defences and into the castle grounds. And so it happened that, in the darkness of the February night, eight carpenters did row down the river to the castle ditch and saw down the palisade. Whereupon, soldiers having climbed past the broken palisade, one of their number, who was a Shrewsbury man and therefore knew the town well, did scale the castle walls and open the gates for his fellows to enter the castle. Colonel Reinking, the Netherlander who was at that time in command of those troops of Parliament, did then make his entry of the town and did quickly secure it for our forces. When the King's men at last offered their surrender, they were given leave to march from the town towards Ludlow.

My love, I know you are afeared that our troops will take Bridgnorth and that there will be many deaths but I told you of the taking of Shrewsbury not to be in boast of my part in that action nor yet to gloat over the trickery with which it was accomplished but rather to seek to assure you that, when our officers decide the time is ripe for capture of the town wherein you dwell, it may not be by bloody battle that we shall succeed. Believe me, we are honourable men and butchery is not within our sphere, if it may be avoided. By then, moreover, you and I will be long vanished from the place, I trust.

It will not be long now, my dearest heart. Pray for me as I pray for you.

Henry Tolliver

Wem. January 23. 1646

My dearest heart,

Why will you not tell me who your father is? It cannot be a secret. Do you think perchance I shall take offence from hearing it? Nay, though he were the King himself I should not fear him nor his name. For that love which beats within my throbbing heart is mighty enough to overwhelm all obstacle that fate may throw at us. Is it that he hath some secret of which you are ashamed to let me know? If it be so, fear not for I am one who knows how to keep secrets for such has been my life these past years that I have durst to bear so many secrets in my seething brain.

It matters not now, I think, for these things of which I shall tell have passed and my small part in their accomplishment is most forgot or else become the story of some other man's success and glory. Being but a common sort of fellow, in my looks and bearing as some would say, I was chosen to be one of those they call a spy though I was a captain in the Parliament's army all the while. My task was to set myself within certain cities or towns in order to discover the arrangements of the King's troops therein and to learn what support there was among the common folk for the cause for which we strove. There was danger in such living because I had to learn to trust some who I would never in another life give a moment's faith to and I had to bury inside my soul the deepest secrets of others who trusted me, not knowing that I was not of the King's party.

Once, when I was in a certain town held by the Parliamentary troops – I cannot yet tell you its name for fear you might have some regard for its people and not know of the terrible things that were done in the King's name – I was witness to much shameful plundering by the King's army. Once entered within the town's walls, the soldiers ran through the streets with their drawn swords, cutting and slashing those men they met with, whether soldiers or no. Then they set their houses on fire and took away all sorts of goods. They broke open anything that might carry bounty, whether locked or no, trunks, chests, boxes, cabinets, bedsteads, cupboards, coffers, and all. Thence they carried away all kinds of clothes, all money or plate they could find, all sorts of boots and stockings, and woollen and linen cloth. They cut the bolster cases and threw the feathers into the streets to be trampled on by horses and men. They threatened all they met with pistols and swords to shoot or run them through, if that they would not give them money, by which means compelling many men to lead them to the places where they had hid their money.

I was lucky to escape their ravages for the house wherein I dwelt at that time was one of those so torched and burnt but I could not fight back for fear of being apprised and, in torture, telling who I was and what might be my reason for being in that town. But the people of that place left me in no doubt that they were not of the King's part when they saw what was done in his name. And they were all the more ardent to hearken to what I told them of the better world our Parliament's forces were fighting to achieve. The King has grievously mistook many of his citizens, thinking them not worthy of consideration and not deigning to hearken to their concerns, but rather choosing to regard them as naught more than fodder for his cannons. He hath trusted too much in the counsel of those his courtiers who do tell him that it is his right as King to rule as he so wishes, never regarding the needs or desires of his people. Master Pierpoint, that was my master when this war did begin, would oft remind me of that famous homily once preached in our churches:

> Almighty God hath created and appointed all things in heaven, earth and waters in a most excellent and perfect order. In heaven he hath appointed distinct orders and states of archangels and angels. In the earth he has assigned kings, princes,

with other governors under them, all
in good and necessary order.

And he would tell me that the King had
disavowed himself of that honour to which
by rights he should have been entitled when
he refused to acknowledge the rights of the
Parliament and sought to raise taxes purely
for the benefit of the throne. Master Pierpoint
would lecture to me on the iniquities enacted
by the King or in the King's name and say why
he and many others had sought to force the
King to hearken to their concerns and, when he
would not, or having hearkened would not take
heed, they felt the time had come to stand
firm against his overweening manner.

He told me especially of the moment when it
was learned on good intelligence that the King
himself was intent to come to Parliament to
seek the arrest of five gentlemen whom he
deemed to be those most opposed to him;
and how the House advised those five good
men and true, among whom was the estimable
Master Pym that my master loved most of
all, to absent themselves before that the
King arrived in the Parliament; and how the
King did command the Speaker to leave his
chair and thereafter did he accuse those five
honourable men of treason but, on casting his
eyes around the House and seeing that they
were not within its walls, declared

– I see all the birds are flown – and demanded that they should be delivered to him; and how the Parliament, enraged by this breaking of tradition and, as they did perceive it, of the privilege rules of the House, refused to do as he bade them; and how the King, seeing that they would not obey his wishes, did flee to Hampton Court.

I can remember all this as if it were but yesterday and yet I was barely then of age myself and had but recently been engaged by Master Pierpoint as tutor to his children. And you, my dearest love, would then perchance have been but a child yourself, whose beauty lay still undiscovered. Did you learn of such momentous things? Did you know how the world was turning? As I sit and sigh inside my tented home and think upon your lovely face, I trow I know nothing of you but your name and your beauty and your sweet kisses that so inflamed the heart that I feared had been turned to stone by this war.

My arms reach out to you as ever – I pray they will touch yours soon.

Henry Tolliver

Dearest Heart,

I write this letter in deepest perturbation, not knowing if I durst ever let you see what I have here writ. For were the King's men to apprehend my letter in some way, if perchance you were to leave it in a place where others might read it, unwitting that you might be in such enterprise, then surely we would be undone. But write I must, for this has been a tale that has churned up my heart for many months like to a whirligig and I cannot keep still my beating heart whensoever I think on it.

Upon an afternoon last August, as I was out riding along the way to Kidderminster looking out, as was my custom, for any of the King's soldiers that might impede my journey or challenge me, I did espy riding swiftly on a white horse down below me in the valley on the far side of the River Severn a cloaked horseman. He seemed anxious to avoid apprising and, whenever and wheresoever he could, he would ride under the trees of the forest thus keeping himself hidden from general view. In my curiosity, I rode along the road in parallel with this outrider, matching his pace as best I could for I was on a not so fleet horse as he, until I saw that he must come down to the ford near a place they call Hampton Loade where a small ferry boat carries people across the river. I rode across the fields until I reached this same place and hid me in a small copse to await this gentleman when he alighted from the ferry boat in order to continue on with his journey. When that he was once again on dry land and goading his horse onward, I did spur my horse out of the copse wherein I hid and challenged him who he was and what was his business. He sought to ride past me without answer but I unsheathed my sword and thrust it in his direction, whereupon he drew back the reins on his steed and waited till I came up to him. He was unarmed but had a package attached to his belt which I did demand of him. He sought to protect it and tried to throw it into the river but I seized his hand as he did so and grappled the package from him, at the same time cudgelling his back with the flat blade of my sword and sending him on his way.

When I arrived back at Wem, I unfastened the package and was amazed at its contents for I saw by the royal seal that it was a letter from the King who was staying at the castle in Bridgnorth at that time. This is the letter (I copied it into my commonplace book):

Bridgenorth, 9th August, 1645.

Nicholas,

This morning I receaved yrs of the 30th. of July, which requyres no answer, but thankes for yr often advertisements: and particularly for those which are moste freedome. In answer to which, I shall desyre you (with ye lyke freeness) to take heede that 358:376 make not much of suspicion ***** for 174:111:29:18:115 ceale 148:316:276:358 [erased] perfectly – and all that are believed to be his particular friends; and I assure you that there is no dispatch yet come from ----------. For newes I refer you to your friendes, only I must tell you that tomorrow I intend to march to Lichfield, and so to Newarke ye next day; but if ye Irish be come, then I turne to Chester. My laste was from Cardiffe, which was written in such haste, that I forgot to bid you send me worde (which now I earnestly desyre you not to forget to doe) how my printed letters, & c., have been receaved at Oxfd. by the severall soerts of people, according to their dyverse humours. This is all at this tyme from yrs

C. R.

I knew not then who was this Nicholas nor what the meaning or purport of this letter for, as you shall see, it is writ in some strange code that I could not con. I took it to the colonel of my troop, whose name I shall not tell for fear, as I said before, that this my letter should fall into others' hands. Colonel _____ gave it to others who were skilled in deciphering these codes. I know not what they learned from this about the movement of the King and his soldiers, although we could guess that Lichfield and Chester would be his next stopping points. Nicholas, I was informed, was the King's secretary that he was most fond of.

It is barely four years since I was a humble schoolmaster teaching Master Pierpoint's young children at Tong Castle, a man with some knowledge of Latin and of the scriptures whose life seemed destined to be spent in such ways. Now I was intercepting messages from the King to his secretary and thinking this to be a proper thing to do. It is not possible to think of this without wishing it were not true and that I was still pursuing my humble calling but at the same time my heart so is churned by this I cannot conceive that schoolmaster and I are but one and the same person.

Is there something in the times that has changed me, do you think? Am I coarsened, roughened, made vulgar by this strife that I have witnessed these past four years? Have I perchance lost the sight of that most fitting commandment of Our Lord to love my neighbour as I would love myself? Would that this past four years and the deaths I have seen, the butchery I have witnessed, the groans of pain and grief I have heard were not true. But then, I catch myself again, but then I would never have seen you, my beautiful lady, my princess, with your dark flashing eyes and that lovely smile that so entices me and wills me I know not in what direction. And not meeting you would have been my bane, for it is only from you that I gain the strength to carry on to see this civil strife to its conclusion, when we can surely at the end be together.

Oh, my love, it is a pain I cannot bear to be without you.

Henry Tolliver

Wem. February 3. 1646

My dearest heart,

You ask what cause I have to rail so against the Bishops of the land and I must inform you of my first master, Master Baxter, with whom I was a student of the ways of God when first I left my home. Master Baxter was the most worthy man that ever I have known and a man of the highest calling who at that time whereof I speak preached the gospel powerfully in Bridgnorth town. He taught me it was best to sing the praises of Almighty God in plain manner without the affectations that bedevilled the church. He would not sign with the cross nor wear the surplice, for which offences as the townspeople did call them he was much pilloried by those who wished to hold to the beliefs that their masters had told them were the righteous ways of thinking.

Master Baxter, though yet young in years, was old in life and had yet suffered mightily in outward labours and inward trials, having borne with fortitude the spleen vented against him for preaching the doctrine of original sin to them in the parish, and telling them that infants before regeneration had so much guilt and corruption as made them loathsome in the eyes of God. Even when he asked them whether they durst say that their children were saved without a Saviour, and were no Christians, and why they baptised them, with much more to that purpose, and even though afterwards they were ashamed, they did still bear false tales against him. He told me he thought the hearts of Bridgnorth people to be harder than the rock on which the town stood and, when he left the town to go to Kidderminster, he shook off the dust from his feet against the ungrateful townsfolk.

Master Baxter knew whereof he spoke, for his own father had been a gambling man, much given to dice and cock fighting, but having seen the ways of our Saviour had reformed his wasteful ways and turned to live a worthy life in God's eyes. He did wear his hair shorn and did keep his clothing plain and simple as was the fashion with those who embraced the Puritan way, which is to say the way God wished them to be. Master Baxter learnt from his father to turn away from the dancing around the maypole and the singing of lewd songs and to devote himself to reading of the Scriptures. He learnt to follow this way of living and scorned the ministers in his father's church whom he thought to be ignorant and immoral men, being more akin to Papists with their altar rails and their incense than he believed was truly God's path to righteousness. He believed that religious persons must talk of God and heaven and read books of devotion and spend the Lord's Day in religious exercises. Never was he afraid himself to rail against swearing and cursing and drunkenness and profaneness as being the enemy to obedience to God, whom he loved.

I did hear Master Baxter preach often when I was still a schoolboy in Bridgnorth and he did give me lessons in God's ways because he said he knew me as one who might one day serve our Saviour in such a way. Oh, had he but known then the turmoil that this accursed war was to bring to our land, I doubt but that he would have told me at that point to gird myself for the many battles that were to come. But how could he know then? The King was still safe on his throne and the world we know was not then turned upside down as now. And I was but a young boy, scarce out of my father's house who had borne my questing mind with fortitude.

My dearest heart, how I do miss you again now in this darkest night, when no moon doth show the way to your bower within the castle walls. These are the darkest nights when I await news of your whereabouts and when you will succeed in trysting with me once again. I pray you are safe.

My love for you is strong and will be so forever.

Henry Tolliver

My dearest heart, my love,

Why did you so turn away from me and let my kisses fall on empty air yester evening? Why are you so distraught and bear grievance against me for that I am telling you truths I durst not tell no man before? Do you not trust that I love you? Do you perceive some blame in me for that I love you so deeply? Surely you are not in faith afeared of me because of what I, a soldier, have executed? Often have I told you that I did not seek this civil strife in which our England besets itself, nor did I seek to be such as would wage war against my fellows nor to smite them with my sword or fire my musket at them, but that the King himself did so provoke his Parliament that this discord could not but be shunned.

Hearken to me, my sweet love, and do not judge me till you have heard all whereof I speak. When I first saw men killed, I was with the troops led by Colonel Brown at Powick Bridge that is near to Worcester, which some say was the first battle of our strife. It was I who did act as guide to Colonel Brown and his troop for I knew the country thereabouts tolerably well and they being from the northern counties knew it not. My first master, Richard Baxter, was also there present, having ridden from Kidderminster where he had been preaching to the townsfolk because there were those in that town who were accusing him of taking for the Parliament's side against the King and being desirous of seeking the protection of the soldiers of Colonel Brown's troop. Right glad I was to see him again, though he was alarmed by the warfare and said that I was foolish to so involve myself in the ways of fighting men for that my duty was to God and to preaching his scriptures. With a heavy heart I told him that my mind was set by all that I had seen and heard, especially from my Master Pierpoint to whom he had commended me but one year since.

You will know perchance that Prince Rupert's troops were better armed than ours and that the Parliament's force was routed by them, with many of our soldiers being slaughtered by the King's men. That was the first time I had seen men killed in battle by other men who were their brothers and bore them no grievance save that they were of the Parliament's division and not of the King's. These were men moreover with whom I had marched through Worcestershire and had shared my evening repast and listened to their complaints and laughed at their stories. They were simple men from the shires who had listed perchance for the pay or perchance because their masters did order them so to do or perchance because they sought to escape from their poor position, believing that to be a soldier was a better life to live. Some were stabbed by the swords of Prince Rupert's soldiers who faced them on Powick Bridge, some were shot as they fled away, some fell in flight and were run through by the King's men following them. Never had I witnessed so much blood that stained the sodden ground.

We retreated to Pershore, my Master Baxter still in attendance but now not wishing to be with the Parliament's army for he said he had seen the vanity of armies and how little confidence could be placed in them. I was angry with him for I had seen my fellows die and railed against him, saying that, if justice were to be the proper cause and if the King would not concede to the just demands of his people and if the King, as he had then set himself, had raised his standard against the people, then it was their beholden right to take up arms against him, until such day as justice were to prevail.

This is what I still hold to, though Master Baxter was loath to agree with me, that this conflict we are engaged upon is a just cause and, though many have died already and many more may yet do so in its pursuit, yet we are right to so seek a resolution to our grievances. Is that why you turn away from me so? Is this the cause of your sudden frozen gaze? Think you that I would not wish every one of those poor men who died at Powick Bridge

229

and at all the other battles since to be alive, ploughing their fields, tending their cattle, dandling their children on their knees, clasping their wives to their sides? Think you I would not rather my life had been so ended rather than any one of theirs? Think you I would not rather that Parliament had found, nay could still find, a better way to conclude its dispute with the King than by this ceaseless disturbance of our civil life?

My love, it were my fondest wish that it could be so and that this war should be at an end, so that we two can be together as one and not kept apart by these tempestuous times. How oft I dream of such a day! How oft I wish for it to be, when I am not sat weary in my tent upon the field or marching footsore from one town to another and you are not locked away within those castle walls! But it cannot yet be so. I am bound by my oath that I shall do whatsoever it is deemed necessary to accomplish that justice which Parliament rightly seeks. If men die in that pursuit, then truly my heart does grieve for them, whether they are the King's men or the Parliament's men, for all men are equal in the sight of Our Lord. Nay, if I die in that pursuit, though I wish it not and have no desire that you should grieve for me, then so be it, for our cause is just. If we kill men in that just pursuit and so bring about a world freed of the King's conceited manner, then so be it, for our cause is just and people all throughout the country will in time see that this is so.

Oh, my dearest, I wish we did not quarrel so. These unsteady times make it so that we cannot speak heart to heart of our love but must forever treat of what matters affect our separated souls. Have faith, my love, our love will be triumphant and we will become old together, looking back upon these troubled times and thanking God that we found each other in them and that our love helped us live through them.

Yours forever,

Henry Tolliver

Wem. February 22. 1646

Dearest heart, o my love,

So your father is that Sir Robert Howard who did proclaim himself for the King in Shrewsbury when that my master William Pierpoint did declare for the Parliament. He is now, you tell me, the new Governor of Bridgnorth Castle. I scarce can contain my beating heart that I should so love the daughter of my greatest foe. Is it possible? Is it true? Is this affection in which I hold you so dear to be torn asunder by this new knowledge that teems through my troubled heart? You - the child of the Governor of that Royalist demesne of Bridgnorth Castle, where the King himself has sometime stayed?

Have you been, nay you must have been, in the company of the King himself, perchance eaten your meal with him and heard him speak? Mayhap he has looked you in the eye and apprised your beauty, for this King has a lecherous look I have heard tell. But there is worse in your letter.

Your father, you say, has been imprisoned for that he had an adulterous affair with a lady named Frances Villiers, the Viscountess Purbeck, who was the daughter of King James's greatest servant Sir Edward Coke, and who is your mother. That I should so adore the offspring of a man who has disgraced the name he was given, who by his lascivious ways has so dishonoured the ancient line of nobility and been in his own right a cause for our Parliamentary conflict!

What of this Lady Purbeck, your mother? You say that she eloped from her husband with your father and did call herself Mrs Wright and lay in privately of a bastard son; for which she was arrested and sentenced by the High Commission Court to do penance for her adulterous ways in a white sheet at the Savoy church in London but that she escaped this sentence by flight; that she then was reconciled to her father who had betrothed her when but a young girl to Sir John Villiers, the Viscount Purbeck, and that Sir Edward her father forgave her, and that she then lived with him until his death; that she then did return to live with your father Sir Robert and that they were both then imprisoned, he in the Fleet and she in the Gatehouse, from where she did escape disguised in a man's apparel and did flee to France.

What kind of man is your father to so involve himself with this woman? What kind of woman is your mother? Did she not think of the stain this adultery would bring upon your father's name? Did she not care for her children? And the stain they would carry through their lives?

There is yet more! You tell that your mother, this Viscountess Purbeck, did later secretly return from France to be with your father in Shropshire at his seat near Clun Castle; that there you were born and raised; and that she was with your father in Oxford when she died last year. Yet your father still loves her and you are with him in Bridgnorth Castle and you say I must not judge him, for he has done no more and no less than we ourselves are guilty of, that is that we, like he and this Lady Purbeck, have been so sore struck with love for each other that the world can seem elsewhere. Forgive him, you plead with me, for he has loved as we do love and so will understand what that love is that breaks the bounds of propriety, that knows no bounds but rather flies in the face of all those who would deny its truth. He, your father, risked all for love and suffered grievously, being imprisoned and losing the one he loved to the dangers of a foreign country. Do we dare risk as much?

Late this afternoon, as I was reading your letter again, I heard voices and the tramp of horses' hooves approaching the old bridge. There was a great commotion as a troop of our soldiers did ride through, their horses breathing clouds and sweating even in this cold time of the season, for they had been ridden at great speed through the Shropshire fields. With this troop, there were sixty or so Royalist soldiers, being the garrison from Apley that the King had supplied for there was a blockhouse there to guard the Severn waterway. In their midst was the aged Sir William Whitmore, who was the lord of that house at Apley, where the King himself had once stayed, and who had mightily supported the King heretofore. This Whitmore was the erstwhile Sheriff of Shropshire and, when the King did raise his standard, he made certain that Bridgnorth was well supplied with muskets and with pikes to keep the Parliament's army away. What a mighty capture this was, for it afforded our troops easier ways on the eastern side of the River Severn and thereby made it more straightforward for me to ride to Bridgnorth to see your lovely face and kiss your honeyed lips.

O my sweetest heart, I durst do whasoe'er I must to make you my own for ever. These temporary times we live through, this strife between men who are brothers and neighbours, these disputes between religious persons, they all, all mean nought in the shadow of our love, that is mighty and that will reign supreme.

Forever thinking of you,

Henry Tolliver

My dear heart, my only love,

My love for you is only outborne by my care
for your life, in this unsteady time in which
we now do dwell. When I did take up arms
against the King and for the just cause of
the Parliament, methought, as wise Master
Pierpoint advised me, that this war would be
but some weeks long, or months as being at
the most, but now it is four long years since
the King did raise his standard in Nottingham
and I took the oath of loyalty to Parliament
and to Lord Essex who commanded our troops
at that time. How little did we know then of
how this civil strife would turn our world
upside down and set man against man, brother
against brother, citizen against citizen.

Now there are pamphlets that come among us
which the common soldiers cannot through
lack of learning read but which those such
as I who can are ever demanded to scan aloud
for their understanding. The words of these
pamphlets urge that there should be no King
and that there is no divine right to rule, only
the common agreement of the wealthy lords
to give the King his place at the main point of
our country; and that those same lords, or
the many of them that have fought for the
rights of the Parliament these recent years, do
not now give allegiance to the King but rather

236

seek to rule the country for themselves from their seats in Parliament; and that these same lords have no more right to rule than the King himself, being the kin of those French lords who conquered England with King William and so, even six hundred years since that time, still bear the stains of those French Papists; and that the people of England should be the rulers of their own country and not the King nor the lords.

These same pamphlets do say that the Parliamentary authority is entrusted unto them by the people for their better security and freedom and that, if the people do perceive that they have less of such security and freedom, then it is the Parliament that has done them wrong and should be dismissed and their places taken by good men and true who will serve the people justly. The writers of these tracts state that the Magna Charta is the great inheritance of the people and the main part of the people's rights and liberties that were taken out of the hands of those Kings, who by force had conquered the nation, by the blood of our ancestors. What betokens the lords to order who shall be able to hunt deer or who shall keep a greyhound or who shall wear velvet or gold clothing? Or what the common labourers shall earn or what punishment they should pay if they shoot but a pigeon? The privilege of liberty, they say, is as the air that we breathe and is the birthright of all men.

So say these writers of pamphlets which are now widely published and which men carry with them everywhere, having taken them from London where there are now many who print these works, encouraging the common people to so strive for their liberty. One of those who is named in these writings, who some say is the leader and main begetter of them, is that Freeborn John I once beheld on Tower Hill when he was haranguing the people at the execution of that wicked traitor the Earl of Strafford. His name is John Lillbourne, who was a captain in the Earl of Essex's army and did fight bravely against Prince Rupert's force as they advanced upon London but was captured and imprisoned by the King's army at Oxford. When he was released, he resigned from the Parliamentary army because he thought the leaders dishonest men who did nought while the poor soldiers fought their battles for them.

These are strange notions that men are discussing now and nothing of what I thought when I first did listen to the preachings of my Master Baxter and the words of my lord, Master William Pierpoint. You cannot see what I see or hear what I hear in the conversations of the soldiers who have been taken from their homes to fight this war for the Parliament and are thinking these new thoughts for the first time and talking of them with their fellows. You think me mad that I do dwell on such matters, for you are led to think all will return as it was beforehand when the King's troops are finally successful and men tire of this fighting. But I think you cannot be right, forgive me that I do so contradict you. I wish that I could take you from the castle and hide you somewhere near our camp fires to hearken to the words that men say as they prepare their food or mend their torn clothes or stoke up the burning embers. They are saying they want to be free and they want to be their own rulers and not to be in thrall to those lords and those bishops and that King who have so grievously stolen from them in the past times and who will do so no longer.

Oh, my love, my sweetest love, who rules my heart, these are indeed strange and terrible times. I fear that we will not see the end of such thinking and speaking for many a long year. This England we dwell in is riven into two parts and, though the one part, being I should say the Parliamentary part, be soon victorious, I do not think the matter will there end, for men's minds have been stirred by these new ideas of freedom and justice. Even when peace comes at last, as surely it must do so, what place will there be for us, my sweetest one, when I am of humble kin and you are of a noble family? Will your father permit his daughter to wed a poor schoolmaster who

239

was his enemy but recently and did fight against him in this war? Will he, whatever the disposition of government that prevails when peace arrives, will he entrust his daughter to a Parliamentarian? And as for yourself, my dearest lady of the twilight, could you leave the comfort and ease of your father's home to share a life of toil and travail with a humble schoolmaster?

No, there is but one solution and that is, if we are to do what we so earnestly desire and live our lives as one, we must take ourselves away from this war, away from this travail, away from this torn and bloodily divided country, away from England. I know of some who have, because of their beliefs and their fears, taken ship to the Americas to start anew their lives in that new country. They have sent back reports of a land where there are no kings and no lords to rule them and take away the products of their labouring, where there is good soil to grow crops and make a life, where there is plentiful wood to build a house and bring up children, where we might start anew on life. What say you? Will you promise yourself to escape from this accursed country with me and to go to the Americas as freeborn man and wife?

I cannot await your answer, my sweet, nor your kisses when next we tryst at Stone Way.

Henry Tolliver

Bridgnorth. April 5. 1646

O my dearest heart,

This is a most fearful time that has arrived sooner than I would it had, for I wished we might have fled afore now and started out for the Americas as I forswore you we should. I had discovered from one in our troop who had been a sailor at Portsmouth the name of a captain that I could approach and seek passage on his ship for us. I knew not then how quick this last attack would happen, nor that all else in Shropshire, especially, High Ercall where Sir Vincvent Corbet's dragoons fought valiantly for many days, would fall so soon to our forces and so much now be invested in the capture of Bridgnorth Castle.

Because I knew the town well from when I served there under Master Baxter what seems many a year since and from other close knowledge, although I dared not reveal that I had been so oft a visitor since then to meet with you, my lovely lady, because of this, I say, our Colonel Lloyd instructed me to show our troops the best way to attack the town so that the castle was seized as soon as it might be possible and so that as few people died as it could be, for he was a merciful man and did not wish unnecessary blood to be spilled. That was why, when our troops came to the North Gate, Colonel Lloyd

241

did call on the garrison of the King's men to surrender. When that offer was refused and when the King's soldiers fired at the cavalry and threw large stones on top of them as they attempted to ride through the North Gate, then was I able to show our soldiers how to climb around the hill by the way they call Love Lane into the churchyard of St Leonard, where my Master Baxter had once preached the holy words of the scriptures.

You will know how that affair turned out, for the King's soldiers did flee from the North Gate back within the castle walls, setting fire to all the houses and market stalls they passed by and sending the poor citizens of the town to find shelter in the woods or by the rocks, where they made themselves tents to dwell in with cloth they had saved from the fire, whilst yet others were forced to seek refuge in the sandstone caves on the hillside. The poor citizens of the town had done nothing to earn such, having provided sustenance and fodder for the soldiers and hay for their horses for many years. The cruelty of the King's men cannot be imagined. Such is the state of our country that men do so punish and deprive their own brothers.

At the same time the King's men fired flaming torches from the castle battlements on to the roof of the church of St Leonard where our troops had gathered and where our gunpowder was stored, so making a great explosion, the like of which I have never before seen and setting fire to all the town's records that were therein stored and also to all the other houses near the North Gate. O, what a mighty conflagration there was that day and night, such as I have never before witnessed and, pray God, I will never again see. It was truly a great destruction of the town by those soldiers of the King's garrison. Colonel Lloyd once more ordered the castle to surrender but that again was refused so, as you know, our soldiers took up position on that hill they call Pampudding Hill and we have been bombarding the Castle ever since.

I tell you all this because, my sweet, I think you may not know what a great destruction your father's side has caused to happen in the town and how it could have been avoided, if he had surrendered as surely he must in time to come. Your father has perchance told you that it was the Parliament's troops that did emblazon the town and drive the people from their homes. Perchance he or one of his captains has told you that the fault lies all with the Parliament's forces for not giving due warning of assault and so bringing about this awful destruction that you can see when you look beyond the castle's walls, but this was not so, for twice Colonel Lloyd did offer him the opportunity to surrender which he did refuse. Does he not know that we have taken

243

all of Shropshire now, without Bridgnorth and Ludlow, and that the King is losing this war? Has not Sir Vincent Corbet told him of what our troops did to his house at High Ercall and that he had to surrender in the end after one month, like it or no, because he had no more provisions for his household; and of how our troops did allow him to ride away from his house without further harm to him and his household? Has not Sir Francis Ottley, that Papist, who is also there with your father in the castle, who did so roughly handle my Master Pierpoint in Shrewsbury back when the King first raised his standard against the Parliament and so bring about this strife, has not he too told how mercy was shown to him when our troops did capture Shrewsbury, whereof he was Governor at that time?

I needs must tell you this, my dearest heart, for that I fear you had doubted my love and believed that I was not just of the enemy's side in this war but as well of the enemy's side that was intent on destroying the castle that is now your home and all that therein do dwell. If somehow you could use your sweet charms to so persuade your father that surrender would be the nobler course to take, it were for the best. This enmity sits ill here and I think may rise between us. Who knows how long this besiegement will continue? I know not now how we may flee from this troubled scene. All is too close. Eyes are everywhere and we must be especial careful. Send me signal of what time I must come to meet you where we oft have met in the past on the Stone Way. It is shaded there and none can spy us in our dalliance, though brief it must be for your longer absence will be noted.

Yours for ever and in fear,

Henry Tolliver

My dearest lady, my love,

Oh how near I was to apprehension this last night! As I came down the Stone Way from our tryst beneath the Bailey walls, purposing to make my way back to the hillside where our camp now is, I heard footsteps approaching up the track in my direction and so, not wishing to be apprised, I climbed behind a hawthorn bush to hide myself until I could see what manner of person this was. How fortunate I did so, for it was an officer of the King's army, in his full armour dressed and bearing his sword in front of him in his grasp, with another soldier that followed close beside him. The officer seemed full of anger for his face was a ruby colour behind his moustache and he moved with haste as if he knew whereof he sought. They saw me not but, as he passed my hiding place, I noted the fierce look in his eyes and I heard him speak to the other man.

- How say you, knave? You saw my daughter outside the Bailey walls? Why did you not seek to apprehend her?

- My lord, I called out to her but I was on the battlements and some distance from her as she slipped through the gateway.

- Are you certain that it was my daughter and not some scurvy kitchen maid? What apparel did she wear?

- My lord, it was your daughter. I would know her way of walking, despite the cloak she wore to hide her face. It was she, I swear by Almighty God.

- I have some time noted her changed manner. She smiles less and seems remote. She feigns to care little for this besiegement we are encircled by. She has been deceived, mark my words, soldier, by the affections of some rogue in the town. We must find her straightway. Make haste.

As he spoke I knew what manner of man this was. It was your father, was it not? He was looking for you and sought to surprise you with me, for he must have gained some foreknowledge of our secret trysts or perchance had guessed at your disappearances. Oh, if only I could have revealed myself to him and spoke to him, as one man to another man, I would have asked him for your hand in marriage. But, these times and this strife being as they are, I could not do so, for he would surely have tried to strike me down as a soldier of the Parliament's side, an enemy as he would know me, one who was besieging the castle wherein he dwelt and commanded those troops still loyal to the King.

247

Was I wrong to think so? Was it indeed your father who passed so close beside me on the Stone Way? Did he discover you or had you already fled back to your quarters? Did he there discover you and seek to know where you had taken yourself? Has some one in the household espied you leaving the castle to meet me and revealed this to your father?

My dearest heart, I trust you are safe and that we are not discovered.

Henry Tolliver

Bridgnorth. April 20.1646

My dearest love,

You were not at our trysting place yester
evening and I can only conjecture that you have
been apprehended by your father and that he
has locked you in your chamber so that you
can never see me again. Is that so? Has he
made you confess that we have been meeting?
Have you told him what I am, that I am a
soldier in the Parliament's army, his sworn
enemy? Does he upbraid you for loving one
who is his enemy, one who seeks only justice
for all men from this tyrant King whose cause
he has espoused?

This silence from you does make me feel
grievous sore, lest it is of your choosing and
not forced upon you by your father. I fear
you love me no longer, for that I have made
you a victim of this conflict, setting you
against your own father and causing you to
forsake him. Is it even so, my sweet? Has
some great thought struck you in the night
and set you to revoke that love which you
did swear to me as I the same forswore
to you? Have you taken your father's side,
thinking perchance that you are in debt to him
in memory of your mother and that allegiance
to me, nay love for me, were foolish and a
dishonour to her name?

O my love, that were not so. Whatsoe'er your regard for your father and your dead mother, it is not they who will be at your side throughout life's struggles. Do you not see that your father is aging and, although you love him and fear to disrespect him, he will not be there to protect you throughout your life? Do you not see that this world is changing around him and that this castle he does govern shall fall soon enough, and too that men have cast off their shackles and will no longer be constrained by the old lords of the counties when they have been fighting so long for freedom? Trust me when I tell you that a new order is coming in this country of ours whose shape I know not but whose voice I have heard around the campfires and on the battlefields and in the sounds of men's shoes as they march. We are surely close to that time when the King must perforce recognise that he does not command this country any longer. All over the Parliament's troops are beating back those armies of the King, are besieging all towns where the King's garrisons are situated, and taking dominance of all places where once the King's supporters held sway. This war, this mighty civil strife we have been engaged on for many years, this endless bloodshed, has almost run its course.

And what of us, my lovely Venetta, for only now dare I pen your name as no longer wary of our discovery, which I fear has already occurred? What of our love? Will you not come to me in the night, as we have so often promised ourselves when locked in embrace and when our kisses so inflame us? Will you not come with me in the night and we can flee, just as we once swore to do? I yet have the name and household of that sea captain in Portsmouth whereof we might purchase passage to New England and I have garnered enough silver whereof to pay for such a passage for the two of us. I know where we may find a horse to speed us on our way, I know the secret paths through this county and through some others where we would not be apprised and besides, this war is drawing to its conclusion and there is little to hinder us by way of obstructions if we were to ride so to Portsmouth.

I needs must tell you that these words I write to you are not mere empty vessels, writ to persuade you of the truth of my argument, but have greater substance than you might dream of. For, beneath the castle in which you sit with your father Sir Robert and those other gentry of the county, as well as all their soldiers and those others of the household, beneath the castle I say there is a work of great moment now being enacted. For an engineer of our troops is even now with his men digging a tunnel through the rock underneath Bridgnorth Castle, purposing, as he has been ordered, to reach a place directly below the church within the castle walls where it is known your troops do store their ammunitions. These engineers have been digging now for several days and it will not be many more days ere they come to the place they intend, for Colonel Lavington has so computed that place. There they will place a huge mine that will so destroy the rock above it that it will cause the ammunitions in that chapel to explode and therefore the whole of the castle grounds will be torn apart in that explosion.

My sweet Venetta, there is not time to spend, disputing your father's words or considering those of mine. Very soon, unless your father does relent and make that surrender which Colonel Lloyd has so desired of him on two times already, then all within the castle grounds will suffer grievously. You must make good your escape now. I will await you at our trysting place on the Stone Way each morn at cock crow and each e'en as the sun sets, praying that you will come to me and that we can so begin our life together. Be not afraid, my love, for I have the protection of the Parliament's army wherever we go in England. I have a letter here in my purse that I did entreat my Master Pierpoint to obtain for me, that guarantees us safe passage. It is signed by Master Cromwell, who men say is our greatest commander in the field and many do say will be the one who will make sure that freedom be not extinguished again, when that this strife does end.

My love, my body aches for you, wishing your arms e'en now were clasped around me and we were riding through the countryside intent on reaching Portsmouth and the longed for passage to a new life together. My soul cries out for your love and begs God in all earnestness to allow you to escape without harm from the castle and from the King's garrison. I pray that you will receive this letter and that our hiding place in the rocks has not been discovered and some other may take this letter and reveal it to your father. I can only hope. I will be waiting as I promised. Pray God we will soon be one.

Yours evermore, my sweetest Venetta,

Henry Tolliver

AUTHOR'S NOTE

For the historical information in this novel, I have drawn freely and heavily on *The Antiquities of Bridgnorth* by Rev. G. Bellett and *Shropshire in the Civil War* by Terry Bracher and Roger Emmett. The story of the More children of Larden Hall is told in two leaflets by Donald Harris, *The More Children and The Mayflower* and *Richard More of Shipton*. The full story of the affair between Sir Robert Howard and Frances, Lady Purbeck is told in *The Curious Case of Lady Purbeck* by Thomas Longueville. However, readers are reminded that my book is fiction and, while drawing on these materials, seeks to use them in an imaginative way.